RAVEN'S PREY

DAVID FRAMEL

DAVID FRAMEL'S
RAVEN'S PREY

Summer 2007

Published by
BisonHurricane Publications
Houston, Texas

First Edition paperback 2007

ISBN 978-0-6151-4777-2

www.davidframelbooks.com

This is for my wife Trish.

My love and my life.
The motivation for all I do.

I love you, Baby.

The soul of Man must quicken to creation.
Out of the formless stone, when the artist united himself with stone,
Spring always new forms of life. . .

- T.S. Eliot
from *The Rock...*"

Death is a shadow that always follows the body.

- 14th-century English proverb

Prologue

A summer like no other. That's what the folks in Raven were calling it, and some of the old-timers were even daring to say the worst ever. A person had to take claims like that seriously coming from men dependent on lengthy pasts for their conversations and feelings of purpose.

"I'd thought '27 was a blistering oven up 'til this summer."

"Ain't nobody can say it's ever been like this."

Stopping by Cleeger's Hardware and Social Circle, passers-by could learn a history that no textbook or professor could recount. It wasn't a legitimate history, but one rich in folklore and personal recollection.

Want to know the real story behind Raven's history? Well, son, pull up a chair, and we'll tell you how things really were. Don't go bothering yourself with the newspaper or town hall records, boy. Those are but the facts, reported to fill space, to meet a deadline, to make a story. The truth of the story lies in the telling. Remember that. It's in the telling.

Surrounded by farming equipment and garden supplies, an oral tradition found a home at Cleeger's. Storytellers had come and gone while listeners were generational. Their assembly ultimately passed on what they believed the truth, the birth, of Raven.

The town no longer had a library. You had to drive twenty minutes into Paul's Valley for that pleasure. *The Raven News*, a twice-weekly newspaper that had served little more than to bring town gossip to print, kept back issues but no real records, and Jimmy Trathor, the editor, a college grad trying to turn a profit on a dream dead in the water, couldn't make heads or tails of the storage room kept by the paper's original publisher since before the Big War.

It was simple. If someone wanted to get answers to Raven's mysteries, its real history, they came to Cleeger's. Usually three or four of the regulars gathered at midday to drink coffee and bring what little life they could muster to the business of Fred Cleeger. Cleeger didn't need this business to thrive as it turned out. A hefty inheritance, frugal living, and the absence of any woman to mess it all up, thank you, had made Fred's hardware business a means to an end. The means being a way to pass the time until his end. Ultimately, Fred enjoyed the status his store had taken on so many years ago. It had been a result of the farming problems facing Midwestern communities like Raven. The government had for a while encouraged, even paid, farmers not to farm. Something about surplus economics. Tell a farmer he can get paid *not* to farm his land for a while, and see if he doesn't take full advantage of that recommendation.

Sun up to sun down had become time to fill, and slowly the men began gathering downtown to share in their newfound idleness. As are men in all things, the desire to be bigger and better led to tales of times past when things were different, when they were slaving to earn a living. Every generation wanted those that followed it to know that life was a challenge, that things had only gotten better and could never get as bad as they used to be. For the farmers of this community, the answer to putting purpose back in their lives was found in each other, and in every subsequent member who joined their elite circle.

Of course, times had changed. Those who claimed a permanent seat at Cleeger's these days were retired, some disabled, but all were ready to give anyone needing it a dose of The Way It Used To Be.

Simon Hartsell, for example. Sixty-eight, a widower, tough as nails. Need to know the story behind the new land acquisitions near Meyer's Creek? Ask Simon. Want to get the lowdown on Jesse Caufield and his messed up family? The telling was as simple as in the asking. Simon, Rucker Thomas, Taft Sindler, Johnny Flaim. Any of the diehards could be of service. Theirs was a brotherhood of knowledge. A circle joined with a resume of experience, a rap sheet of hard times. All were data banks of the town history, information passed down through the ages that totaled Raven's unique past. With most of the civic records locked away long ago, the stories issued through The Circle gained substantial credence, as did the communicators. No one, though, measured up to the patriarch of the group. If events were questioned, one source was the final say. If you sought the definitive, you asked Mason Givens.

Givens had lived during most of the town's recorded history, so if he said the summer was the worst on record, on *his* record, then you believed it. Mason didn't concern himself with what the National Weather Service may say about summers in the past. He had lived it.

"Heat's never been this bad. Don't need to be told any different. You going to take the word of someone you don't even know who got their information from who knows where, or do you believe me?"

It was hard to argue with the living history of the Raven township.

Not that anyone would dare breech The Circle to chance confrontation and invoke the wrath of the likes of Givens.

Over time, The Circle had gained the status of a holy place. One paid reverence when passing. If the day's storyline caught your interest, you stood at the perimeter of the purposefully placed chairs and didn't interrupt. If you had a question, you held it until the speaker paused to refill a pipe or change position in his chair. There was no denying they were great orators, captivating in a lot of ways. Since Cleeger's saw little business during the day, a sense of calm would descend on the gathering. A clouded light would filter through Fred's windows that had not seen a day of cleaning in forever (the men of The Circle could probably relate that history if asked) and create a somber mood. A few storytellers would rarely look up, as if they were pulling recollection out of the very slats of Fred's dirty wooden floor. It was their style, and their voices carried without pushing beyond a conversational volume, the audience sensing an importance in each word.

"You'll hear them tell you '27 was the hottest day on record for Raven, but it ain't the same heat. Yeah, the temperatures were greater, but it wasn't a confining heat like this." It was Mason Givens, arms folded over his chest as always, chair on the slightest lean, his voice commanding respect.

"I remember Momma putting us out on the back porch at night to sleep because the house would get unbearable. We'd go down to the creek at high noon and just lay in the water, but some days that didn't even help," Mason pondered, staring up at a place just behind and above the audience, as if a motion picture played before him - his trademark.

"Seemed like that summer would never end. Even as a youngin' I recall wishing the summer would end, even if it meant getting back to school."

Givens shifted his weight, readjusted the lean in his chair, swiped his forefinger across his sweaty upper lip, and continued.

"This summer is different. The heat closes in on you. It's heavy, like the air could tip a scale. And you know, back in nineteen and twenty-seven, there'd be a little wind stirring on occasion. We've had nary a gust in four weeks."

Fred's ceiling fans and window unit worked non-stop this time of year, but the heat managed to work its way through the walls to hang unhindered about The Circle. Things were probably not much better at home, but these men would have gathered if Fred's store had been a desert by comparison. It was who they were. Being defined at seventy plus years old had its importance.

Those in attendance nodded their heads in agreement. They had all suffered the summer's reign. Beyond their sharing, the gallery remained small. The Circle had few bystanders this day. The heat and noon hour had kept visitors away from Cleeger's. Raven stood immobile under the weight of the midday sun.

Driving through town, a passing motorist might have felt the lethargy, the stillness, and been compelled to turn the cool air up another notch. No dogs barked, no children screamed in play. It was a deadness, a point in time in which everything functioned at a rate that assured nothing more than to survive. The nights brought no respite, no evening breeze to chill seeping pores.

Air-conditioners worked overtime when they were working. Many had failed under the extreme conditions, and there was little hope for immediate cures to ailing equipment. In Raven, the residents bore it, carried the weight of oppression on their shoulders yet another day, looking for the cold light at the end of the summer tunnel - the coming of fall and its cool cure for what appeared terminal.

The men of The Circle waited too, hoping this, the worst of all their collective experiences, would soon end. But it was early June, and the prospects for a quick remedy were unfathomable. The heat was here to stay, and even Raven's old-timers could tell it was going to be hell.

1

Pete Thompson couldn't sleep. Tossing and turning in damp sheets most of the night, he had forgone any further attempts to doze off and got up for the day. The sun had yet to make its appearance over a Raven horizon, but the temperature seemed to have remained high long after evening's arrival. With the sun's departure went the sharpness, the brightness that pierced the eyes and bent the head in retreat. The nights held to the heat, as if the entire town were under a dome.

He scratched the neglected stubble that shadowed his slack jaw line and crossed the short hall in his trailer to the bathroom where he splashed lukewarm water on his already moist face. The mirror over the medicine cabinet cast a hazy image as he toweled off, his reflection appearing to be part of an unsteady air current.

Flopping in his overused recliner and lighting a cigarette, Pete contemplated his objectives for the day. Scavenging the highway and local trash bins for aluminum was bad enough since being out of work, but the prospects of spending the day under the intolerable June sky was unwelcoming at best. His job and self-respect had been terminated at the Raven Power Plant not three months earlier following a disagreement with his supervisor. Friends had been few when it was time to turn to others for help, and after spending the better part of the first month in Raven's only drinking establishment, The Watering Hole, Pete had sunk into a depression that led him to scouring the county for metal and beer cans to feed his liquor habit.

The trailer was his outright, a product of a failed marriage and dashed dreams, and his pickup was too old and beaten up to be the subject of any monthly payment. For him, enough money to drink and pay an occasional utility bill was all that was important for now. He knew a big score was waiting; the chance to be someone lay just ahead.

At present, having enough to survive until the Fates declared his outcome was Pete's only concern, but the prospects for future gold mines of sellable scrap were growing thin. He knew he would have to do something soon, but what, he didn't know. Going back to a job, working with authority snapping its whip and barking its orders was not for Pete. He needed some way to get a stake, and his past week of contemplation had led him no where.

God, when will this heat let up, thought Pete, as he threw on some clothes in the corner of the room and made his way out the door.

He had no idea where he was going. Burning gas in the truck looking for opportunity was a waste in his mind, but what little motivation held him together told Pete that sitting at home would not bring any financial security. What he needed was somewhere, somewhere out there. It was a matter of finding it.

Pete had been down every avenue of self-employment options. Nothing seemed right for him. He was smart. Full of ideas. Damned supervisor had seen that and canned him out of spite. *I would have had that bastard's job*, he rationalized, *and he made sure I was gone before proving myself the better man to the higher ups.*

Life had always been that way for him. Never getting dealt a hand that he could work with, always having to pick himself up after a blindside knockdown and move on.

His ex-wife had been a part of that too. Packing up and moving to Lincoln without a warning one. Yelling over her shoulder about drinking and *mental abuse*. What the hell did she think he was supposed to do? Let people just walk all over him while he was trying to make his place? They had been through some tough times, but all he asked was that she hang on; he would land them a stake that would free them for life.

But she had lost faith. *Lost interest*, in the words of Pete Thompson. *She would regret the day*, he had told the walls of the trailer many times, sometimes screaming the words and hurling a beer bottle for good measure. She would regret the day she walked when she learned the fortune he had walked into. It was out there, waiting for him, and damned if he wasn't ready to make it his.

Slipping behind the wheel of his old Chevy, Pete started the engine with a bang from the exhaust pipe and considered where to start the day differently. There was no denying the weather would be the same, like Hell. That was where he was living, Hell on earth.

The statement hid a validity of which no one was yet aware. Like all the residents of Raven, his life was getting ready to take a dramatic turn. The temperature would be the least of their worries.

Main Street didn't really come to life with the dawning of the new day. It was as if it forced itself into some semblance of motion. Dottie

Pickering bothered over a sidewalk that really didn't need sweeping in front of her antique shop. A creature of habit, Dottie had donned a broom and flipped her "Yes, We're Open!" sign for years. A few lights began to snap on at Red Miles' Feed Store diagonal to Dottie's, and it wouldn't be long before Noah Carpenter would be opening the doors to his grocery. It wasn't much, but then again Raven hadn't really been much for quite awhile.

Originally a booming cattle town in the late 1800s, Raven had seen a changing economy and big city growth put an end to its days of hustling residents and financial prosperity. Most of the town's businesses had shut their doors during the Reagan administration. *Damn Republicans. Put one in office and the working class suffers.* The public school had long since closed down, and what children remained were bussed to neighboring Davenport to attend school. Rural America was feeling the pinch; a separation from the technological advances pushing its citizens into the twenty-first century. Small communities were like dinosaurs, their residents nearing extinction.

Pete chugged through town without the slightest interest in the goings-on of his fellow Ravenites. He was on a selfish mission of personal salvation, and the problems of his community, of the entire country for that matter, held little water where he was concerned. The road led a mile and a half east to Route 10, which Pete negotiated north for a few miles.

Travis Tritt told Pete through his ancient AM radio that it was a great day to be alive, and briefly, Pete had to side with ol' Trav. If he could find what he was looking for, whatever he was looking for (because Pete wasn't sure himself what he was after or where he could find it), then everyday would be a great one.

Route 10 would eventually take him out of Raven through Coal County to Lioneville and Hermitage, but Pete hoped something would catch his eye before he got too far from home, and he certainly wasn't going to venture far from Raven if he could help it. Granted, he was on a trek to find his destiny, but he was donating a day's wages (measured in Pepsi cans) and a tank full of gas to follow this whim. *And that's what it was, wasn't it? A whim.* He had no direction in what he was doing. *What was he thinking?* Good fortune didn't jump out in front of you as you sauntered down the road waiting for its arrival. He knew better.

It didn't take him long to let a lack of sleep and the heat frustrate his efforts. Having left Route 10 long ago and taken a few back roads that skirted Raven east in his journey nowhere, he found himself on a little used road on the southeast corner of town. The narrow, gutted asphalt eventually curved to a point where he lost his sense of direction, causing a hot, frustrated Pete to begin looking for a place to turn around.

Get back to town and try to salvage some of this day, he thought. Salvage the day in salvage. Not a means to the glitzy lifestyle he had promised himself, but it would get him through another day until he figured out what he was going to do. One thing he knew, though, was that this had *not* been the direction to take.

He told himself he had to stop being so damn compulsive in his life. Jumping at every idea, reacting to everything, had not been lucrative in the past. It had, in fact, lost him his wife, his job, and any hopes for a dream realized at a youthful age. Now, at thirty-three, Pete was not looking forward to starting over. He was in need of saving what time he had left and making it bearable.

Unlike this weather, he thought, as he spied a gravel road and slowed to make a turn and head back to a more populated part of town. Even for Raven, this was deserted. After checking the road in the direction he had just come (*Why?* he asked himself. *No other fool had a reason to be out here*), Pete threw the Chevy in reverse and began to turn the wheel when he noticed the sign. To the side of the road, overgrown slightly with weeds and faded from long exposure, a homemade placard caught his eye.

It wasn't its location that drew Pete's attention nor was it the sign's worn look. No, it was the message it conveyed. Simple, but for Pete, most effective. Out here, traveling nowhere in particular, with no purpose or goal in sight, Pete read his fortune: *Opportunity Awaits! 1/2 Mile!*

"What the hell..."

Pete sat for the longest time and considered the situation. What could possibly be of opportunity here, now, down this old road? Based on the obvious long-term effects of the weather, Pete could imagine the sign's origins from twenty years ago. Maybe it promised the chance to invest in acreage or housing at the beginning of Raven's struggle to survive. It probably was the doing of an old woman who wanted people to join her in stuffing envelopes or selling Avon. Either way, it was too late for chance to touch the lives of this dying community. Pete asked himself why he hadn't let that logical thought steer him from squandering half the day on this goose chase.

He released the brake and let the truck continue its backward approach to the asphalt when the sign drew his attention again. He stopped, pondered the insanity of it all, and finally let the thought of missed opportunity put the truck in drive for him and lead toward the promise foretold down the gravel ribbon of road.

If after one mile he encountered nothing but boarded up barns and abandoned homes, a frequent sight in Raven, he could simply count it as the final leg of his ill-fated mission. And if, by some wild coincidence, the sign led him to the chance of a lifetime, well, he couldn't bear the thought of missing out.

Of all people, Pete was reminded of a poem from high school that had actually stayed with him. Little about school had made an impression on Pete, but every now and then in his English classes, a piece of prose or poetry would strike a nerve. Something about a *dream deferred* being like a sore that infected the whole body. He certainly didn't want to hang on to a hope, only to wish he had found the courage to act on it down the line, regardless of its prospects, when it was too late.

Asking a little more of the old truck, gravel bouncing off the wheel wells as he flew down the old chat road, Pete began to feel a rare excitement, one he hadn't felt in many years. He blasted the radio, the song's beauty lost in his amateur voice. Maybe this would be his pot of gold, his calling. The answer lay less than a mile away.

■

Pete took the gravel lane slowly; not sure what he was looking for, he didn't want to miss it. He considered the possibility that an additional sign would guide him to his destination, but after what had to be a half-mile over the jarring, elbowed road, he held no hope that anything awaited him. The conditions made the already-beaten Chevy bounce and roll side-to-side, adding to his crawling pace and building anger. Whatever shocks were left on the relic got a workout as Pete managed to keep rolling, all the while envisioning an axle breaking or, better yet, getting stuck.

What in God's precious name was he doing out here? It was crazy. Next hair-brained idea he had, he was going to ignore it and stick to what he knew. No doubts when hauling scrap metal. No jungle-like travel when he headed to the nearest dumpster. And for what? The beckoning of a sign calling to a yesterday decades ago? Pete resolved to turn back at the first opportunity that presented itself.

The glare of the sun on his dirty windshield and the cloud of dirt the Chevy's tires kicked up made finding anything a challenge. He figured he had at least come a mile, even at this snail's crawl, and he was yet to see a single barn, shanty, or outhouse for that matter. Nothing. If it weren't for the sound of his struggling vehicle and the mere presence of a road, Pete would have thought himself in a different dimension.

The land to either side was overgrown and stark, long-since abandoned. What puzzled Pete was the lack of fencing. Not even a stray post or stranded link of barbed wire poked from the tall weeds.

Sweat now pouring from his face, causing his shirt to cling to his back, Pete glanced a clearing ahead to his right. As he neared the gap in the high-standing growth in the road's ditch, he had expectations of a structure to come into view, but nothing emerged as he wheeled the Chevy into the open area. Here there appeared to be a drive that continued from the road and stopped some fifty yards ahead. Needing a break from the truck's interior, Pete climbed down from the cab and surveyed the oasis of clearing.

A few pieces of broken glass, a small strip of rubber, possibly from a bicycle, were all he noted that even suggested someone had once been there. The clearing and the road itself were enough to tell him that the area had been occupied at one time, and even a house could have been moved from there, but now there existed such an *emptiness*, a feeling of isolation Pete had never experienced before. Alone most of the time and living a mile from his nearest neighbor, he had thought himself an authority on the subject.

He circled his truck to the tailgate and took a few steps up what must have been the driveway when his puzzlement grew, not over his surroundings, but his presence in this vacancy. He stood with his hands on his hips, a picture of loss. *This is not what I need to be doing right now,* thought Pete. *It's time to just get back in the truck and rock-and-roll myself out of here.*

As he headed back to his four-wheeled oven, Pete couldn't help but notice another odd thing. Silence. He stopped and let the shuffle of his feet subside in the gravel. There were no sounds. Not a bird or a cricket. Nothing. The quiet added to the stark landscape and his thoughts of having entered a place out of the ordinary.

Feelings of confusion and the sensation of being engulfed by the stillness put Pete in a mild panic. He couldn't explain away the dread that was building inside him, and now the very air he was struggling to breathe had a noticeable heaviness, a quality that squeezed his lungs and fought to give up its oxygen. It was all wrong. Really wrong.

Time seemed to slow at that moment for Pete Thompson. Leaning forward to hurry the final yards to his truck, he felt his reality, like the journey down the old beaten path not five minutes ago, come to a crawl.

For Pete, the gods on Olympus had pointed their remote control, the slow motion button depressed.

He felt compacted, pressed from all sides, as the air thickened and congealed around him. Pete recalled when he was a kid and his friends would gather at Old Man Parson's pond to splash and play during summers past. Once they had stripped to their underwater and trudged in, everybody settled to their chins to cool off. He remembered how difficult it was to swing his arms under that water as he would stir the cooler level below.

That's how he felt now, as if he were in a pool of water limiting his every move. Exhaustion overtook him quickly, and Pete stood helpless in the driveway, still a distance from his truck.

The sensation of enclosure began to work deep into his temples, triggering a dull headache. He noticed his knees and shoulders bending under the weight of the unseen force. Hands between his thighs and the pain increasing throughout his body, Pete began to cry out in his mind at the agony.

What's happening to me? God, somebody help me! But no one was there to help, and even if there were someone nearby, he knew he couldn't muster the energy to force a shout from his throat. Even that was restricted as the pressure increased around him. He imagined briefly that this must be what the bottom of the ocean was like - a crushing, unyielding force.

It had come upon him so quickly, and now the pain in his head was torturous. He grimaced and bowed to the weight as it assaulted him from every direction. In the last instance before Pete Thompson slipped into a merciful and permanent unconsciousness, he sensed a presence, an intelligence. Something was opening up to him, receiving him as a child to its mother's womb. In his excruciating pain, Pete welcomed the reception, and the puzzling feeling of joining a greater self.

■

Had a bird or a squirrel been witness to Pete Thompson's ordeal, they would have seen him come to his statuesque halt on the driveway in the clearing, the air about him shimmering like the heat rising off the macadam on a summer day. His appearance, hunched over and irregular, became distorted and chaotic until he was nothing but a blur. This image hung for a moment in time, and then, with a rush of air and a barely audible pop, he instantaneously vanished without a trace.

2

"Tim. *Tim, answer me!*"

"What?"

"You get in here right now and finish cleaning this mess up. I'm not here to follow behind you."

"In a minute."

"Right now, mister!"

"Ah, all right."

For Carrie Hammons the day was starting in the wrong direction. Lunches to make, kids to get ready, and she still had to transform herself before heading to her first appointment. The kitchen would have to wait until this evening, as the whole house seemed to be doing lately, but she was damned if Tim was going to start some irresponsible habits around a home already going through neglect, a neglect she wouldn't allow for much longer.

Dragging into the kitchen with an air of defiance, ten-year-old Tim Hammons grabbed his breakfast plate and glass and haphazardly placed them in the sink.

"Oh, no, you rinse those and put them in the dishwasher."

While her son dramatized every motion and mumbled under his breath, things that ten months ago would have landed him a grounding and facing the wrath of an involved father when he got home from work, Carrie pulled what she needed from the pantry to make lunches.

"I don't know why you have to buck me at every turn, Tim. You know how hard it's been for me to take care of you and your sister, this house, and manage a job I just started. I know you're mad at what's gone on, but you've got to help with this."

Tim lifted the door of the dishwasher and started out of the kitchen, his eyes downcast. "Sorry, Mom. I'll get Sara ready."

Carrie slathered bread with peanut butter and stared out the murky window at the brightening day. It looked like another hot one as her eyes followed a winding path across the browning backyard, over the chain-link fence, and into a wooded area lanced by a rising sun.

Showing real estate had not been in her plans a year ago, but Carrie had recently found herself without a husband or a way to pay the bills, so she had taken Mr. Shephard's offer to point out the "luxuries" his properties offered to prospective buyers. It wasn't really something she enjoyed doing, and the money had not proven to be very good, but it was all she had. She stepped to the refrigerator and poked around for a couple of apples. She could hear Sara arguing with her brother that he was not her boss, and she didn't have to get ready because he said so.

"Mom, Sara won't get ready for school."

Carrie's shoulders, already slumping from the events of the past months, dropped a little more as she headed to the hallway to deal with her children. Turning the corner to her daughter's room, she found a defiant Sara sitting on her rumpled bed, arms crossed, blonde curls hiding a pinched face, head down. Her brother, with all his good intentions, had given up and gone to his own room.

"Sara, get dressed for school before you miss the bus. There are just a few more days of school left, and then you have the whole summer ahead of you. You know I can't take time out to drive you to school today. I have an appointment."

"You always have appointments."

Carrie realized that the adjustments the kids were making were slow in coming. Both were showing their frustration with the absence of their father and the routine they were used to, but there was nothing she could do about it except hope they worked it out.

"Mommy always has appointments so you and your brother can keep your rooms and have clothes to wear. Your dad isn't here to help with those things for me."

A cheap thing to say, especially to a seven-year-old, but Carrie, too, was going through some adjusting. The sense of abandonment and loneliness and the pain of waiting for answers had been more than she could take some days.

Walt had disappeared one day last August following thirteen years of marriage. It had not been a breeze by any means for Walt and her, but they had made a modest living for themselves, raised two children, and had what Carrie deemed a fairly successful relationship. They had probably been in somewhat of a rut recently, in every way conceivable, but Carrie had assumed all marriages of their longevity had suffered the same way. And then, out of the blue, without warning, he was gone. No letter, no phone call, nothing. His office in Cedar Hill had no knowledge of his whereabouts.

The day after his disappearance, Carrie, desperate for answers with no where to turn other than the police, sought the advice of an old family friend, Bill Curtis, an attorney who had handled some of their legal matters and who spent an occasional Sunday watching football with Walt at their home. Bill had no clue of Walt's plans, would be surprised if he had gone to any extremes to remove himself from his family's life, and suggested she call the authorities.

Days had turned into weeks and answers were few and far between. Carrie had exhausted all hope, and what tears she had left, she guiltily shed more for her future than her past.

Raven police, in their limited wisdom and manpower, learned from MarDel Resources that on the day that Walt vanished he had planned on spending the morning checking one of Coal County's few remaining oil rig sites just off Route 42 before coming into the office to finish some paperwork.

Whether he ever left the drilling location was not known, but his car, a '92 Caprice, was found at the site. There was no evidence of foul play. In fact, the car, the location, everything, had not proven to be out of the ordinary. It was as if Walt had parked his car, left his briefcase and keys in it, and simply vanished. An APB was put out for Walt, but there was never any news.

It was Bill who suggested she fall back on her earlier career and call Shephard Realty in nearby Paul's Valley to generate some income for the family until Walt's whereabouts was determined. The life insurance company that carried Walt's policy was going to need a great deal of time or proof of his death before they would issue any kind of settlement, and even Bill admitted that it would be years before a decision could be agreed upon given the circumstances.

After much self-searching and the depletion of most of their entire life's savings, Carrie had gone to see Mr. Shephard about a realty job. Though she had not shown homes in years, it would be simple to renew her license and jump back in the realty saddle. Ross Shephard, as a favor to Bill she would learn later, started her at a nominal base salary.

Commissions were initially impossible because he had put her in charge of homes in the Raven community. There was no company willing to represent the sale of homes in the area (the population had decreased seventeen percent in the past two years), but Shephard jumped on real estate opportunities no matter how far-fetched. Getting people to move into the town and purchase a home was a different matter entirely.

Nonetheless, Carrie had persevered, and after locating a few couples in Raven, "a laidback town free of crimes and worry, which is why I choose to call it my home" (a plug she had relied on more than once), she established herself in the company and impressed Mr. Shephard with her determination and creativity.

"She could sell sand to an Arab," he always told his associates.

Once she had the kids kissed and out the door, lunches in hand, Carrie settled into getting herself ready for the day. A nine o'clock showing in Paul's Valley, Shephard's home turf and the only location within miles of Raven where new home construction was underway, was to be her first opportunity to make a sale, in her mind, worthy of her abilities. Mr. Shephard had given her the chance after weeks of cajoling.

"I need you working Raven, Care."

She hated when he called her that.

"No one can move those properties as well as you."

"Mr. Shephard, I have always appreciated the opportunity you gave me a year ago to come in here and try to start over, but I need some better commissions. I would have to sell ten homes in Raven to come close to making what one home sale in, say, Ridgeview Estates or Meadowbrook would bring me. Give me a few locals. Please."

Her desire to step up in the real estate world was more motivated, though, by a sense of pride than money.

She was, for now, getting by, and though she wanted more for her children, they were managing. What it was that she needed was an elevation of her own self-worth, a feeling of importance. Being bragged about in the office was fine, but the recognition stopped there. Her name on a yard sign in Paul's Valley would be a start, a visual symbol of her arrival. She wanted to show people that, though she loved her husband, she could go on without him and be the breadwinner of the family. Walt Hammons did not define her. Deep inside she resented Walt for leaving her to manage life without him, whether it was his purposeful doing or not. Regardless of the reasons, she wasn't going to let it pull her down and make her look reliant and weak. It was not the way she had been raised.

She still had properties in Raven, some had been with her from the start, but Paul's Valley communities offered the first potential for desirable commissions, and she was going to throw everything she had into these sales. She had met her clients, the Martins (Rob and Cindy, he a mechanical engineer and she an interior designer) just yesterday, and their salaries and desire for a place to call home had made Raven the last place to start looking. Carrie was to meet them at the office where they could discuss some of her new properties.

Stepping from the shower and surveying the mirror, Carrie saw the last year weighing heavily in the lines around her eyes. A new business suit awaited her, bought with money she really hadn't earned yet, so she went about the task of turning herself into something professional. Her brown, wavy hair framed what many saw as an angelic, childlike face, lightly freckled with fragile lines, one that falsely announced weakness. This was accompanied by a slight figure, though shapely, what she believed her best feature, something she took pride in when she considered her age.

Not unattractive for a thirty-two year old mother of two, Carrie was better at turning clients heads with her pitch, her "nasty slider," as Shephard called it. Combine these qualities with a genuine interest in people's happiness and satisfaction, and she had what she believed was an effective, comforting sales approach. It would be beneath her to bat an eye or pout a lip at a male client, especially if a wife accompanied him, so she allowed her natural self to be her tool.

She never misled people, never made them believe something that wasn't true. If a house had structural concerns, she told them. If a house had a history of electrical problems, the clients were always informed. But at the same time Carrie effectively and convincingly pointed out the positives, allowing the imperfections to be covered over like spackling on a wall. She painted a picture for her clients of what wonders they could accomplish given time and elbow grease, what magnificent opportunities lay in the buying of an old home. Forget "fixer-upper." These homes were diamonds in a rough compounded by years of failed upkeep. Previous owners had failed to see a home's beauty and lacked the desire to let it show. As Carrie's audience, prospective buyers were encouraged to be the ones to resurrect what once was, to care enough to make a difference. And it worked because Carrie believed what she was saying, believed it with all her heart.

Each home she sold was a piece of a whole, and she dearly loved her hometown of Raven. In her mind a beautiful home lay just under the surface of what she was showing, as if years acted like masks over its true self. There was a history that had smothered what once was a freshness and vitality that cried out for reconditioning.

Standing in the living room of a rundown Raven home, clients would gaze at Carrie as worshippers before an evangelist, captured by her voice and enthusiasm. Returning Raven to its glory days was beyond her powers, she realized, but she hated to see the neglect and sense of emptiness that was overtaking the community. She wanted people to love the town as much as she did, to help her in securing its life for years to come.

After adding the final touches and passing her own personal inspection, Carrie headed out the door and made her way to the very car her husband was last seen driving. An eyesore of a Ford Escort also sat parked in the driveway (she really needed to sell Walt's car, she knew), but on days when she was hauling clients, the Caprice was her only option. She didn't like getting behind the wheel of the car for the feelings it created, but the impression it gave versus the Escort with its rusting paint and little passenger comfort made the choice for her. And on a day like today when Carrie could feel the sweat beginning to invade her makeup, a failing air conditioner was a risk she was not willing to take.

She had to be at her best, taking the Martins on a preplanned parade of the homes in her jurisdiction. It may take a day or two, but if everything went as planned and she was at her best, she could soon be celebrating a personal triumph.

Driving out of Raven and headed to Paul's Valley, Carrie could almost feel herself leaving behind the past and heading toward a refreshing future. She was going to make it; she just knew it. Walt or no Walt, she was headed in the right direction.

3

The offices of Shephard Realty were located in the heart of Paul's Valley, a progressive city fifteen miles outside of Raven. The city had seen a surge in population over the last few years, in a large part due to the failure of investment in small towns. Rural communities were becoming run-down and unable to provide adequate police and fire protection and draw interest from construction firms and various industries. The resulting lack of employment and small business opportunities in what once were thriving agricultural areas had left long-time residents, families that had spent generations living off the same land, to seek jobs and subsequent housing in the larger suburban communities. It was a matter of time before towns like Raven would succumb to a dwindling population and be nothing more than vague sketches of what they once were.

The temperature outside had already topped ninety degrees by the time Carrie pulled into the parking lot, and the forecast was for a three-digit day again. Carrie had arrived at her office a few minutes before her scheduled appointment with the Martins, grabbed a cup of coffee from the small kitchenette, exchanged niceties with some of the other realtors, and settled into her chair to evaluate her plans. When 9:10 rolled around and her clients had failed to make an appearance, Carrie saw her newfound hopes crumbling around her, but before anxiety could take a firm hold of her, they arrived.

Settling into chairs next to her desk, the Martins seemed eager to begin the locating of their dream home.

"Well, Rob, Cindy, let me detail for you some of the options we have at our disposal, and then I can take you around to some of our choicest homes."

Carrie was a stickler for following a playbook, knowing ahead of time her direction and intentions.

"It seems to me that your price range benefits us in selecting from a variety of properties. Tell me, are you looking for something contemporary or possibly older?"

"We had hoped for a new construction - progressive. Something large, two-story, covenanted. We would appreciate you steering us clear of the low-income riffraff. We enjoy our privacy and want to be in an area that is clean and free of children running everywhere with no supervision," said Ron, and Carrie was not surprised to hear his response. He had struck her on the phone as a young professional, interested in living the good life and wanting a home that would visually impart that knowledge to passers-by. His wife exuded an equal sense of self, a haughtiness and pride that left Carrie disliking her from the beginning.

"Yes, we definitely want to settle in a private community, one free of the problems you see today in longstanding areas, like crime and filth. If you could start in the newer additions in Paul's Valley, we can begin our selections from there."

Cindy Martin's speech and manner reeked of self-importance, and Carrie began to reconsider having begged Ross Shephard to let her work with such clientele. The Martins had described Raven without knowing it, and she had taken it personally. Her Raven was most of what they had said and more, but she loved it just the same. It was what helped define her, and at a time in her life where uncertainty existed at every turn, a sense of belonging and security was welcome.

"I have just the area for you, and I have already identified some homes that may intrigue you," she said.

Carrie fumbled with some papers, gathering both her facts sheets and composure before continuing. "If we don't find what your looking for today, we can schedule a time to look at some other areas in and around Paul's Valley. The possibilities are tremendous, and I can assure you that we will find what you are looking for." Smooth, efficient, and appealing, Carrie so wanted to give in to the desire to hand over the Martins to a realtor who had no dignity, but instead allowed her need to achieve to override any malicious thoughts. Ross Shepard was right - his Care could do anything, and she could now include belittling herself to advance.

■

By lunchtime the Martins had not seen anything that met their uniquely conceited interests, and Carrie's frustration had on occasion made its way to the surface, though she was able to mask it with verbal suggestions that she was disappointed in herself in not getting them to their Utopia more quickly. They separated with the plan on continuing the search the next day, this time in a few new home communities Carrie swore would fulfill their quest.

She returned to the office mentally and emotionally exhausted.

"Well, Carrie, how did it go today?" It was Kevin Gardner, young, aggressive, especially around women, with a childish good looks that only pushed him to push himself on others, and yet eager to make himself famous through, of all things, real estate.

"It could have gone a lot better," Carrie sighed, hoping Kevin's questioning would find a quick end. "I still have Pine Ridge and Shannandale to show them. Maybe something will catch their eye there."

"Tough ones, huh? Well, just show them that Hammons' magic, and I'm sure you'll have them eating out of your hand. Always works on me," Kevin offered, though Carrie was used to this by now. Ten years younger and full of himself, Kevin had always seemed like a big child to Carrie, eager to play but not yet of legal age. She wasn't the only one in the office that had to stave him off with a polite change of subject, but just once she thought she might take him up on his advances just to see what he would do. She had already surmised he would run like a frightened deer, curious but ultimately too fearful to follow through. She had yet to even consider the idea of dating since the disappearance of Walt, and she wasn't sure she would know what to do given the opportunity. Years off the circuit, Carrie was still tentative about putting her availability back in circulation.

"You are so full of it, Kevin. How did your open house go in Meadowbrook this weekend?" she said, changing the subject.

"Got qualifying going for the Tucker home, and I think I have a live one on that new ranch house on Sandy Springs Drive," he said, with a confidence that Carrie often envied, but felt she was well on the way to matching.

"Great. Glad to hear you're doing well."

"Thanks, Carrie, and stay after it. You'll do fine. Remember, if you need some help, I'm just down the hall. Maybe we could even do a joint open house in a few weekends if you're up to it," he said, pushing ever further as always.

"With my kids, it's hard to do the weekend thing, but I'll keep it in mind, and thanks for the offer," she said.

"Okay, whenever. Going out for lunch?"

"No, I'm staying in to make a few calls before I have to head back to

Raven. I have a new property over there that needs my attention. Signs. Walk through. You know." Carrie wondered if he was ever going to give up for today.

"Yeah, I know. Okay, well, I gotta go. Later."

Later. Much later, Mr. Kevin. She genuinely liked him for all his irritability and boyish immaturity, but she just couldn't find a place in her life right now where she could enjoy the flattery and adolescent behaviors of a self-centered, man child. Let some other woman find that crap inspiring. She didn't need a man to tell her she had worth; that job was open for only one person - herself. As soon as she was able to manage a firm pat on her own back, she might be more open to the approaches of people like Kevin, who use a person's own pride against them. She was far from a feeling anywhere near boastful, so for now, she secluded herself within a wall of denial. Like a caterpillar in a cocoon, she would stay in her shell until a transformation had occurred.

After making a few calls in response to messages and calling the children's school to verify end-of-the-year parent-teacher conferences for that Friday (a subject she dreaded, as both Tim and Sara's academic performances had taken a turn for the worse following their father's disappearance), Carrie left her office to survey the new property Mr. Shephard had informed her about with a memo on her desk that morning. She was familiar with the area, but the house address did not ring any bells. She had been born and raised in Raven, went to high school, met Walt, and started a family all within its friendly confines, but had to admit when she didn't know every square inch of town.

She walked back out in the heat to her car and felt the incredible weight of the humidity on her. It was unbelievable how heavy the air felt, as if it were condensing like a trash compactor, closing in all around her. By the time she was in the car, she was grateful for the air conditioning and realized the Escort would have to stay parked a few weeks longer if the heat continued like this. No way it could provide any relief under these conditions.

As she made her way out Highway 74 south toward Raven, she settled into the drive with a melancholy that was unexpected. She had hoped to be leaving Paul's Valley today with a huge commission staring her in the face, and, more importantly, a feeling that she had succeeded at the next level. But the Martins had been fickle, voicing what Carrie had deemed as picky complaints about various aspects of the homes she had shown them. The need for more earth shades, the lack of a kitchen island, deeper walk-in closets. These were minor in her estimation, changes that could be affected by people with the money to buy the house in the first place. It only added to the frustration that began in the office. The Martins were going to be hard to please, she realized. Every realtor's nightmare – a couple that can't seemingly be satisfied and injects the realtor with the feeling that he or she has in some way failed them. They put their hopes in the hands of a professional dream fulfiller, and she was falling short.

But she was Carrie Hammons, the incredible realtor who could sell sand to the Arabs, wasn't she? She was the golden child of Shephard Realty, right? She had established a foundation for herself and now it was time to climb the ladder. Carrie gathered her resolve and decided she would not cater to their martyrdom. She would find them a house, and they would damn well like it. They would thank her for their good fortune and spread the word to all their other high and mighty friends that Carrie Hammons, Realtor Extraordinaire, would save them from a life of searching for that defining abode. She would be their liberator from living in a place that was beneath them. She'd give them their image, their statement in brick and stucco, and they would be forever grateful.

God, she hated herself sometimes.

■

Highway 74 passed directly through Raven, literally splitting it down the middle. As the road passed the city limits marker, the speed limit radically decreased, and an aging sign proclaimed you were "Welcome to Raven. Stay awhile." The sign had been erected long before Carrie was added to the town's head count, and over the years it had been the object of gunfire, violent weather, and city maintenance crews. It now stood at a slant, overgrown with weeds and faded into near oblivion, a symbol of the town it introduced. There was little left of Raven to welcome anyone to, and Carrie regretted not being able to do more for the town except encourage a few buyers to invest in the dying old boy. Real estate was like the pulse of a town, and if properties were becoming available at a rate three times faster than were being purchased, she knew it was only a matter of time before that clock stopped ticking, before Raven was a spot of sweeping dust storms, ramshackle barns, and empty storefronts. The fate of Raven was that of other towns outlying the growing big cities and increasingly favorable suburbs, one of isolation and eventual death. It was inevitable, and Carrie hoped she could continue to do her part to keep it alive long enough to see her children grown up, but the prospects looked bleak.

Raven was the home to a population of 294, a group of diehards hanging onto the dream of living in a small out-of-the-way community where life was laid back and at a slow pace. But America was growing beyond that, it seemed, and the promise of convenience in the bigger communities, the opportunities and advantages that they held, was beginning to heavily outweigh the prospect of small town living. Carrie and Walt had often considered moving to Cedar Hills where Walt would be closer to work and the children nearer their school, but Carrie had always been the naysayer when the conversation had arisen.

"I don't know, Walt. We have everything that we need here. Your job is only thirty minutes away, and the kids ride a bus to school no matter where we live. I just think we would regret giving up the peacefulness of Raven just to be closer to a shopping center or restaurants," she would say, ultimately ending any further conversation on the matter until Walt would bring it up again. He was destined to live the big city life, she had pondered, which may very well be what he was now doing. Tired of waiting for Carrie to agree to his lifestyle change, he had left everything behind that reminded him of little backwoods Raven and set out to experience the high life. *Well, enjoy, Walt. If that's what you wanted. I'll take my hometown anytime.*

But as she made her way through the dying heart of her beloved Raven, Carrie wondered if she was hanging on to a sinking ship, and for the first time she asked herself whether she was truly willing to go down with it.

4

Like many other small towns in the Midwest, Raven was witnessing a transitional period that was bringing to an end all but the most zealous communities. Farming and ranching, though still a modest income for many men bent on continuing the family business, reliving the days of a booming agricultural period or simply wanting to remain in a pastoral climate free of the hustle of corporate America, were seeing a change in its management and operation. Large agricultural companies were finding it profitable to acquire huge portions of acreage, construct processing and distribution centers, and farm huge quantities of product for a fast-growing consumer population. No longer needed was the small farmer, whose output was so small and ability to produce in variety so limited that the skeptical market often doomed a farmer after a few seasons of low-yielding harvests. What had been in generations for many years was sold. Families, unable to look the other way as their children suffered and banks foreclosed all around them, uprooted their lives and allowed themselves to be whisked away on the highway of economic and technological advancement. Left behind were memories of a time when the Midwest flourished, when a man could stake himself a piece of land and provide for those he loved. The result often had a domino effect that could be felt throughout a community, as local suppliers and small businesses that had relied on a steady income from small, independent farming and ranching operations closed their doors. Towns were dying, holding to a few of their inhabitants who were either retired or maintained jobs in larger communities while still choosing to live in rural locations. It hadn't happened over night, nor would the devolution of Midwestern America come to a halt. Time was chipping away at the cornerstone of this country's foundation, and soon ghostly images of towns that once were would dot the landscape for hundreds of miles.

The very power service that Pete Thompson had been fired from and would seemingly not be returning to had, for the past year, been terminating electrical power to areas on the outskirts of the town. Service was being stopped on a daily basis throughout the community, so the plant had justified severing and collecting lines and power sources in areas uninhabited for years. At a time of financial belt-tightening, the company was shrinking its supply area and recovering materials that could be utilized elsewhere. Transformers, power boxes, even sections of reusable power line, were being dismantled and confiscated as replacement. The company was seeing little in the establishment of service and even less in renewal, so workers part of the skeleton crew that still existed spent most of their days in a teardown mode.

In an area just east of Highway 74 before it exited town south, Ed Stevens slowed his Raven Power and Utility truck to a dusty stop in front of a ground transformer box that stood unneeded in an area vacated for many weeks. The green box was one of a few that had once routed electrical power for some twenty small homes, an automotive repair shop, and a rustic family restaurant spread out over a mile square area. Today no one needed to turn on a light, plug in a space heater (they were crazy if they did in this heat), or power a neon sign. It was another example of Raven's narrowing inhabitance.

Ed opened one of the truck's two storage boxes, wincing at the burn administered to his bare hand by the hot metal handle, and filled his tool belt with the necessary equipment for the removal of the transformer. He had already completed a successful operation that morning just a mile north on Chestnut, collecting some expanses of electrical cable from a few empty properties, and he was eager to yank this box and head back to the plant for lunch and to be out of the heat.

Hoping Erma had packed him something other than egg salad but hungry enough to eat anything, he figured there would be little to keep him busy later in the afternoon, so he viewed this job as his last for the day. He preferred lately to get his outdoor work done in the mornings before the real pressure cooker of day hit. Raven Power was unraveling just as sure as the town was, he knew, but until he was without a job, he gave little thought to what he would do in the future. For now, Ed's future was waiting in a metal lunchbox, and with a concerted effort, he could be enjoying its contents within the hour.

The supply of electricity to the box had been shut down long ago, so Ed would be able to work quickly without fear of injury. He had enjoyed his job much more since Raven was disassembling itself. A loner by choice, Ed was free to relax at work, rarely dealing with new customers or fellow utility workers. He liked setting his own pace and not meeting the demands of others. Ed whistled as he walked to the transformer, glad to be a part of Raven's crumbling state.

He had been settled down to his business for about twenty minutes when he noticed a change in his surroundings. It was subtle; nothing he could put a finger on. What he first registered was the undisturbed quiet, which he liked; in fact, he welcomed it without questioning its oddness in an area one would expect to be teeming with insect and animal life. Under his makeshift tent, he paused and listened. Like other utility workers during the summer that were working in this part of the country, Ed had thrown up a four-legged folding canvas that cast a comforting shade over himself and his work area. The heat was another story, but canceling the direct sunlight for the duration of his efforts made the work more bearable. What caught Ed's attention he couldn't readily put into words. Nothing had changed in his sensual estimation, but he perceived a difference in the air, as if a door or window that was part of his external conditions had been closed.

Ed waited while he considered this, his right hand holding a screwdriver as his left held back various wires obstructing his view. Bent over the open box, he began to recognize a change in his breathing, once steady and now somewhat labored. Erma would jump on an opportunity to ride him over his health if she ever thought he was suffering some physical ailment.

"I told you. It's that snack junk you eat. And all that beer! No wonder you don't feel well. Should have listened to me," she'd gloat.

Yeah, and if I listened to you, what little enjoyment I have in life is out the door. I'll stick with my potato chips and Budweiser, thank you very much. Just keep your mouth shut.

Ed quickly took a mental inventory of his body, seeking anything else that appeared different. He was sweating, but who wouldn't be on a day like this at nearly high noon? He thought he felt the start of a headache coming on, but the hunger pains he had felt earlier coupled with the extreme temperatures were probably the reason for that.

He decided to stand and stretch his body. As Ed emerged from under the canvas, he saw a distortion in his line of sight, a slight wavering of definition and sharpened images. *Probably stood up too quickly,* he surmised. With every intention of placing his arms over his head to relieve the soreness his body had adopted while seated hunched over the transformer, Ed felt a resistance to his movements. It was as if he was trying to push the ceiling in a room only slightly taller than the top of his head.

Stunned and worried by this seemingly instantaneous failure of his body to respond as it had all his life, Ed lowered his arms. He recognized a slowness, a clumsiness to his movements as he now tried to bend his knees and turn his trunk. Was this a heart attack? He wasn't sure what happened when you had one, but it was all Ed could rationalize coming upon him so quickly. The optical problem he had upon standing was now a full-fledged dizziness, manifesting itself in a field of vision that appeared distorted, as if he were looking through opaque glass or murky water.

Ed's movements were limited now as the panicked thought of running overtook him, but as in a dream where flight is necessary, he felt like he was standing in lead shoes and unable to lift his legs. His head pounded, threatening to explode and send cranial shrapnel over a large area. He began to bow also to the pressure of a great weight enclosing him like a titanic hand, squeezing him tighter and tighter, and forcing his body into a fetal position. His mind screamed with pain, but his mouth wouldn't work, the unnatural gravity compressing his lips, his tongue, even his throat. He cried out silently as well at the unfairness that he be taken so suddenly, without warning. He was dying, would die, and no one could help him way out here.

Erma. What about Erma? What would she do? *Help me, Erma. Help me...*

Ed crouched, fully enveloped by a force he logically determined was an internal flaw in his makeup, a failure of his life system. The intensity of the pain, the obscure messages his senses were delivering him, all reinforced his conclusion that what he was experiencing was a manifestation of a physical problem. There was nothing outside him inflicting the unmerciful torment. His body had fought the good fight, but had thrown in the towel.

He surrendered to his fate with this conviction, his mind crying out for Erma and about the injustice of it all, until he mercifully lost consciousness. Ed Stevens - husband, father, practicing Methodist, and devout conservative - would never know that he soon blurred and vanished.

5

Carrie turned west off 74 on Vandalia, two blocks before Main Street, and made her way down the two lane residential street until she came to her newest property, a three-bedroom nightmare in the middle of an already dwindling block. The house had been a For Sale by Owner for six months prior to Shephard Realty's assumption of its disposal. It was no doubt in need of more than improvement; rehabilitation was a better description, with hanging shutters, peeling paint, missing shingles, and a garage door crying out in its awkward state for replacement. Free of landscaping or any visible decorative qualities, the house struck Carrie as another great challenge. Given the state of home sales in Raven, she didn't see much promise in a quick turnover.

She stepped out of her car into a purgatory of heat to which she had no compare, fully aware that what awaited her inside the closed-up house would be far more stifling than anything she had experienced all day. Right out of Greek mythology, Hades had come looking for Persephone, and his search had started in Raven.

The homes she had visited with the Martins had been air-conditioned, made comfortable for buyers able to make the hefty monthly mortgages they demanded. This house had probably not been aired out in weeks, and it was now her job to assess the property's attributes as a preliminary function in her representation of it. The owners were seeking $65,000, but were flexible within $10,000 of that amount. Shephard asked all its clients in Raven to be optimistic about their sale price, but at the same time to be aware of the lack of new buyers to the area. If a home even sold (usually for eighty percent of the original asking price), realtors like Carrie considered it a gift from heaven. And with each passing month the frequency of sales lessened to the point that a home such as this one would probably end up property of the bank, abandoned by owners unable to hold on to it any longer.

Carrie crossed the driveway, splintered with deep fissures and marked here and there with pocks, and stepped on the porch, key and notebook in hand. Taking in a deep breath in preparation for the blast of hot air she expected to hit her, she turned the knob and pushed the door inward.

Coming from the sharp light of afternoon into the dull shades and shadows of the house put Carrie in a brief moment of unease. She stopped in the foyer and let her eyes adjust to the interior. Glancing to her left, she met the eyes of a person standing not three feet away. Carrie gasped in panic and flung herself backwards, striking the opposite wall with her right shoulder. In the instant that she reestablished eye contact with the intruder, she realized the same painful fate had befallen her companion in the short hallway. Leaning against the wall with a look of dread on her face, Carrie ashamedly stared at herself in a long mirror.

"Damn. Damn. Dammit," voiced Carrie, relieved, embarrassed, and angry all at the same time. Smoothing down her new outfit, already showing visible signs of a full day's work, yet unperturbed, she continued through the foyer and into a small living area. It, like the rest of the house, was crying out for a cosmetic overhaul. The carpets, wallpaper, and wood trim were heavily aged; the ceiling and areas around the door frames slashed with settling cracks that meandered in their paths.

Her eyes now fully adjusted, Carrie surveyed the rest of the house, making notes and as always trying to find an appealing selling point for the house. It would take an appraiser to determine any structural damage or other problems that she could not assess on her own. What Carrie was able to determine without the help of a professional was that the house, like all the other properties she was in charge of managing and selling in Raven, had a welcoming quality she couldn't put into words. There wasn't a doormat that announced it or a sign in the yard that professed it, but all the houses she had similarly inspected and judged had exhibited a quality, a warmth, that she just couldn't put her finger on. True, she loved her hometown and wished everyone had the same opinion and desire to live there, but this was something more. As she crossed the threshold of every house, walking from room to room and making herself acquainted, Carrie would begin to feel a sense of security and comfort, as if the houses were appealing to her to make them hers.

She obviously never voiced this feeling in the office, sure it would become a source of amusement for everyone, but it was an intuitive reaction she couldn't deny and maybe this was the secret to her success with homes in Raven. She certainly hadn't set any sales records over the past few months, but she had amazed Ross Shephard by selling even one home. Residents were moving out in droves, the town offered nothing in the way of schools or business opportunities, and public services were on the decline, and yet Carrie was able to get people to move into the community.

"What's your selling point, Care?" he would often query as another Raven property sign made its way back to the office.

"I just tell them it's a nice place to live. There's more to a town than just shopping malls and pizza parlors." She often took a defensive posture when describing her successes in the failing town she called her own.

"Everything is so peaceful. There's no rushing around trying to get somewhere. Crime is non-existent, and people just care about each other. There are no strangers. It's like a big, happy family."

Every empty home reinforced that feeling of belonging for Carrie. Each house was like an orphaned member of the community, and it was her job as a member of the family to find someone to care for it. She wasn't always lucky; in reality, most of the homes she was trying to sell had not found there way into the arms of a loving owner, but she was proud of the success she had had up to that point.

It wasn't a matter of money obviously. She made a paltry commission after the final selling price had taken its inevitable nosedive. Realtors in the office questioned her sanity about expending so much energy on sales that were far from lucrative, but this didn't bother her at all. She viewed it more as a community service, and in a private way, in terms of helping a dear friend. She couldn't explain the importance Raven had for her, but it was one thing in her life that had remained a constant, steady and true. When all else had failed her - her parents, friends, and Walt - there was Raven to welcome her home. It was a companionship she understood at a deeply conscious level, and she was sure others like her had felt a deep passion for their hometowns. She would do what she could to see her close friend along.

Having familiarized herself with 201 West Vandalia, Carrie locked the front door and returned to her car. Giving the house a final glance through her gleaming windshield, Carrie pledged her commitment to its occupancy. "I'll do what I can, old girl. Be patient."

■

When Carrie swung into her own driveway that afternoon, mentally exhausted and physically taxed after a day in and out of the smothering heat, Tim and Sara were still an hour from arriving. She always tried to get home before they were due off the bus, and on days when appointments made that impossible, she would call the school and have the two stay in aftercare until she arrived to pick them up. She was thankful for the care program at the school, hating the thought of the kids coming home to an empty house, but there was an hourly fee that often bit into her checkbook. Not that she would ever forego the aftercare to save some money, but there were weeks when she wished the kids were old enough to care for themselves at home until she could get there. That was quite a few years off, so for now she planned her days and her expenditures to accommodate the added costs.

Once in the house, she rifled through the mail, thankful for the lack of bills, and had every intention of going about her usual evening routine. Laundry. Dinner. It all needed taken care of, but after her day of frustration in Paul's Valley and being straddled with yet another reminder that Raven was on a downward spiral, she was just not in an industrious frame of mind. All she really wanted to do was get out of her weathered wardrobe and relax. The needs of others could be put on hold for a while so she could catch her second wind. The kids would be barging through the door in no time, and her opportunity for a break would not come again until after they were in bed.

Having changed into shorts and an old t-shirt, she made herself a glass of iced tea and, grabbing the newspaper, settled into a corner of the sofa to unwind. The coolness of the house, uncomplicated by the scorching temperatures outside, was a testament to Walt's placing importance on the quality of certain things in their home, like the heating and cooling system.

"A first-class carpet or expensive wood paneling won't mean anything if we are freezing or have no hot water. We can't skimp on things like that." She was thankful for his practicality as she curled into the cushion and read her paper in comfort.

National news was always the front page of *The Raven*, even if some horrific or monumental event had happened just down the street from the news offices. Jim Trathor tried to give his paper a big city flare, but ultimately he would have to depend on the events in and around Raven just to sell the thing. Like Carrie, most of the residents had delivery subscriptions and would simply pay young Bobby Rollson once a month when he came knocking at the door. In many homes the paper might miss being read in favor of the larger city paper, but people seemed to view receiving it as a part of residence in Raven, which was probably the only thing that kept Jim's business afloat. He wasn't really putting to print anything people were eager to read, but then again, he would occasionally come upon what he thought was a choice piece of gossip that was his duty to circulate, like his paper.

Carrie often skipped national concerns, gave cursory attention to the rare local story (usually involving some business closure or land sale), and turned to the gossip column. Jim's name for this section always made her giggle - *All the Rave*. What the column lacked in subtlety it made up for in entertaining observations. It was common to find the private life of a Raven resident exposed in all its glory, usually in a tone suggesting a depraved situation. Names were never used, probably to avoid a slanderous retaliation, but if you had lived in town for little more than six months, you could always tell whom Jim was picking on.

It's very odd to this reporter that a local thrift store owner found himself locked out of the house and yelling at the top of his lungs for admittance at all hours of the night on more than one occasion this week. Maybe Sy Arnold needs to move last call up a few hours at The Watering Hole so Raven wives aren't so upset.

Let's see, with one thrift store in town, to whom might he be referring? Carrie loved it. Not that she ever thought the ramblings of a man who probably got his information third hand was reliable but because it gave her the feeling that there was life in the old town yet. Good or bad, as long as couples were disagreeing and neighbors were in dispute, it was life. She hoped Jim would always keep at it. The more life the better as far as she was concerned.

A few minutes after four, Tim and Sara came barreling through the door, Sara practically falling to the floor in an attempt to get by her brother and show Carrie a piece of paper.

"Look, Mommy. I got an S plus on my handwriting. Look. Isn't that good?"

"Oh, yes, honey, that is great. I told you if you take your time, your penmanship is beautiful."

Carrie forever had to gloat over the work that Sara brought home. Not that she minded. She was happy to have a child who took pride in her work. Tim, in contrast, had struggled in school, and over time he was simply happy a day of it had come to an end. It wasn't for a lack of trying that had led him to a less than stellar academic career so far. He overachieved in many situations, but as Walt had said many times, Tim just didn't bring a lot of cards to the table to play with. It was frustrating for both Tim and Carrie, but she had learned that school would never be his forte. He would have to find something else that brought him personal pride. Carrie encouraged him in a variety of pursuits, but up to now, he had not found anything that brightened his outlook and made him feel successful.

"How was your day, Tim?" she asked.

"Okay, I guess." Carrie recognized the tone of a disappointing day.

"Well, I would suggest that if anybody has work to do for school tomorrow, they get after it now because we are going to be eating later, and then we are going to tackle this house together and try to bring it back to some kind of clean."

"Ahhhhh..." Collectively.

"No ah's. Tonight we dig out from underneath this filthy place."

Both kids headed to their rooms, hoping to display the appearance of following instruction. Carrie knew, though, she would eventually go down the hall to find Tim playing video games (a gift from his father that Carrie had fought for weeks. *Walt, he can't have distractions from his schoolwork. It's hard enough as it is to get him to show any interest.*) and Sara at her small tea party table writing her alphabet and trying to improve on perfection.

As she headed to the kitchen pantry to find dinner, whatever plans Carrie had for a smooth, productive evening were about to be sidetracked by the ringing phone. Few people called her at home since friends were scarce, and she expressly forbade the office to ever give her number out to clients. She had always believed that once she was home, work was put away until the next day. It was the only way she felt she could manage a job, her family, and her sanity. Stepping over to the end table near Walt's old recliner, she picked up the receiver.

"Carrie, it's Bill."

"Hi, how are you?"

"Doing fine, just fine. Thought I'd call and see what's up at the Hammons homestead."

Bill was the only person who ever checked on her anymore since the business with Walt had died down. Carrie was often reluctant to bother Bill with her problems, but he never seemed put out or bothered by anything she brought to him.

"The usual here. More work than time. How about you? Still sending the bad guys away?" she said, poking fun at Bill's law practice that dealt not in criminal cases but corporate actions.

"You know I am. I have a job to do. Protecting the streets of cities like Raven from ruthless corporate takeovers and insider trading. Seriously, how are you doing? Holding up on the job all right?"

No matter how much she cared about Bill and loved him for his genuine concern, she was not the least bit interested in discussing work.

Work was just that, and she had hoped to put it aside for the evening.

"It's okay. Got a few properties in Paul's Valley that Ross is giving me a shot at. Different type of clients though. I guess I can't complain."

The conversation stumbled along for another few minutes, in a large part due to the lack of enthusiasm and contribution she was putting into it. Eventually Bill read his old friend's frame of mind and pushed it no further.

"Well, I'll let you get back to it. Just wanted to make sure you were still around. Haven't heard from you lately," he said, trying not to show his disappointment in her unresponsiveness but coming across somewhat dejected nonetheless.

"All right, Bill, and thanks for calling. I've been meaning to touch base with you, but between the kids and the job, you know, it's been pretty tough. I'll give you a call soon and maybe we can have lunch. What do you say? Break away from the big wigs and their million dollar problems and have lunch with a friend?"

"You just name the time and day, lady, and I'm there. Talk to you later."

Bill Curtis had been a college buddy of Walt's who had chosen a more profitable direction than his old roommate. Walt often said Bill had made his own breaks, and when the two returned to Raven to pursue their individual careers, it was Bill who was living his dream life. A nice house in one of the Valley's older yet high-priced additions, fine cars, a wife of impeccable class and beauty. Everything that might make the next guy envious, but it turned out to be a fairy tale. Bill's wife left him after he had established himself as one of the finest young lawyers in a five county area, taking half of everything plus a tidy alimony. His vision of a perfect life came crashing down around him, and he credited friends like Walt and Carrie with providing him a stability he could fall back on. Today he seemed well adjusted, making money hand over fist and at the top of his game.

Carrie often wondered if he kept tabs on her because of their long friendship or because he was subconsciously repaying a debt from long ago. Either way, she felt a deep gratitude to Bill and made it a point to get together with him when she could. She liked his company and for some reason had denied herself its pleasure lately. Carrie vowed to rekindle the friendship.

6

The disappearances of Pete Thompson and Ed Stevens weren't ignored, especially that of Stevens, whose wife Erma was in touch with local authorities immediately after Raven Power officials contacted her as to his whereabouts. Stevens' truck had been located with little effort as his day's itinerary led to the partially dismantled transformer. Thompson's absence was not as readily identified, but within a week, friends used to sharing their misery with Pete at The Watering Hole cycled from inquiries among themselves to a twice daily pilgrimage to his trailer. Had he not been a creature of habit, frequently seen knee-deep in various dumpsters or walking Route 10 and Highway 74 north and south, most acquaintances would have thought little of his AWOL status. A call to the Raven Police Department made getting back to the Hole for a cold one a little more guiltless.

The decline of Raven had affected among other things the size of its police force. A staff of three full-time and two part-time officers had shrunk due to financial constraints to local sheriff Sam Butler and patrol officer Cody Hawkins. Hawkins, a young, inexperienced reminder that law enforcement had taken a turn for the worse in Raven, spent most of his work time driving the streets and back roads of town in the late evenings, hoping to sniff out major crime in his own fantasies, but realistically providing for Sam Butler a badge at night so he could find solitude at home at the end of the day. It was not uncommon for Cody to call the sheriff three or four times a night to ask his opinion on the need for further investigation, the potential for the sheriff's involvement, or a handful of other problems that ultimately Sam said could wait until morning. Cody was never deterred, and Sam rarely chastised him for his efforts. What Sheriff Butler understood was that Raven was on its way to deciding whether it wanted to continue supporting his office, relying wholly on county officers should tax revenues go down any further, so he welcomed any opportunities for the community to see his two-man team in action.

Sheriff Butler recognized the importance of the Thompson/Stevens situation to his department, and at a time when he did little more than serve foreclosure notices and write the occasional speeding ticket, it was an unpleasant but welcome change of pace. Erma Stevens had come to his office the day following her husband's vanishing trick, pleading with Sam to do whatever was necessary to find her Ed. She just knew that someone had brought him to harm. He hadn't returned to work at the end of his shift or come home that night. Raven Power had a truck missing and an AWOL employee the following morning that they were calling about, and she had no answers.

He went out to see her that afternoon, having sent her home earlier in the day while he did some checking. Sam knew the Stevens well; they attended the same church and the wives served together on various town committees. It was unlike Ed to fail to return to work, let alone be out all night, and when his boss contacted the sheriff's office to confirm the recovery of the abandoned truck, Sam realized he had a legitimate missing person.

Erma answered the door frantic and disheveled, and when she saw it was Sam, she broke down in uncontrollable sobs. Luckily for the sheriff, a neighbor, Gale Thomas, wife of The Circle's very own Rucker, was there to lead her to the couch and offer comfort.

"He's dead, isn't he? You...you found him dead somewhere, and that's why you're here," she moaned, holding her face in her hands in a lost agony. Gale tried to quiet her with reassurances.

Sam was quick to calm her as well, though he figured the news he did bring would just complicate matters.

"Now, Erma, stop crying. I didn't find Ed dead. I don't know where he is yet, but we don't know that he is dead." Sam's words came discomforting to his own ears.

Dabbing her eyes almost robotically with her apron, Erma spoke in halting gasps.

"Then what's wrong, Sam? Where is he? Why hasn't he come home? They haven't seen him at work, and you know Ed. He's a good worker. He would never skip out on work." She was right in everything she said, which made it all the more difficult to console her with theory and speculation.

"I don't know where Ed is, Erma, but we'll find him. I came over to let you know I heard from Mike Tyler. They found his truck just south of town off 74. He was over there pulling a transformer. I'm on my way to check it out, but I thought I'd check on you first."

Erma stared long and hard at Sam, her eyes red and wet with dark circles beginning to show. This was a woman whose entire existence centered on her husband. When they weren't together, he was all she talked about. Ed had once confided in Sam his concern about his wife's overbearing attachment, but he seemed to love her so much that the concern came across more as bragging. The sheriff readied himself for another outburst of beseeching and sobbing but was unprepared for what she offered.

"Find him, Sam. Find my Ed."

She said it simply, rationally, as if it answered all their questions.

"I will, Erma. I'll do everything I can," said Sam, rising in front of her from his chair. "I promise."

Before leaving, Sam patted her hands that kneaded a corner of the apron incessantly. She kept her eyes on her work, as if she had given her instructions and was on to other business. He gave a nod to Gale and made his way out the front door.

Climbing back in his cruiser and pointing south, Sam felt helpless for the first time about the disappearance. He had made a promise to the wife of a missing friend, unsure whether he could keep it. One deputy and few resources meant he would need a bit of luck on figuring out this case. He hoped some of the answers would be found at the site of the rescued truck.

■

Two power employees were waiting in a truck of their own near Ed's when Sheriff Butler arrived. He hoped that the scene had been left just the way it had been found but knew that was wishful thinking. By now both men had probably looked through the truck, walked all over any footsteps or tire tread evidence, and generally contaminated any possible leads in solving the disappearance. Sam had specifically told power officials to instruct their recovery crew to stay away from the truck and immediate area. As he pulled to a stop along side their idling truck, Sam concluded the men had remained in their vehicle since arriving.

"Howdy, Sheriff."

Sam knew the driver and had seen his partner on occasion.

"Boys, if you will wait in your truck...in fact, why don't you go on back to the plant, and I will let your supervisor know I am treating this as a crime scene and will need the truck to stay here for awhile," Sam said, not sure if a crime had been committed but ready to clear the area from any further public interference.

"If you say so," said the driver, quickly rolling up his window to preserve the air-conditioning at battle with the summer day as he backed off the shoulder and onto the road.

Sam climbed from his cruiser and spent the next thirty minutes surveying Ed's truck interior, the work station at the transformer, and the grounds at a twenty-yard perimeter from the site. He found nothing. The cab was undisturbed with an array of clipboards, maps, and utility pamphlets. Directly in front of the driver's door and leading to the work location, Sam saw a single pair of intermittent footprints resembling work boots, though he could not be sure whether they were Ed's or another power employee's. The makeshift canvas tent stood silently over an open transformer box, a stool, and various tools.

Sam determined that taping the area off as a crime scene was necessary and set about doing so after contacting the State Bureau from his cruiser. Involving the SBI was a requirement in missing person's cases, but he wasn't confident that the state lab would be able to find anything substantial here to help explain Ed's disappearance. He was a simple man, genuinely happy in a job he took seriously. The sheriff knew that unless someone had abducted Ed or tricked him away from the site, he would not have left behind company equipment or an agonizing wife.

When Sam finished enclosing the truck and the rest of the area in yellow police tape, he radioed ahead to the station, hoping to find his deputy preparing for his shift. He quickly filled Cody in on the events of that morning and the location of Ed's truck.

"Do you need me out there, Sheriff? I can bring whatever you need, maybe direct traffic until you have secured the area?" Cody said, rushing through his questions in anticipation of a major news breaker in his own jurisdiction. Sam had to laugh to himself as he imagined Cody standing in the middle of the road last traveled by the men he had sent back to work half an hour ago, hands on hips, ready to steer traffic clear of the crime scene.

"No, Cody, you stay there and spruce things up a little bit. We may have some important visitors shortly from the State Bureau. I assume they will send a couple investigators, and I need you to lead them out here," Sam said, squelching any plans of Cody's to turn the situation into a circus. "I'll wait here until you arrive."

Sam racked the handset and waited in the car, as thankful for the cool air blowing from the vents as the power employees had surely been. It was going to be a long evening. He still had the call regarding Pete Thompson to deal with, but the sheriff had already determined that tracing the whereabouts of the town scavenger was not a high priority. Pete was known to leave for days at a time, usually off on a wild, get-rich-quick scheme that eventually led him back to Raven and his collecting.

They always come back, Sam pondered. Raven was full of people who had struck out for a bigger and better life only to return to their native soil. The town held a magnetism he couldn't explain. He often felt it himself, cruising the streets and back roads of the community. It was like a hook set deep in your gullet. You occasionally received a little slack and found yourself outside its boundaries, but inevitably you were reeled back in when your presence was long overdue. Call it homesickness, love of your roots, whatever. Sam honestly thought Raven had a hold on its residents, and they would forever remain in its clutches.

He settled in for the long wait, and soon phoned his wife to let her know he would be late. While he talked to her, Sam was struck with the realization that Erma Stevens wouldn't be receiving a similar call from Ed.

7

Carrie met Bill for lunch at a popular delicatessen the following week in Paul's Valley, making good on her promise to herself to get out and do some living for a change. Life had been nothing but the kids and the demands of her job, along with the doubts and fears that accompany trying to manage on your own for the first time. Things were much better than they had been a year ago, and for the first time in she didn't know how long, Carrie relaxed and enjoyed herself. She had always been comfortable around Bill Curtis in social situations, and though she was somewhat unsure of how she would behave after so long in a more private setting, those concerns were abolished within minutes of sitting down.

The deli was loud, experiencing its usual lunchtime fare. It was bright, airy, and exceptionally cool in light of the record heat and number of customers seeking a remedy to their appetites. Carrie had always liked the restaurant with its down home flavor and colorful accents. She actually found herself relaxing in the hectic atmosphere, content to leave her frustrations and demands beyond the window they sat near, relishing a moment of peace with a friend. Since Walt's exit, she had not been able to find time for anyone or anything, especially herself. Bill was just the person with whom to break her loner status. Ten years older than Carrie, he had retained a youthful, athletic appearance that made him appealing for other reasons.

"Well, I'm glad you finally decided to grab a bite with me," Bill chastised with his steady smile and easy manner. Carrie had always been aware of these pleasant qualities, but for the first time they struck her in a different way.

"I've just had so much going on. It's not that I haven't wanted to do this. It's just that I've been so busy, I never feel like I have time to do anything like this," she confessed, holding Bill's steady stare in her own. "This is really nice. I could make a habit of it if you're interested."

"Lunch with a beautiful woman? Who in their right mind would pass it up?" he said.

The reference to beautiful brought a flush to Carrie's cheeks that she hadn't felt in a long time. She felt like a schoolgirl for a passing instant, basking in the glow of admiration. Unable to respond to his innocent flirtation, Carrie could only look down in her lap and smile.

"So how's the job? Ross treating you all right?" Bill asked, turning the awkward moment back to a more comfortable dialogue. "You haven't told me anything since you started over there."

"It's getting better," she said. "I've taken on some new properties in a few of the new additions out here, and of course my Raven homes keep me busy."

"You don't honestly have any luck with Raven, do you?" Bill asked matter-of-factly, but to Carrie in a tone as skeptical as the responses she received in the office. Yes, she was having luck with Raven. It meant just a little determination and the ability to see the advantages living there offered. The prospects of selling a house in her hometown had challenged Carrie to succeed in the beginning; now it was a matter of duty. She had adopted a belief system in which she alone was responsible for ensuring the continued habitation of Raven, and she was willing to spend most of her realty time to this purpose.

The homes could not sell themselves on looks and location alone, though. It took a champion of their cause, and though Carrie was unwilling to admit these things to her friend Bill Curtis, it was her reality.

"Bill, not all of us are able to buy the luxuries of a Paul's Valley or Lioneville," she said. This may have stung him a little, sitting comfortably in one of the more elegant homes in the area, but she had to make her point.

"Raven offers affordable living and a small town environment. We are close to schools, shopping centers, hospitals - you name it. Why wouldn't it be a place to settle down?"

Carrie had jumped on her soapbox without the conscious desire to be there, but Bill had breached the subject. She had spent so much time over the past year defending her job that it had become second nature. If he thought he was going to make her see differently or come close to winning this battle, he was sadly mistaken.

"I didn't mean anything by that. I just figured there were, you know, nicer places that people would want to move to," he said, obviously balking on the word *nicer* but unable to choke it back down.

Carrie looked at him in stunned surprised, as if he had just informed her about the brutal death of a friend. This was not going the way he had hoped. Bill hadn't realized the importance of Carrie's job as it applied to Raven. Desperate to take the subject a different direction before the entire afternoon was hopelessly lost, Bill tried to smooth over his comments.

"I didn't mean it that way, either. I don't know what I was saying. Tell me about the kids. How are Tim and Sara doing?"

His attempts at recanting and leading the conversation down a different path were received with half-hearted attention. In a few brief minutes, Bill had managed to build a wall between them. It may be a long time before he could expect another lunch with Carrie Hammons. She had never been so fully absorbed by a cause the whole time he had known her. Walt was the extrovert, the talker, and the driver behind the family's actions. Carrie had always been reserved, lost at times in the background of a world painted by her husband. She had her children and a home, and it had seemed to Bill that she was happy to care for those things in her life, though he suspected she did it with a quiet yet fierce pride and determination. That sense of service was displaying itself here in the face of their discussion regarding her efforts in Raven. Bill didn't find it odd, but for some reason he couldn't explain, it was troubling.

Carrie spent the remainder of their lunch languishing in disappointment and self-pity. What had started out as an enjoyable encounter that promised more of the same had turned into an ugly exchange. Bill was like the rest of them when it came to Raven, and that had been her greatest letdown. She was yet to find anyone that understood what she was trying to accomplish, and now she expected she never would. Sometimes even she could not fully comprehend what drove her.

Selling homes in the ritzy subdivisions had initially been a dream come true. But after a week of subjecting herself to the likes of the Martins, who were yet to be happy with anything she showed them (Carrie suspected that nothing she ever suggested would ever satisfy them, and soon she would have to admit this to Ross Shephard and let someone else have a crack at them), Carrie sought the warm embrace of Raven and its simple surroundings. It meant the struggle with money would continue indefinitely, but she refused to wake up every day hating to go to work. If she had to earn a living for the family, and thanks to Walt she did, then she was going to enjoy going to the office and scheduling meetings with people who might understand the inner beauty of Raven, the appeal that drew others like them to call it home. After the financial abilities of clients were determined at Shephard Realty, Carrie was usually called upon to offer assistance when low-cost was a priority. And happy to accommodate she was, eager to make a couple the newest in Raven dwellers. It was all very natural to her thinking, and she never thought it strange.

■

When she left Bill at the deli, half-heartedly agreeing to call him the first thing next week so they could get together again, Carrie drove into Raven for an afternoon appointment. She had made it a practice in her daily plans to reserve her showings after lunch in Raven so she was close to home and more than likely to beat the kids home. The sharp radiance across her windshield lessened visibility, but for a veteran of Raven streets, the turn onto Vandalia was second nature. This would be the first showing of her most recent acquisition, and though she had been unable to find a great deal of salable qualities, she thought the house worthy of ownership. The price was right and the repairs were manageable without needing a professional. She hoped her clients saw in it what she did.

Turning into the driveway of her newly adoptive project, Carrie began to rehearse her approach. The exterior of the home was its worst feature by far, so she had to get the family inside quickly if she was going to have any luck. If they wandered too long outside, they may be turned off before ever seeing what Carrie considered very livable. A blast of heat hit her square in the face as she climbed out of the car, but she actually welcomed it for one of the few times this summer because it could be the catalyst she needed to ensure her clients quick entry in the home. She had viewed the house many times since its acquisition, and the cosmetic scars were still quite conspicuous. A coat of paint was a necessity and would probably improve things immediately, but the condition of the garage door and general lack of repair across the expanse of the house were points not in her favor from the outset. The heat wave had kept yard growth to a minimum throughout the county, so any further possibilities of the house turning people away were limited to itself.

Carrie opened the front door, crossing the threshold of stifling heat and brightness to a puzzling coolness similar to a cave. Like every other house Carrie had managed in Raven, she had spent many afternoons cleaning and assuring everything was just so. No matter how unbearable today had been, the house on Vandalia held a comfortable temperature without the assistance of central air or even a window unit. Shephard

Realty required its customers to maintain the electricity in their homes, but the thermostats were kept at levels that would not burden the homeowner with a huge bill. Every time Carrie spent time in the Vandalia house, she never once heard the air come on. She had even opened blinds and curtains to awaken the cavern-like quality of the house, but that had not affected the climate at all. And now, glancing at her reflection in the foyer mirror, which still brought a slight smile to her remembering face, she felt that familiar caress of air.

Carrie walked the entire house, noting the condition of the carpet, looking for telltale spots of dust, canvassing the walls and ceiling, and reminding herself of everything positive the house had to offer. The kitchen was large for a three-bedroom and, if she determined her client was a cook, she would concentrate a majority of her efforts there. The living area and bedrooms were adequate, but a family larger than four would probably be cramped. Of course, the reason her clients were seeing this house was for financial considerations, so they couldn't be expecting its walls to conceal thousands of square feet. Carrie had already provided her initial portrayal of the house in a meeting yesterday in her office.

"Now I don't want to lead you to believe that this house is a castle, because certainly for the price it is not. There are some minor needs on the outside - paint, for example, but nothing costly or time-consuming. What I want you to pay attention to is the interior beauty of the home, and keep in mind what you are getting for the price you are able to pay. With a few swipes of a brush and turns of a screw, you will find you can have a lovely home in a quiet neighborhood where your kids can play safely and grow up free of the hectic nature of the big city."

She was happy as always with her pitch, dishonesty never being a requirement when talking about Raven and its properties. The town sold itself, in her mind, and her role was to act as the go-between, to make the public aware of the pleasant living that awaited them. She often bubbled with enthusiasm over the prospects of adding to her community, and this sometimes confused and generally turned off some clients, but most found themselves caught up in the passion she displayed and believed that they too could come to love the town the way she did.

Having arrived thirty minutes before her appointment to assess what final touches she could apply to the house and her speech, Carrie finished her trek standing in the living room, the center of the property and what she considered its best feature. Of workable size, the room opened in four directions: to the bedroom hall at her left, the kitchen to her right, the foyer behind her, and a patio door in front that led to a small, fenced backyard. A ceiling fan turned slowly above her as she revolved below it, stirring a satisfying breeze while she surveyed the textured walls and polished wood trim. *It certainly was a gorgeous house*, Carrie thought. She was sure that no one could deny its allure and be eager to make it his or her own.

As she circled slowly in place and took in her surroundings, she sensed a peaceful euphoria she had never felt before. For Carrie, everything was right and perfect with the world as long as she was here, wrapped inside the comforting walls of the house on Vandalia Avenue. She closed her eyes and breathed deeply of a clean freshness that relaxed her and pacified any doubts she had regarding the impending arrival of her clients. Spreading her arms unabashedly as she turned, Carrie was swept gently up and away by a comforting embrace that freed her from her earthbound state and carried her skyward. If this was what drug addicts and thrill seekers experienced during their personal adventures, then Carrie was willing to become addicted to this perfect union. In her mind's eye, she saw herself floating among the clouds, free of fear and, surprisingly, loneliness. In time she sensed a presence with her, a guiding force that filled her with wave after wave of soothing pleasure.

Wrapped completely in this protective sensual shroud, Carrie was unaware where she was or how she had soared there, but she knew she didn't want to leave this feeling of utter peace. And now, as her ascension reached an apparent zenith, she heard a voice. Soft, pleasing, coming to her in breathless whispers, the voice spoke its intentions.

"Carrie. Sweet Carrie." Soothing. Gentle.

"Listen to me. I need you to bring them. Make them come to me, Carrie. Help me. Make them come. I need them."

Carrie tried to speak, but questions that flooded her mind were unable to exit her lips. What? Why? Who are...? But nothing came forth. She was unable to perform the slightest motor skill. She just was, existing as the sensations rolled over her in a tidal ecstasy. Response, physical action, nothing was in her power. Never before had she felt such helplessness, but the pleasure of the moment made even her own will an expendable concession. Physical pleasure had never been like this for Carrie, at any level with anyone. Whatever was happening to her would make a lasting impression.

■

Carrie was startled to consciousness by a knocking at the front door. She looked about the living room in confusion as she lay on the earthy carpet, the sun streaming in the patio windows. Getting to her feet quickly, uncertain of what had just transpired, she smoothed her slacks and gathered her composure. *Was it a dream?* she wondered, walking toward the incessant knocking that echoed in the narrow foyer. *What happened to me?*

Baffled and still slightly unsteady, Carrie checked herself in the mirror and opened the door inward, sure of only one thing - the need to sell the house.

8

Forensics failed to provide Sheriff Butler with any helpful information after obtaining various samples from the truck and the grounds in and around Ed Steven's work area. Latent fingerprints proved to be those of Ed and previous employees who had operated the vehicle, but everyone had checked out. There had been no signs of a struggle, no second set of tire tracks or footprints, no physical evidence of any kind to assist the sheriff's office. Sam was starting at square one, and as maddening as it was, he knew his department would ultimately be held responsible should Ed's whereabouts be undetermined. Sitting at his desk in his office mulling over a strategy with Cody Hawkins, Sam was very conscious of his earlier promise to Erma Stevens and the likelihood of ever making good on it.

A fan oscillated in the corner of the tiny room, creating just enough movement of the air to make things bearable. Cody, stiff-backed and ever attentive, sat in a chair across from the sheriff, hanging on his every word as Sam sifted through the lab's reports, hoping to find something to go on.

"Nothing. Absolutely nothing to work with. Those boys went over ever inch of the truck and a fifty-yard perimeter. Nothing," he said, shaking his head with a defeated look. "We have literally no where to begin."

"Would Mr. Stevens be the kind of man to leave town? I mean, just say the hell with everything, and get out of Dodge. Not tell his wife or nothing?" Cody asked. For every situation that presented itself to the deputy, he could be counted on to embellish the possibilities in the unspoken hopes that Raven would have a real detective story on its hands. It was something Sam had learned to expect.

"No, no. Not Ed. He was a devoted father and longtime resident. I knew him personally, and I could never imagine him being able to hide something like that. It's just too unbelievable."

That was not totally true, but Sam Butler would never admit his private knowledge to just anyone. Ed had complained on many occasion that the job, his wife, the small town life, it held him down, crushed him in its weight of normalcy and predictability. Just once, he often reveled, he'd like something out of the ordinary to run headlong into his life and shake it up a little. Not an earth shattering transformation, but something that would break the monotony briefly. Sam had wondered aloud if that meant a job change, hitting the lottery, or, dare he say it, a chance encounter with another woman.

"Well, hell no, Sam. I could never do that to Erma. Wouldn't figure any gal would be willing enough to look my way anyhow. No, what I'm talking about," and it was here that Ed would look off in a dreamy way, as if seeing a vision that had played out a thousand times before in his head, "is something so unexpected yet welcome that I could go on it for years. You know, like meeting the President or saving someone's life. Stuff like that."

Not the daydreams of a man willing to leave everything behind for a life-altering experience. No, Ed would not walk away. Someone had helped misplace him.

"I'd like to start with people close to him – family, friends, fellow workers. We have no leads and maybe we can learn somewhere to start. It's important that we leave nothing to chance, Cody. Every statement is worthy of consideration."

Sam knew his deputy would handle himself professionally. It was one thing he never worried about with Cody. His fear was that the boy might overlook an important piece of information because he had not found it noteworthy.

"Standard investigative procedures. We need to know whether anyone noticed anything odd about Ed's behavior over the past few weeks. Anyone different he was seen with. A change in daily habits. Shoot, I want to know if he'd added an extra spoon of sugar to his coffee. This one's important to me, Cody. I need your best work."

Whether he understood the true measure of the case, Cody didn't offer, but there was no denying the commitment he had to Sam.

"You can count on me, Sheriff. I'll help you get this figured out. If I have to put in extra hours, I'm ready to do my job," Cody said.

"Well, that's good because it is going to mean additional hours. Ed Stevens is not our only concern though. I've been out to Pete Thompson's place, and he's nowhere to be found. His friends have still not heard from him. I want to believe he just up and headed to greener pastures, but he left everything he owned behind. Can't tell that he could have thrown a few things in his truck, but just like Ed, it's uncharacteristic."

Sam gave less consideration to the Thompson case for, professionally, all the wrong reasons. No family member was hounding him to find Pete. He had no job, no involvement in the community. Few people even noticed he was gone. Sam told himself that was not why he had put Pete on the back burner. It was Pete's lifestyle to remain unseen for days at a time, especially if he had found a few days work out of town. Eventually he had accepted it as another missing person's case, but up to now, driving out to his trailer had been all Sam had done in an investigative capacity. He planned on looking into it more once he got Cody started on Ed's case, maybe heading over to Pete's favorite hangout and asking some questions.

Having issued the deputy his instructions and watched him exit in a vaguely military fashion, Sam tucked the lab findings in a folder and filed them along side similar folders in a cabinet next to his desk. The number of records dealing with missing persons was not enormous, but when Sam considered the size of Raven and the recent additions to his files, it brought lines of concern to his brow. In the past eighteen months, five people were now missing, their locations unknown. Though all active investigations, the sheriff's office had exhausted all avenues. Sam had ultimately put the first three on the national wire, and feared Raven's most recent two disappearances would end up the same way.

What puzzled Sam about each case, and Ed and Pete were no exceptions, was that they all had similar profiles. The missing party literally vanished. No one saw them leave or remembered them in a suspicious situation. They apparently left on a whim without taking a thing or telling anyone, as if they just decided to skip town at a moment's notice. And what was the most mysterious about all the cases was that not a single usable lead had ever been discovered. It was like they had been teleported to a faraway land, unable to contact those who would be affected by their loss. No sign, no reason, just gone. It was bad enough that residents were leaving town in droves to avoid the likelihood that Raven would close shop, but vanishing in thin air? Sam could only shake his head and rely on steady police work to provide an answer. *If* an answer was out there.

■

While Sam Butler searched for an explanation to the events that were beginning to fill his case drawer, a possible answer to the dilemma awaited his witnessing only a mile from the station. As were many older communities in the Midwest, Raven had been laid out in a manner that gave meaning to the term *block*. A "main street" acted as the chief thoroughfare for the town, with equidistant neighboring roads lying parallel to it. Crossing these paths at a right angle were a like distribution of paved, blacktopped, and even partially bricked streets, creating a grid that, simple in its design, allowed for easier zoning, utility access, and, for those new to town, a sense of direction and site location.

Streets running north and south were numbered, descending as one headed east. The east/west roads were named, and though they were in alphabetical order, the titles assigned had failed to follow a theme or subject matter, what one would expect in a town so perfectly divided. The street signs of Raven did not reflect the names of trees or Presidents or a collective idea like desert names (Oasis Avenue, Palm Tree Lane, Camel Drive). Following the alphabet was apparently the best the town fathers were able to do. Best not to be too exotic, it seemed. Leave the exotic names to the big city boys.

It was on the corner of Fifteenth Street and Miller that Sheriff Butler needed to be instead of stuck in his office debating whether to make the drive to The Watering Hole to keep at least one of his promises, made to himself regarding the Pete Thompson investigation. In his backyard contemplating the state of his prize tulip beds, Roland Densmore wiped his beaded brow and shook his head. The lack of sufficient rain coupled with a heat he couldn't remember in his thirty-five years in Raven had done its job on the tulips. Roland asked for little in his life, and the tulips, which had moved from a hobby to a passion, were now being taken away from him.

"Dead," Roland professed. "Dead and gone."

What water he could provide the flowers seemed to evaporate quickly, leaving him with dry, brittle dirt and the sobering image of plants hanging their heads in agony. The forecast had not promised a change, and Roland had given in to the prospects of a failed year of strikingly beautiful yellow and red tulips. Jimmy Trathor had featured him last year in the paper about this time, providing a humbling photo of the man and his organic children. It had become his trademark, what people recognized as an accomplishment, and Roland had leaned on this single moment to carry him through to the next.

Jimmy would certainly not be out this year to waste film on a browning patch of colorless and wilting flowers. *Game over. Hit the showers, big boy. You just didn't have it this year.* It was enough to drive a serious gardener crazy. How was he supposed to operate under these conditions? Who would expect anything from him when he was fighting a lack of rain, killer temperatures, and unbearable humidity?

Roland bent with his hoe to try to discover a rich life waiting only centimeters below the surface, but as he pulled the tool toward him, it only skimmed the solid surface, taking a faint chunk of dirt here and there in an effort to do its duty. It was useless. Better to let the beds die out, till the soil in the fall, and hope for better circumstances next year. Turning his back on the source of a great deal of pride for many years was difficult for Roland. The plants were the one thing in his life that brought satisfaction, but there was no beating the weather.

Before heading back inside his terminally empty house, he walked across the crunching lawn to the backyard shed to relieve himself of the hoe. As he put it back among his other tools, he realized that he would not need to make a return visit to the shed for quite a while. Mowing, weed eating, turning the soil, nothing was necessary at this point in what would surely be a storied summer in Raven's history.

Roland turned from the closed double doors and walked toward the back door of the house when he stopped in a dizzying rush of vertigo. His eyes had lost focus in that brief second, and he held his head forward in this right hand and let the sensation pass.

Wow, thought Roland. *That was weird*. He had not been outside for more than five minutes, having declared his death sentence on the flowerbeds very early in the game. He squinted his eyes hard, once, twice, and then lifted his vision back to the house again. Better, but a lingering pain remained at his temples. The heat was certainly not healthy to plants or humans in Roland's estimation, and he figured he better get inside, fix himself a cool drink, and let the living room recliner take some of his ills away.

Within his next few steps, Roland felt a tremendous weight descend upon him, leaving him bent over and moving as if in wet cement. He was in fair shape for a man of his age, so the sudden physical symptoms he was experiencing made little sense to him. He was not prepared for the rapid progression of agony that overtook his body - the throbbing temples, the cloistering, enveloping heat, or the inability to draw a deep breath. Roland stood puzzled and very afraid, unconditioned to responding to his present situation. A scream stuck unwillingly in his throat, which was readily constricting the passage of air in or out.

His vision failing, the pressure increasing across his entire body geometrically, Roland resembled the very flowers he had just passed sentence on, bent and lifeless. Inside his raging mind, he cried out in desperation, begging for an end to the excruciating pain that racked his body. The world he knew, a world of simple tasks and retired labors, was emptying into one of fire and unmerciful pain. Roland knew nothing of the landscape that lay before him. Only minutes ago crossing the same yard he had traversed countless times for many years, he now saw blackness, a wasteland of nothingness at his feet, and seemingly beyond.

In a final crescendo of all-encompassing physical agony, Roland sensed a drawing of his very essence from the tortured shell that had once been his body. In the split second before he was no longer, Roland envisioned something tearing him open like a package and feasting on what lived inside.

9

With the dishes put away and the kids off in their rooms seeking further entertainment before the close of the day, Carrie sat at the kitchen table with a few department store flyers, seeing nothing of interest as she mindlessly flipped the pages and thought about the events of the past few hours. She was caught up in a whirlwind of activity the moment she stepped in the door of her own house after work, getting laundry going, welcoming the kids home and dealing with the subsequent battles that followed, and finally getting dinner started.

As the relentless sun seared the horizon and marked the end of another oppressive day, Carrie sat and allowed the moment to wash over her. She had ignored her thoughts as they repeatedly sought answers to her day's enigma, but now, with her labors accomplished, her mind drifted to the house on Vandalia.

Once she had opened the front door of the house, the fog that had enveloped her mind was instantly swept away and she was able to conduct her business in earnest. Surprisingly, she was at the top of her game, giving a tour and presentation that would have made the King of Siam want to live in an outhouse if so similarly introduced. It was only moments earlier that she had been startled to consciousness on the very living room floor she now crossed, painting a beautiful landscape of possibilities that awaited the potential buyers if they made this house their own. Reviews of her performances were usually not revealed until clients had a day or two to "talk it over," but Carrie was rewarded when she was told the couple had to have the place. *Had to*, not, *it's nice, we'll think it over and get back with you*. They were to meet with her the next morning in her office to get the paperwork started. Carrie had not felt her typical pride in a sale. What came over her was more of a relief, as if it was crucial to her well being that she sell the house. It was undeniable that she had pushed the house, an approach she had never taken before and, in fact, had promised herself to avoid. But a feeling of fear and dread drove her if she failed, and so theatrics and embellishment took over for the first time. Some realtors traveled this road, acting like the stereotypical used car dealer. It had always been what Carrie hated in realty, the pushiness, and if necessary, the lies to cover the truth about a home's misgivings. She felt dirty and in many ways criminal, and Carrie could only blame herself. Placing blame on the events prior to her appointment would be a cop-out, she knew. And what of those events? She had little memory and less desire to recall.

The other part of her day that led to this moment of self-searching was lunch with Bill. What had started out as an innocent, relaxing opportunity to do some catching up with a friend had turned into a verbal free-for-all and ultimately miserable meal. She still held some resentment for Walt, that was obvious, but the sight of Bill had given her a target to vent some of those feelings.

She saw his good intentions now, but as she sat at the table across from him and listened to his views on Raven, Carrie was overcome with an anger and protective reaction that had surprised even her. She had to resolve in her own mind all this business with Walt. He was gone, apparently of his own device, and she was left to pick up the pieces. Friends of his like Bill, true friends who wanted to believe that something unlawful had led to Walt's departure, were not the enemy. If she was going to continue an adjustment (here it was a year) then the time to start was way past due. She knew her attack of Bill had been in keeping with her feelings about Walt and Raven lately, but the time to take the next step was now. Anger was what kept her unhappy. Making Raven the only thing good in her life would keep her lonely. It was important that she fix both soon.

The ring of the phone would make the fixing begin sooner than she had thought.

"Hi, Carrie. It's Bill. Listen, about today. I..."

"Stop right there. Let me say something first," Carrie said, hoping she could say the right things to explain her behavior. "I overreacted, and for the life of me I can't tell you why. I don't even know myself. If you want to tell me I am a nut, and you can't imagine being in the same hemisphere with me ever again, I understand. I can't apologize enough other than to say I am sorry and hope this hasn't jeopardized our friendship."

Carrie bit her lip and waited. The sales pitch was over. She meant what she was saying to Bill and wasn't sure how crazy and moody she might have been today. If he told her the prospects of getting together in the future were probably a bad idea in light of everything that had gone on, she would not blame him. The fact that he held onto the silence a little longer made Carrie doubt he had heard the sincerity in her voice.

"Wow. I...I don't know what to say," Bill stammered, the words that had poured from Carrie evidently taking him aback. "I really was just calling to tell you that *I* was sorry for the disaster lunch turned out to be."

"What?"

"Yeah, I overstepped my bounds on the Raven stuff, and I should have just kept my big, capitalist mouth shut. You're the realtor. You know what's best for you and your clients. I promise to stay out of your business if you'll forgive me."

"Bill, you have every right to express your opinion. I have always wanted it in the past, but today I...I don't know. Can we just forget about it?" Carrie said. She was reaching out to a friend, one she recognized as just that, and it had become important to her that he stay that way.

"Friends?" he offered.

"Friends."

"And to prove it, let's try lunch again first thing Monday, what do you say?" Bill said.

In this moment of feeling accepted, in feeling valued, Carrie's response was still surprising to her, but she had a need to talk further about herself, specifically what had happened to her at the house today. She didn't know if Bill would have the answers, but she had leaned on his common sense and helpfulness when things had not been in sync with her life before, so she thought it only natural that his assistance be requested now.

"Bill, I have no idea what you have going this evening, and I hope I don't sound too silly all over again, but could we possibly make that get-together happen now, at my house? I need to talk about something that went on today, and I don't think it can wait until after the weekend."

"Well, I was planning on cleaning the cat's litter box and paying a few bills, but your offer sounds so much more entertaining. I'd be glad to come by. Say thirty minutes?" Bill said.

"Thanks, Bill. Thanks a lot. See you in half an hour."

Carrie hung up the phone and sighed a breath of relief. At least she had not destroyed a friendship in the course of the day. Remarkably, Bill was not only going to come over to give credence to their status, but he may be able to shed some light on her experience. She found comfort in the former, but wasn't sure if Bill could perform one of his little miracles on the latter.

She looked down at the glass tabletop and through to her legs in the chair. Had she really floated above the floor? Where had she gone, physically and mentally, in the course of those few minutes? She hoped Bill could provide her with some answers without thinking she really was crazy.

Carrie was readying the kids for bed when Bill arrived. They each had to see him, especially Sara, who had always had a strong affection for him and was instantly in his lap with a hundred questions when he was around. Walt used to allow it for a brief minute or two then would ask Carrie to get her busy with something else so the men could talk or enjoy their game on television. Bill, on the other hand, always made the most of his time with Sara, and Carrie had often thought he would have made a good father if he had ever had children. A house full of screaming kids had never been a part of his ex-wife's plans from the start, so Bill had seemingly relished these occasions when visiting, showing a general interest in everything Carrie's daughter had to say and encouraging her to tell him as much as possible in their limited conversations.

And now, here, with Sara in serious discussion about a certain toy she had played with at school as she sat securely on Bill's knee, Carrie fought the impulse to remove the child as Walt invariably instructed and let Bill the adult determine when enough was enough. She knew Sara would go all night if given the opportunity, so she tempered her decision later with the suggestion that Bill tuck Sara in bed for the night.

"And read a story?" Sara asked, looking up from her perch with eyes that couldn't be denied.

"And read a story," Bill said.

Carrie objected to his having to do anything since it was her invitation to talk that had brought him there, but he insisted.

"I don't mind at all. I want to," he said, and as he carried Sara piggyback down the hall, Carrie berated herself for ever coming to words with such a kind, gentle man.

While Carrie made coffee and straightened up the den, she could hear Bill softly relating a tale from one of the many children's books on the shelf in Sara's bedroom. For an instant she had a sense of completeness, as if Walt were back home and the family was back to normal. It had all been taken away so quickly, without warning. She knew the only thing that would end these fits of reminiscence would be some sort of closure, some answer to the abrupt change her life had experienced. Until then, visions of the way it was, accompanied by resentment, would continue to attach themselves to her thoughts.

Bill soon joined her, settling in on the couch across from her in his relaxed manner.

"You've got some great kids, Carrie. And that daughter of yours.

Whenever you tire of them, let me know, and I'll take them off your hands," he said with genuine honesty.

"You say that now, but give yourself one night of arguing and resistance, and you would have them roped and gagged on my front porch the next day," she said.

Bill could only laugh at this, which Carrie encouraged considering the serious nature of what conversation lay ahead, if she could even bring herself to tell her tale.

"Okay. We got off on the wrong foot today, " Bill said, crossing his arms as he leaned back in the corner of the couch. Let people who studied body language tell you that it was a sign of defense. Carrie saw a man open and forthright. "Tell me what needed discussed immediately, and I'll sit here and listen. I checked my opinion at the door."

Carrie was so thankful for Bill, his help always coming at no charge, without expectation of reimbursement. With that in mind, she couldn't understand why now she was hesitant to breach the subject of her experience prior to her clients' arrival this afternoon. Maybe because it sounded so insane she feared Bill would be thinking only the worst about her mental health. If she couldn't fathom what had happened to her, how could he? He wasn't a doctor or psychologist. She wasn't sure if even those professions could help her. She didn't know what she needed, but short of going to a priest for exorcism, her choices were not clear.

"The fact that I value your opinion is why I needed to talk to you. I had something happen to me today that, I don't know, scared me a great deal. Would you like some coffee?"

Bill leaned to the coffee table in front of them and held his cup as Carrie poured.

"You know I would do anything in my power to see that you and the kids were all right," Bill started. "I realized you probably needed some period of, well, adjustment, following Walt's disappearance, so I have tried to remain on the perimeter while you sort things out. I let you know a long time ago, before the job, before anything, that you could count on me. No strings attached. You and Walt were, are, my friends. I don't forget friends."

If Carrie wasn't feeling any guilt for summoning Bill with little warning before, she felt it now.

"And that is why I've turned to you," she said. "I have really no excuses for the last year. Brooding over Walt. Not even sure if he simply left. I didn't want to drag anyone else down with me. Make my problems theirs, you know what I mean?"

Carrie felt the cork on her emotions beginning to loosen, the months of frustration and bitterness seeking release, nearing the surface.

"I thought I was dealing fine with everything - the job, the kids, the house - by myself. No help, thank you. I envisioned the world standing in amazement as I juggled it all alone. But then today..."

She broke briefly at this point, fighting back the flood that stood poised to engulf her. Bill took her hands and let the moment pass uninterrupted. Within a few seconds, she was collected and he let her continue.

"Bill, something happened to me today that makes me think I haven't dealt with life very well lately, if ever. I don't know if I'm losing my mind or what, but I can tell you I'm worried, and I need a rational answer before I really lose it." Carrie sipped from her cup and tried to steady her nerves.

Up to this point, Bill had listened patiently, failing to show any reaction that would divulge his summation of her dialogue.

"Tell me what happened" was all Bill offered, giving Carrie every reason to believe he was there for her, to help and not to judge. He looked at her with interest and concern, making what Carrie was about to tell him more manageable.

"Okay, here goes. But remember, as my friend you have to give me a twenty minute head start before you call the guys in the white coats."

By the time both of their cups' contents were cold and forgotten, Carrie had recounted her afternoon in the living room on Vandalia. The story had not come easily, as she stopped many times between tears of confusion to gather herself. In the end she was able to tell everything, and in the telling recall some things she had not remembered. Bill was intent and silent throughout, giving her the time necessary with little reaction.

When Carrie was finished, she sat expectantly, kneading her napkin and wondering just how crazy she had come off in her storytelling. She looked at Bill and tried to see what he was thinking. He didn't make her wait long.

"Carrie, first of all, you don't need to be troubling yourself with thoughts of insanity or that you are incapable of handling your responsibilities. From the story you told me, I think we are talking about someone who has worked herself to death trying to prove she can get along without anyone's help."

"But I haven't been tired, sleepy, anything like that," Carrie said. Bill shook his head and continued.

"That's not what I am talking about. You have been pushing yourself so hard - making something of the job, keeping the house and family going - that you took a little siesta, a break from your reality for a while. Like a daydream, only you did it in the living room of a house you were selling." Now it was Carrie's turn to shake her head, but Bill was insistent.

"You may not feel physically tired, Carrie, but you have gone through a mental workout over the last year. It seems very natural to me that you could doze off while taking a break and dream of still another demand being put on you. It's how your life has been. Nothing but demands."

Carrie was not sold on the idea.

"No. I didn't lie down on the floor and get a catnap in before my clients showed up. I was walking the house, standing in the living room. Only horses sleep standing up."

"But you said yourself that you were lying on the floor when the knock came on the door. You were resting, Carrie. Taking a break while you waited for your clients to show up. The subject of your dream is understandable. I wouldn't worry," Bill said, his assurance hard to deny. "If you had dreamed that the house had four legs and walked down the road, I would still blame it on mental fatigue. When is the last time you took some time off for yourself?"

Carrie remained skeptical. "I don't know. It seemed so real, so there. And then I pushed that house down their throats, like I had to sell it or else. Still, I was on the floor when the Lipscombs arrived."

"Of course you pushed the house," Bill countered. "It was a natural reaction to your mind's demands, demands that you have put on yourself for too long now."

"Are you sure I'm not crazy to have had a...a dream like that, with a voice telling me to help it?" Carrie said, needing answers when she was unable to provide her own. She wanted to believe what Bill was telling her, wanted to accept the theory that she had gone too long too hard, that her mind had taken the vacation she was denying it. She hoped he was right.

"Crazy? You are the last person I would label with that adjective. It's a testament to your sanity that you have survived this past year without throwing in the towel." Bill was confident and evidently trying to pass that on to Carrie. "No, Ma'am, you're not crazy, but you are if you don't find some time for yourself. Start doing things with *you* in mind. No job, no kids. Let me watch them one night and you just get away. Seriously."

"I couldn't ask that of you. You've done enough already," Carrie said.

Bill once again disagreed. "You could and you will. Really, it's for your own good. Find a night next week and take care of Carrie."

She was struck with a feeling of gratefulness that, unlike her just told story, she couldn't describe. Bill was once again there for her, even after the tirade she had thrown over lunch. He really was a special person. A friend.

"I'll tell you what. Make that an evening out with you, and I'll consider it," she said, feeling the flush on her face again but too relieved to be ashamed.

"You've got a deal," Bill said.

Carrie realized with his response that they might have ushered in a new phase of their friendship.

10

Raven had been the object of many changes over the past decades; changes similar to those of other towns its size, but the increasing frequency of citizen loss made it unique in its devolution. During the weeks following Carrie's "experience," two more residents were reported missing, including Roland Densmore, who failed to empty his mailbox or attend two community gatherings, enough to create suspicion and request an inquiry by local associates. What Sam Butler had on his hands as sheriff was an epidemic of frightening proportions, limiting the number of explanations while increasing the inevitability of outside law enforcement intervention. If he were unable to make any progress within the next few days, the sheriff knew his hands were tied, and he could only imagine the result - state authorities would descend upon Raven to take over the investigation from the incompetent local officers. This was the last thing he wanted at such a critical juncture in the town's future and the future of his office. County patrol units, though not always at a beckoned call, would look very attractive to a town steeped in a financial bind and riddled with unsolved crime. There was certainly no valid reason to keep funding a department that was not performing its duty, and the public outcry alone would guarantee this. He needed answers, and he needed them quickly.

Sam elicited the aid of an acquaintance from his days at the police academy for some fresh ideas as to the cause of his predicament. The years and the opposite directions of their careers made Sam uncomfortable in conversation, but he was determined to sacrifice pride to move forward. Steve Edwards, former special investigator and currently head of the state bureau's missing person's unit, had been a young and eager recruit when he and Sam parted ways twenty years ago. Though contact between the two had diminished over time, due in a large part to Edwards' rise in the ranks of law enforcement, Sam had kept tabs on his classmate for just such a problem. You could never have too many associations in the business, and Sam hoped this one would pay off.

After a few forced pleasantries, the men got down to the purpose of Sam's call. He outlined the numerous cases as quickly but accurately as possible, combining the chief qualities they all shared. Edwards listened intently, interjecting questions here and there as Sam told his story.

"It's a baffling situation, Steve. I hope you can help," the sheriff said. It had not taken long for Sam to assume a submissive posture, and he hated himself for it.

"Glad to give you my thoughts, but you realize that if you are unable to come up with some usable information regarding the location of these missing persons, my department must involve itself. It's a wonder you have allowed things to go on this long as it is," Edwards said, in his best voice of reprimand.

Sam fought the will to hang up. "I hoped something would break before now. At least if I had a body or proof of crime, I could justify the state's involvement. Right now all I have is the unknown whereabouts of eight people, three of those in the last month.

"And you say the basic facts are the same in each instance - no evidence of foul play, no eyewitnesses, no history or explanations pointing to their leaving town? One minute they're in Raven, the next minute they're gone." Edwards didn't sound convinced. "You're sure you haven't missed something?"

Sam regretted the call already, but he trudged on.

"I have had your crime lab boys down here three times recently. They've found nothing. I've interviewed, retraced, and put out bulletins. No one has turned up. I'm beginning to believe in E.T."

"E.T. in Hicksville, USA. Who would have thought?" Edwards laughed in his condescending voice. "Case closed."

Sam remembered his old friend as being free of humility, but the years had really elevated his opinion of himself. He knew that the only thing that had kept Edwards and his gang of death stalkers out of Raven had been a lack of substantiated evidence that a crime had taken place, let alone a homicide. Sam was sure he would have a hard time dealing with the likes of Steve Edwards in his jurisdiction.

"So, what would you suggest at this point?" Sam asked.

Edwards breathed heavily, possibly stumped by the request, which brought a flash of a smile to Sam's face. *The big shot has no advice*, he thought.

"Short of letting my boys down there for a crack at your information and checking out the potential crime scenes, I would say you have two options," he said. "It doesn't sound like that many people in such a concentrated area would just up and leave their families and possessions behind. First, step up patrols. Visibility keeps prospective criminals at bay in most cases. Have your officers pull extra duty for a few weeks to establish your presence."

Little did Edwards know that Cody was it, a fact Sam was unwilling to confide.

"Second. Make a general public announcement seeking any information regarding the disappearances. It means exposing your department as ineffectual. There is even the chance of a hysterical reaction, but most of the community is probably up on the news anyway. Use your local paper if you have one. Assure them there is no reason for alarm. Remember, it is sometimes all right to admit to the public when you need their assistance. Local authorities do it all the time."

But not you state people, huh, Steve? No, you guys don't rely on anyone.

"In the meantime, keep my office posted on any new developments. You're at a crossroads here, Sam. Something will break quickly once you get the wheels in motion."

Sam was afraid he was right. Admission of what sounded like incompetence, though, was sure to put the final nail in the department's coffin. *Here lies the Raven Police Department. We failed to serve and protect.*

"Well, thanks, Steve. I'll stay in touch."

Leaning back in his chair after one of the most humiliating moments in his career, Sam closed his eyes and tried to relax. He felt helpless, more so than before deciding to make the call. What he had been told was obvious. Sam, good buddy, you have nothing to go on, especially with your primitive knowledge in investigative procedure. Kneel before the people that pay you and beg for their help. Forget your pride, your dignity as sheriff, and admit when you can't stay in the game.

Sam retrieved the phone and called Jimmy Trathor.

■

Carrie tossed her purse on the bed and headed into the bathroom to remove an evening's worth of entertainment and revelry. She had spent another fabulous few hours with Bill, this time at Paul's Valley's popular nightspot for drinks and dancing, something she hadn't done even when

Walt was around (he didn't like dancing or crowds). It had taken her back to a youthful period in her life when letting loose and kicking back were not only possible but also meant to be. She had missed out on most of the party atmosphere surrounding young adulthood, the carefree lifestyle of limited responsibility. Instead she found herself married and pregnant before settling down had even crossed her mind. Walt had rumbled through her life at an impressionable time, and she got caught up in his runaway dreams of family and success. Still in college and just beginning to taste the pleasures that freedom offers, Carrie failed to recognize the true sacrifice she would be making, the pushing aside of years of growing as an individual to share in the visions of a man she truly knew only superficially. Not that she hadn't loved Walt and been proud of the life they had created for themselves, but there were often those moments of regret, of longing for a missed part of her life. Tonight, Bill had provided a way for her to recapture some of that abandoned time she had considered lost forever.

Switching on the light, Carrie scrutinized herself in the mirror. Everything had held together remarkably well considering the activity she had put it through. Hair, make-up (she had excused herself midway through the evening to see what needed touching up), and dress had proven resilient, up to the challenge of physical activity both the music and Bill had demanded. He wanted to dance every dance, reluctant to sit until her insistence dragged him from the parquet floor back to their table.

"You have to give me a break every now and then. I'm out of practice and definitely not as young as I used to be," she had said. Bill showed the advancement of time on his own face, out of breath with sweat beading his forehead, but he was determined to spend more time on the crowded floor, as if the heat of the day were not enough.

"Okay, we'll take a quick break, but not for long. Listen to that beat," he gasped, seemingly not the least bit conscious of his exhaustion.

Carrie closed the bathroom door and turned the shower faucet to hot, letting the water warm up as she removed her clothing. The kids had been asleep for hours according to the sitter, and she didn't want to wake them as she readied for bed. A shower had sounded wonderful after leaving Bill at the front door. He was gracious enough to drive the babysitter home after they returned, eliminating another awkward moment like the one they had experienced only four nights previous.

Their relationship was growing, the comfort and ease they felt with each other's company obvious, but there still hadn't been a physical sign of affection. That first night out, a simple dinner at the only formal restaurant still operating in Raven, Mattie's Place, had opened the door to an ever-deepening friendship. Carrie thought Bill was fumbling with the thoughts of showing his increased interest the same way she was, but the timing had never been right. They had now been in what she considered a dating capacity for two weeks now, either lunch, dinner, or in tonight's case, dancing, and not a single brush of the hand or peck on the cheek had resulted. It was a trying period for both of them; neither having been out since becoming single, so Carrie realized it would be a while before they moved to the next level, if they went there at all.

Bill seemed taken with her, but she was beginning to wonder. *Maybe he needs more assurance from me,* as she readied two towels and then stepped into the shower.

Once adjusted, the water felt fabulous, and she lingered under the spray until the water tank began to signal its demise. She shut off the water and reached for one of the towels, her arm moving through the concentration of steam that filled the entire bathroom. After toweling off and putting her hair up in the other, Carrie gathered her robe from the back of the door, put it on, and stepped out.

The mirror was completely fogged over as Carrie glimpsed and then stared into its murky haze, immediately struck with a surprisingly comfortable feeling of déjà vu. She made no move to swipe the mirror's surface or open the bathroom door to allow the steam to escape. There was no reason because the familiarity of the moment brought no fear.

Carrie stood rigid, her eyes fixated as a peacefulness overtook her. The relaxing shower was only a prelude to the pleasure this experience conveyed. It was just like the Vandalia home, the sense of floating without a care, a feeling of detachment from the physical world, and ultimately the recognition of a presence and the feeling of not being alone. It was almost instantaneous, and soon everything around her was forgotten. Nothing mattered but that she drifted with this tide of welcome sensation. How much time was passing she could never say, but she wasn't concerned.

She gave herself willingly to whatever had come over her, like a lover surrendering what remained of her individuality to become one with another. And again, a voice, intoxicating, sending soothing vibrations across the length of her body with each syllable.

"Carrie. I need you. I need more. Bring them to me. I must have them to survive."

The appeal was genuine, and Carrie felt the need described as if it were her own.

"Help me, Carrie. Help me. I will die without them."

The richness, the sensual allure of the voice was so satisfying to Carrie that she was left wanting when the communication ended. As before, she couldn't respond, was unable to transmit the myriad of questions that filled her mind. She was but a receiver, though she believed she had not heard but felt the intimate voice. Whatever the meaning was behind the message she had been given, the speaker chose not to discuss.

Carrie roused on the floor of the bathroom disoriented but unharmed. She lay there for a few minutes, collecting her thoughts and finding her memory of the event intact. She eventually sat up, pulled the already cockeyed towel from her head, and walked into the bedroom where she dressed for bed. The ability to perform normal tasks after such an incredibly abnormal adventure never crossed her mind. Carrie climbed under the covers confused, yet refreshed and invigorated at the same time.

She lay in the dark for several minutes, reliving the moment, and questioning whether she should bring this to Bill's attention again. He had been very dismissive of her story before, passing it off as the daydreams of an overworked single mother. She had known better then but had chosen to appear satisfied with his summation to bring peace to their friendship. Now, more than ever, she recognized the truth in what she recalled, the significance of the experience. For a reason she failed to fully understand, something or someone needed her to help it, to provide for it. Provide what? Who were they, and what use could she be? So many questions, yet so little to provide answers. Carrie resolved to find those answers, but how she didn't know.

11

A week after the Lipscombs moved into their new home on Vandalia, word had already reached each ear residing in Raven that the police department was requesting any help in the substantial number of disappearances that continued to threaten the community. Since Sheriff Butler's appeal had appeared in the paper, one more unexplainable occurrence had increased the list of missing persons. Butler continued to fatten his files, but he failed to get any closer to an answer. His phone was a never-ending cycle of rings, from either local residents in fear or suspicious of their neighbors to interested news organizations. By now state investigators were planning a workable time to take over the cases, as tales of Raven's unique troubles were spreading nationwide. As a result, Jim Trathor was a wanted man, the journalistic key for every major news source that did not want to go the final step and send its own people to the site. Stories were quick to circulate as to the reasons behind the growing list of missing persons. Whether it was a serial killer who disposed of the bodies without leaving a trace (Sam always laughed at that one because even he, a small town cop, knew serial murderers wanted their deeds made public) or a bout of hysteria that was forcing people to leave by droves, the truth remained that Raven was dealing with a special situation that needed resolved. The puzzling decline of the population was systematically deciding the fate of the town's existence. There would soon be no one around to qualify Raven as nothing more than a spot in the road if the rate of disappearances continued.

The recent events and media attention had not escaped the eyes or ears of Raven's own historical society, The Circle at Cleeger's. Mason Givens, as was his ceremonial right, oversaw the discussions everyday at the back of the store, and it was the collective opinion of the group that something unfortunate had befallen their town and it wasn't going to stop any time soon. One of their very own, Taft Sindler, retired and widowed, the perfect recipe for Circle attendance, had not shown up at the hardware store for three days when the most recent call went out to add a name to the list. Though the loss of Jesse Caufield earlier did not instigate discussion (the group had chewed on theories for weeks, including Johnny Flaim's idea that due to the heat, people were spontaneously combusting throughout town), the Circle was determined to find an answer with Taft's departure.

Some of the talk had become so heated lately that Fred Cleeger had on more than one occasion told the men to quiet down while customers were present. Passers-by may discount the conversations as harmless, a pursuit best suited for those in society caught in their twilight years, but for Mason Givens companions, it was vital to Raven's future.

"We're reaping what we've sown, I'm telling you," Mason said, sitting in his familiar chair in an even more familiar pose, arms crossed, head slightly tilted with his chair. It may not have been a stature that demanded respect and undivided attention, but he got it anyway. His voice, even at a whisper, caught the ear like a fish and reeled it in.

"When people let a town fall apart, have businesses closing, and folks are out of work, all the stuff we've seen happening here, there is retribution. There is payback."

No one ever questioned the words of Mason. His look was like ice; his comebacks were usually biting. Like Shakespeare's Petruchio, if he said the sun was the moon, you were his Katherine and went along with it. Veterans of the Circle understood this, though not all days were exclusive to their presence. The occasional newcomer would come across the group or hear of the Circle's daily passing of time and join in. It was days like today that the green among them would taste the wrath of their leader.

"Payback? Who'd care enough to wipeout a couple dozen people because the town is collapsing?" Ned Garrett, in Cleeger's to buy a new watering hose, had fallen within earshot of the conversation. Up to this point, he had listened without comment, but now he chose to demonstrate his youthful ignorance.

Mason looked hard at this new arrival with downcast eyes, the only movement that signaled he had even heard Ned's rebuttal. Ned, a moment earlier confident in his observation, now cringed under the elder man's stare.

"*I'd* care, son. Raven's been my home for more than half a century. I'd care. And if you knew what few of you youngsters knew these days, you'd put more of yourself in your town."

Ned reddened, belittled after just seconds ago strutting like a rooster.

"I just meant...it seemed unlikely to me that...just for a town?"

It came out with far less confidence than the words that had preceded it. Ned was cooked, basting in the juices of embarrassment, as the rest of the onlookers offered no support. He had jumped out there with such self-certainty. Let him sink or swim on his own.

"I know what you meant, son. You and every other kid cock sure of life. Well, let me tell you. There's things out there you haven't seen, haven't dealt with. Things you know nothing about. So as soon as you know-it-alls have been educated about life, then you can stick your nose in. 'Til then, mind your place."

Mason left little doubt about his feelings when he spoke, and for the amateurs like Ned Garrett, it was a hard lesson to take. Ned shoved his hands deep in his pockets and stared at his shifting feet on the dusty floor. He stood by idly for a few more minutes, eventually slouching away down the aisle to end both his shopping and his misery.

Such was the fate of those that challenged the wisdom of the Circle - a swift, unforgiving dose of reality, guaranteed to be hard to swallow. The men continued their exchanges as always, leaving no stone unturned as they solved the riddles of life's important mysteries. The relevance to Raven being the only tool by which to measure its seriousness.

■

The searing sun cast a short shadow at the feet of Ned Garrett as he stepped off the sidewalk in front of Cleeger's. He squinted at the storefront windows, contemplating a return to face off with Mason Givens once again, but thought better of it and crossed the street to his car. It was midday, and if Raven's downtown had what could be called a busy time, it was now. Most residents commuted to outlying areas for work, but those that held jobs in town usually came to Main Street for lunch. A café and small burger stand were all the town menu offered, but some came to Raven's heart just to pass the time, to spy old acquaintances, or cruise the remaining shops until their break was over.

Ned pulled out of his space and headed up Main, topping off his anger with the realization that he had left without a hose, his whole purpose for coming. Working night shifts at the glass factory in Elroy, Ned spent most of his afternoons piddling around an empty house or filling his hours in town. Sleep didn't come easy to him, though he would get in three or four hours on his return home each morning, just in time to kiss his wife Jill good-bye as she headed to work. He hoped for a day shift soon; it was his option when the next spot came open. Until then he would deal with it.

He hadn't planned on the confrontation with Mason when he walked into Cleeger's, the excuse of replacing gardening equipment as valid in his mind as any other reason to bail from home for a few hours. He had read the police department's appeal for information in the recent disappearances, had even spoken briefly the day before with Noah Carpenter at the grocery, but the gravity of the situation had not pressed him until overhearing the men. What had they said? Something about the town's downfall as the motivation for revenge. Revenge carried out by whom? It had struck Ned as totally off base, a thought hatched from the ponderings of a bunch of, well, senile old men, who had nothing better to do then fabricate an exaggerated version of the cause of Raven's plight. He thought checkers was the most aggressive thinking a senior citizen undertook, and now he understood why it should stay that way.

Mason had been quite convincing, yes, but to honestly believe that detective novel stuff? What a fool. The town was closing some of its last chapters, true. Its existence was almost played out. The fact that people were turning up missing was purely coincidental. Raven was losing residents by the droves in legitimate form; most were relocating before the town doors were shut permanently. It was obvious to Ned that some people were leaving without any hoopla. There had been many nights prior to leaving for work that he had told Jill their future lay somewhere else, and they ought to consider getting out now as opposed to later when it would be more difficult to sell the house. He had to admit he had too much invested to walk away from everything, the house, most of their possessions, but who could say what value other people placed on those kinds of things. Maybe these folks who everyone was talking about as missing just wanted a clean start, to wash their hands of Raven and its deteriorating conditions and find a fresh place. Nothing to remind them of the disappointments they left behind. Just get up from the chair, grab the keys, and go.

Ned's thoughts sounded pretty convincing to himself, until his rational mind was reminded that many of the missing had abandoned their cars, their families, even their final paychecks to follow his make-believe road to fulfillment. That seemed extreme, he had to admit. But he couldn't buy into the tall tale of a lunatic reeking havoc in a small sandbox like Raven because no one wanted to play anymore. It was a ridiculous answer to what he thought needed a logical approach. Whatever the cause, he gave it no more consideration as he pulled into his driveway.

Waving at Mrs. Longdale across the street who was checking her mailbox, a task she performed unerringly ten to twelve times a day until she struck pay dirt, Ned bent to peer into his own box on the curb when a wave of dizziness struck him. It was a distortion of the eyes and a wave of sickness in his stomach. He righted himself with a jerk, squinting his eyes against the sun as he searched for steadiness. Like a drunken sailor on a tossing ship, Ned searched for support with his flailing hands but found none as his knees crumbled beneath him and left him sitting in the road next to the curb. He was confused and a little scared as he started to stand, then thought better of it. He tried to let the feeling pass, but with each wave of disorientation, and the start of a throbbing in his temples, he began to think he was in trouble.

Panic crept into his mind, pushing his rational thoughts aside as he tried to scramble to his feet. They couldn't find purchase though, and as Ned finally pushed from all fours to a standing position, he stumbled headlong across the lawn a few yards and crashed painfully into the ground face first.

Help. He needed help in the worst way. He turned his head toward Mrs. Longdale, and for the first time noticed the difficulty in simple movement, but her back was to him as she shuffled back up her driveway to await her next gold rush. He tried to call out, but when he opened his mouth, a faint crackle of his vocal cords emerged. *I've got to get to the phone. Call for help.* Pushing himself to his hands and knees, he found himself in a struggle that took all his strength. From there he could go no farther, the exhaustion he felt was instantaneous and complete. His head hung toward his chest as he fought for each breath, and the pressure behind his eyes increased at an alarming rate. Over his entire body he began to become aware of a crushing pressure, forcing itself upon him from all directions. It felt like a vice exerting itself slowly, attempting to condense him in a small package.

He was going to burst, could feel the approach to red line, as all the bodily liquids housed in his shell of a frame sought escape. He was being reduced and consumed, was sure of it, though why he came to that conclusion he had little time to ponder. Ned looked again for assistance, but could see only waves of image, color, and light. In a last gasp of air, thick and acrid in its make-up, Ned Garrett witnessed the truth of Mason Givens words. He saw, and he believed.

June Longdale made the last few feet to her screen door, and grasping the handle, started to pull it toward her. Something made her stop momentarily, and looking over her shoulder, she examined the scenery before her. The dry summer heat had sapped everything, leaving a withered and brown landscape. Shimmering in the noon sun, the pavement of the street looked like a river bottom with a clear current passing over it. The illusion was so great that June swore that river rose into the Garrett's front yard, giving a rippling effect to the lower half of the house, their driveway, and the statuette propped near the walkway. June turned away and went into the cool comfort of her home, her brow narrowed to a set of creased lines as she wondered when Ned and Jill had decided to add a yard figure.

12

The temperature in Raven would eclipse the one hundred degree mark for the fifteenth straight day as Carrie negotiated a final turn into the parking lot and began what she envisioned would be an incredible day for her, Shephard Realty, and most importantly, Raven itself. The properties in Paul's Valley all but forgotten, Carrie was focusing her attention more than ever on pushing the homes no one else was willing or thought were possible to sell. She found she was unable to concentrate on anything else lately - her home, kids, even the recreated relationship with Bill. Armed with yard signs, newspaper ads, and a fevered desire to succeed at all costs, Carrie was devoting more and more time to the venture.

Ross Shephard and the other realtors had congratulated her uncanny success, at the same time whispering of her puzzling motivation. There was no commission large enough in the Raven area to warrant the effort she was putting forth. Shephard himself, the last man to suggest to an employee of his that they were unnecessarily burning the candle at both ends, had stopped Carrie during one of her short visits to the office gathering some paperwork to make sure she was all right.

"Carrie, I've noticed your solid commitment to the Raven properties, and I just wanted to, well, make sure everything is going all right. I mean, you're in and out of here so much I never get the chance to check in with you."

She stood over her desk, an explosion having covered its surface, sifting through papers and obviously trying to remember something.

"What? Oh, Ross, yes, I was looking for some appraisal copies. Is there something you needed?"

Carrie never looked up from her search, a harried look on her face belying the professional appearance she exhibited.

"I've got two appointments on adjoining properties on Thirty-second in less than an hour. Another after lunch. I don't think I can help with anything pressing today."

"No. No. I was just wondering if you have everything under control, and from the looks of it, I guess you do. I saw you moved three places last week in Raven alone. An incredible job."

Shephard watched as Carrie continued her hunt, appearing to talk to herself as she went. He wasn't sure if he was getting through or not.

"Carrie? Carrie?"

"Huh? Oh, sorry, Ross. It's just that...I have appointments. I need to get moving," she said, having found her lost treasure and now ready to set sail.

Shephard pressed no further. "Of course, you get on your way. Can't keep a Shephard client waiting. Good luck and let's move another one."

He punched the air with a right cross in emphasis of this last part, an awkward motion for a man of his girth, but Carrie was unaware as she grabbed her purse and headed out of the office.

She darted out the front door and to her car as Shephard watched the bright outdoors engulf her receding figure. He stood for a few minutes and contemplated what he frankly considered her *workaholic* behavior. Though she was a fine person and energetic worker, he had never seen the fire she had shown lately. Her appearance was never disheveled, but he could tell the schedule she was keeping was wearing her down. It would probably be a few more weeks, and she would be in his office explaining her need to take a break for a while, to gather herself. Her triumphs would earn her that time off. He certainly wouldn't dismiss a realtor having the unbelievable streak she was having. Not much money for either of them, but it kept the Shephard name out there, a recognized winner in the real estate game. Carrie was becoming a prime engineer in its operation, and if she was happy moving Raven homes now, he knew she would be valuable when that well ran dry and more profitable homes were in need of happy mortgagers. Until her inevitable collapse, he would give her free reign. She would either come to her senses soon or Raven's mysterious allure would end. Shephard nodded his head as he turned back to his own office, confident that time would take care of everything.

■

Carrie had failed to recognize the changes that were taking place in her approach to life in general. If anyone had been able to stop her train of thought for two minutes, a train on a non-stop trek to preserving Raven, they would have told her of their concern about her recent disposition. Off the job, she was constantly preoccupied, as if she were in a permanent daydream. Her own house was showing signs of neglect. Usually a stickler for cleanliness and order, Carrie gave little time to chores she once thought vitally important. Tim and Sara were more frequently arriving to an empty house, something that would have bothered her a week ago. When she was home, she drifted around the house from room to room, unable to sit still and acting like there was something she had forgotten to do. She talked to herself in low, questioning tones, a behavior Bill had noticed on more than one occasion. Just when they seemed to be moving in a direction of their shared choosing at a speed comfortable to both, Carrie was beginning to show disinterest.

During a dinner date following a busy day of open houses, Bill confronted her with his concerns, hoping to dispel his own fears that she was no longer a willing partner in their relationship.

Carrie played with the food on her plate, and as Bill chose his moment, he realized that he hadn't seen her appetite as poor as it was now. Even her clothes were showing a subtle hang in their wear, as if she may have dropped a size in the past few days. The list of changes was not earthshaking, but his growing care for her would not allow him to sit back and let her deteriorate along with their friendship.

"Carrie, there's something I wanted to talk to you about."

She continued rearranging her plate. Bill thought it very odd she had made such a transformation in a matter of days, going from the warm, talkative person he was growing closer to by the day, to this, a withdrawn, preoccupied stranger.

"Carrie, what's going on? I've tried to understand your attitude lately, but I'm lost. What's happened?"

She put her fork down and straightened the napkin in her lap.

"Nothing is wrong. Nothing has happened. I have a lot of work on my mind and it just needs my attention. I can't walk away from the office and leave everything there. This working thing is new to me, remember?"

Her tone was sarcastic, almost hateful.

"You have learned how to adjust and separate one from the other. I'm not there yet."

It sounded convincing enough, if, unlike Bill, you had not been spending so much time with her and had something to compare it to.

"No, Carrie. I don't buy that. Look. It's me. Bill. I know you too well to believe that. Work is not the reason for your moodiness, your lack of interest in everything else. No way. Tell me what is up with you."

A defensive look spread across her face, and Bill was taken back to a lunch date not too far in the past. He recognized the creasing of the forehead, the curl of the upper lip, the stiffening of the back. She was poised to lash out, and he braced himself for what was being foreshadowed.

Pushing her plate toward the center of the table and nearly breaking a water glass with the force, Carrie reddened in anger. Bill shared her coloring, though his was for a different reason

"How dare you tell me how I feel, or question what's wrong with me. I have enough to worry about without you boo-hooing that I'm not giving you the attention you think you deserve. You're just like the kids. *When are you going to have time for me?* Well, I'll tell you something, and this goes for everyone else that is tossing their demands my way. Get in line, buddy. I don't have enough time to take care of myself let alone the rest of you."

Bill could feel the stares of the other restaurant patrons. Carrie's soliloquy had reached a volume few could ignore, and for a minute he was convinced everyone, waiters, cooks, busboys, had stopped what they were doing to take in his predicament. She glared at him, hands pressed firmly to her hips, every muscle in her lithe body straining. Bill realized he had to defuse the situation before she really exploded. The evening was over; it was now a matter of getting up and out of the restaurant without further undo attention.

"I'm sorry. I didn't mean to upset..."

"No, no, no. Don't blame yourself. It's my fault that your self-centered ego failed to get its necessary strokes. Please, allow me to remind you just how important you are."

She said this with a thick dose of cynicism, twisting her face in a fashion that nearly repulsed him.

"Come on, Carrie. Make me feel wanted. Make me feel special. I need you, Carrie," she said, tossing her head left to right. "Well, listen here, little boy. Carrie is tired of giving. Carrie is tired of being the one with all the answers. *Carrie is tired.*"

And she did look tired to Bill as he sat stricken under the cloud of guilt she had cast over him, all the while letting her frustrations rain down. Her eyes finally dropped and she simply slumped motionless in her chair as if she were trying to recover from the tirade she had just levied. Bill let the silence work its way between them, hoping their audience would consider the show over and go back to their own conversations. Surely, anymore out of his mouth would set off another verbal explosion, so he calmly stood up after a few more minutes, unfolded a few bills from his money clip, and then stood over her waiting. He wasn't sure how long she would leave him in this unpleasant position, but he considered it more appealing than his previous station.

Methodically, Carrie placed her napkin on the table, gathered her purse, and pushed her chair back. She allowed him to take her arm as they headed for the door, her head bowed in either shame or exhaustion.

Neither spoke on the way to Raven. Carrie sat with her hands in her lap, looking out the window at the stretch of highway before them. Bill wanted to say something, but the fear of offending her outweighed the need to speak.

He wasn't sure what had just happened moments ago, but he was sure there was more to the situation than he was able to figure out. In the past few weeks, he had grown to feel for Carrie in a way he had not felt for anyone in a long time, possibly ever. A man of little emotion, more in tune to logic and thought, a byproduct of his upbringing and career, he imagined, Bill had experienced an awakening of feelings he had considered dead and gone. Through Carrie he had revealed a side of himself he had planned on putting away permanently for fear of it being damaged again. But she made him feel so good about himself, so alive, that it was only natural he come out of his self-imposed emotional prison and feel the light of, well, love. It was love. He had to admit it. The comfortable nature of their coupling had made falling in love with her a simple act. He had thought of what it would be like to take her in his arms and hold her closely, kiss her passionately. Sure that she felt the same way and would welcome his advances, Bill knew he would be acting on his feelings soon, but now this. Whatever had triggered her outburst was important for him to understand. Now was not the time for passion. As he had surmised after that lunch months ago, Carrie needed an opportunity to work through things before she could be approached about their future. He was confident she would be willing to talk with him about tonight's issues within the next few days. What he had to determine when that conversation took place was why. Why the about face? What was it that sent Carrie, a mild, gentle, loving person into a tyrannical fit of accusations and denial? He had to find the key. Once he had that, he hoped he could open a door and shed some light on her frustrations.

∎

While Bill was depositing Carrie at her front door, perplexed about her behavior, Sam Butler remained stumped over his own problems. Never in his years of law enforcement had he come across a group of similar cases that failed to reveal a shred of light that would point him down the dark path of investigation. Lawmen were like scientists. Presented with a problem and list of facts, they would give birth to a hypothesis. After making an educated guess, they would test this theory under a variety of conditions. Trial and error. Ultimately, they would either discover the answer to their problem or debunk their original explanation. This in turn opened doors to other possibilities.

With the growing case files of missing persons, Sam had none of the scientific variables at his disposal. The facts he had were slim to none, except that people were gone. There was no forensic evidence to even begin to postulate. He couldn't test because he hadn't been able to even get a sniff of a possible answer. He was, putting scientific principle aside, grasping for straws. He'd like to say he had come to a dead end in his search for the truth, but he hadn't even started down a discernable road yet.

The result of all his questioning, lab analysis, and public appeal was a big fat zero. The need for outside help was inevitable, a landslide ready to crash on him, and he could do nothing to stop its arrival. The thought of Steve Edwards and his starched band of suits taking the reins turned his stomach and could signal an end to his department, but he saw no other options available to him. The public outcry to end Raven's predicament had grown to a deafening crescendo, and Sam had decided that tomorrow he would make the hated call to the State Bureau to rescue his sinking ship.

On this apparent final evening, he sat at his paper-covered desk across from an expectant Cody Hawkins searching for the Holy Grail of Law Enforcement, a clue. They had poured over stacks of information together for more than three hours now and were getting nowhere. Not that Cody had necessarily been any help. Sam used his deputy as a sounding board, as a sympathetic ear, but he never expected to get any usable ideas from the green officer.

"That's it then," Sam shrugged, leaning back and rubbing his eyes with balled fists. "I can't think of another thing we haven't looked at."

His outward disappointment masked an inner relief that the search was over. Someone else could worry about the depleting population of Raven. He was done.

Cody had sat in his alert position the entire time, asserting his usual gung-ho comments during Sam's silent reflections.

"Maybe we could go back to the crime scenes, Sheriff. There may be something out there we missed."

"No, Cody. Number one, we don't know whether any crimes were even committed. Two, the lab boys have been over everything, and I went behind them the whole way. No, I'm telling you, unless we get a solid hit on our APBs, unless someone comes in here with a story better than Russian espionage or alien abduction, we are at the end of the line."

Sam stopped and looked seriously at Cody.

"We owe these people better, too. Let the bureau see what they can come up with. There is nothing more we can do."

He was mentally and physically haggard. Since recognizing Raven's growing problem, Sam had worked sixteen-hour days, seen little of his wife, and had nothing to show for his efforts. The people of Raven had been patient, but fear would soon begin to seep into the daily actions of his charges - locked doors, streets free of children at play - and it would riddle him with guilt. He had always been counted on to maintain law and order in town, in the process providing a sense of security. Gone now was the cover of safety, the protective blanket that wrapped itself around the citizens. The unexplainable vanishing of nine people had laid bare a vulnerability that Sam was helpless to correct. For his friends, his neighbors, his own family, he had to relinquish the reigns and admit his failure.

"I'll make the call in the morning. For now, make your rounds, and let's hope the night goes problem free," Sam instructed, gathering his scattered files in preparation for tomorrow's takeover.

Cody stood, hitched his thumbs in his belt, and remarked, "Sorry, Sheriff. I wish I could help us." He sounded honestly remorseful for their situation.

"We did everything we could, Cody. Now get on out of here and keep your eyes open. We may get lucky yet."

After the deputy exited to his cruiser, Sam picked up the phone to tell his wife he was coming home. Home for how much longer, he didn't know.

13

The State Bureau of Investigation descended upon Raven within hours of Sheriff Butler's call. As Sam had privately feared, Steve Edwards accompanied the initial agents, evaluating the situation and rubbing salt in his personal wounds at the same time. Edwards had adopted an air of superiority that was better seen than heard since his days at the academy, and this further deepened Sam's frustration and anger. Dressed the part of a special investigator, from the fitted suit to dark sunglasses, barking orders to lesser clones that responded to his every word, Edwards established his dictatorial presence with little delay. The offices of the Sheriff's Department were quickly commandeered as the SBI command center, and Sam reluctantly turned over all files and documentation pertinent to the numerous missing persons. For the duration of the SBI's stay, Sam and his deputy would have to work out of the old chamber building at the end of Main Street.

Edwards had previously formulated a special task force for such a crisis, drilled it on proper procedures should the present scenario arise, and had it in place within a matter of an hour. As Sam suspected, he and Cody would play second fiddle to the state team, making themselves available for questions involving the town's layout and fulfilling any minor orders Edwards voiced in his signature hail of commands to his team.

"I want the town map placed on this wall. Get the forensics lab on the phone. Hoskins will do. Let's set up a crime board with the missing - names, ages, addresses, everything relevant. Group them by time of disappearance and geographical location. Let's see if we can't establish a pattern here, gentlemen. I'll bet on a workable profile."

No one questioned Edwards, which indicated his clear leadership qualities and spoke well of his underlings. Like it or not, Sam Butler had been replaced, and there was little else he could do but catch a ride on the wave of activity Edwards had pushed forward and hope to retain some measure of usefulness. Who knew? A situation may call for local input, and Sam wanted to be available should the opportunity to stay visible present itself. At a time when visibility was a challenge in Raven, for even the common citizen, he hoped he wasn't forgotten.

■

Carrie gave little attention to the added activity taking place at the Sheriff's Department as she passed through downtown on her way to the pharmacy. She had been having trouble sleeping the last few nights and wanted to find something to help her doze off. Whether it was work, her recent troubles with Bill, or just a temporary bout of stress and anxiety, Carrie was weary and needed rest. She had stayed up the night before watching infomercials (sitting in front of the television had a mindless quality she disliked until recently), waiting for sleep to cloak her in its dark midst, but even that had proven fruitless. The feeling of complete physical and mental exhaustion was undeniable, but if she retired to her bed, she found herself back in the living room following thirty minutes of tossing and turning.

As she pulled into a space at Miller Drug, Carrie began to worry that this last resort may, too, be a waste of effort and expense. The last few days had left her shaken and confused. Her job, and particularly the properties in Raven, had monopolized every thought, every impulse. It was as if the many aspects of her life had been sloughed off like a useless skin, replaced by a singular purpose. What had held importance to her as a single parent, those things she wanted to maintain in her life as a message to herself and the outside world that she could make it, now meant very little. Why, she couldn't say.

The repetitious vision she had experienced in the bathroom nights earlier had been the pivotal point in her transformation. This she recognized, but the reason why it had held such mastery over her was unexplainable. What she was able to grasp was the undeniable sense that she was needed, in a way she had never felt before. Her life had filled itself over the years with those she clung to, dependent on their insights and wisdom in order to sustain her. Friends, family, even a co-worker in an after-school job had been sources for advice and reassurance. But this...this was something herculean in its magnitude. Carrie felt a great burden rest itself squarely on her shoulders that night after she seemingly floated above and beyond the world she knew. The experience took her not only to another dimension but placed her in charge of a task that spelled life or death. For what or who she didn't know, but it was her duty to perform her job at the highest possible level. Maintaining the habitation of Raven was her sole function now. She was depended on, and it was clear where any blame would be placed should she fail.

The store windows reflected the bright midday sun, and Carrie could feel the rays drawing strength from her, sapping what little energy she had left. Her dragging body expended what had to be its last ounce of reserves to push her out of the car and into the pharmacy.

Miller Drug was the only drugstore in Raven, and its owner, Roy Oster (he had bought the business from retired Cecil Miller fifteen years previous), prayed on this reality. Overpriced and generic free, Oster's guaranteed customers would pay dearly for their afflictions with each prescription and shelf purchase.

Announced with the familiar chime of a bell, Carrie crossed in front of various floor displays and headed to the back of the store to inquire about some sleeping pills. Lacking animation and anything resembling personality, Roy Oster, a spooky man of fifty-two with melting features and a gruff countenance, stood behind the pharmacy counter and surveyed Carrie's passage to his medical lair. His elevated position and lofty gaze gave him the appearance of a wise man, the holder of great knowledge, who held the secrets of the ages in his mortar and pestle. In truth, Oster was a self-centered loner who used his monopoly on pharmaceuticals within a radius of fifteen miles to extract dependence from locals. He commanded respect and gratefulness because he was the only game in town. Given competition, and a few Ravenites made the pilgrimage to the Valley or Cedar Hills to avoid dealing with Oster, Miller Drug would fall victim to the unwelcome creature that had laid siege to many businesses in town, a lack of patronage. Carrie secretly wished this on Oster, though she was grateful on this day that he was open to the public.

Looking up at Miller Drug's lone wolf and employee, Carrie greeted the pharmacist and made her request.

"I have a couple of brand names on this wall," Oster gestured with his eyes and a slight shrug to Carrie's left. "Most are effective, none addictive, but I'd recommend not taking any sleep aid for more than three nights. They can alter your sleep patterns and disrupt your natural predisposition to rest."

Carrie could have gained the same information in a medical manual, but she was grateful with Oster's response and appreciated his occupational knowledge. It didn't change how she felt about the man -

he was a patronizing bore - but she couldn't help but admire anyone who approached his job with a passionate commitment to perfection. Oster certainly knew his medicines.

"Thank you, Mr. Oster," Carrie said, convincingly free of any distaste for the man. She had found it hard in life to mask her emotions, but even that quality in her was changing.

She located the sleep aids, settled on a name familiar to her commercialized subconscious, and returned to the counter with her purchase.

"I think I'll go with this, and thank you for the advice on its use," she said, fumbling for money through a purse that provided a too small space for its contents.

Oster never looked up from whatever occupied his attention.

"Why I'm here. People often think just because something is bought off the shelf, it can't be harmful. Well, they're wrong. Sometimes dead wrong."

Carrie had to add weird to her list of undesirable qualities in Oster's possession. It was no wonder few liked him. She believed the measure of a person's worth was in his friends, and this exchange had explained his situation clearly. Social skills were not genetic; they were environmental abilities learned over time. In Oster's case, Carrie thought, he had missed every class.

Oster rung up her purchase and followed her visually out the door (though Carrie had no proof of this, she could feel his stare). Before she left, he added, "Remember. Three days. No more."

She left the store somewhat shaken, happy to return to the oppressive temperatures outside versus the dark foreboding that had laid hold of her in the store. It was for a few hours of restful sleep she had come, and she left feeling more uptight than ever. A more rational Carrie would have recognized the changes taking place within her and sought answers. Bill would be of value at a time like this, acting as both a sounding board and advice-giver, but she was determined to maintain secrecy and deal with it on her own.

It wasn't a fear of Bill's reaction; she could handle a critical evaluation. What kept her silence was a subconscious fear that telling someone would put at great risk the object of her increased work ethic. Bill had already demonstrated his scorn of Raven and its future. It angered her that he had chosen to stand in defiance, challenging her righteous path. If given enough information, he might jeopardize her efforts, lay waste to the successes she had already enjoyed, and foil any future endeavors. It was imperative that her mission - and it had become a mission of late - continue to its final act, and disbelievers like Bill be ignored. She was not completely sure what the end-result of her valuable work would be, but she was convinced that the role she was playing was crucial to the all-important outcome.

Carrie headed home relaxed in her choices and committed more than ever to securing the future of Raven. She could live without Bill and his negative attitude, a person with whom she had felt a strong bond forming, but now as an obstacle to her progress. She didn't need him. She didn't need anybody. All she wanted was some sleep, and to awake the next day ready to fulfill her calling. She was determined to answer that call - for herself and Raven.

■

Steve Edwards settled into the sheriff's chair, remarking to an empty office that even a town as small as Raven could afford better seating for its elected officials, and began the painstaking review of Sam Butler's files. He expected to verify early in his evaluation of the records that Butler had mishandled every investigation, that the missing link that tied all the cases together awaited the discriminating eyes of a seasoned professional lawman. What he discovered instead was a well-kept inventory of each case, complete with timetables, copies of lab analysis, and notes taken during interviews. It was unquestionably fine police procedure, and though Edwards was pleasantly surprised by his findings, he was disappointed that faulty police work was the reason answers remained in the dark. Butler had followed procedures by the book, even evaluating job and family histories of each individual to expose potential clues to his or her disappearance. It was sound work, and Edwards realized his quick fix would take longer than expected.

He looked up from the paperwork briefly and scanned the office. What drew men to this type of environment never ceased to amaze him. Functioning with few of the technological advances available to law enforcement today, small town officers were reliant on footwork and conversation to solve their legal problems. Maybe that was the attraction - old-fashioned police work. Today's police graduate was knowledgeable about the advantages of the computer as well as procedure. Communication devices, weaponry, advanced field equipment - all offered the modern detective a greater means of enforcement and discovery. Though confident in his ability in and modern approach to resolving Raven's dilemma, Edwards wondered whether the primitive tools of Sam Butler had scratched a surface impervious to further digging.

If the answers lay hidden, Edwards was sure he was the man to uncover them. He would start with a thorough and detailed re-examination of the cases from the beginning. Having ridden into Raven like the proverbial cavalry, he represented the hope and salvation for the remaining inhabitants of this quiet community. Before his stay was completed, the citizens of Raven would once again walk their streets in safety, praising the name of Steve Edwards, their deliverer, the man in the white hat.

14

Bill Curtis was not satisfied to simply leave Carrie alone to work out whatever was happening to her. As a lawyer it was not in his make-up to stand back and count on others to take care of things. The transformation he had witnessed was nothing like the outburst she had experienced at lunch so many days ago. This new identity she had assumed was frightening in many respects. In the years he had been a friend with her and Walt, Bill had always observed a Carrie void of emotional displays, unassuming in her approach to social situations. Walt was an extrovert, the voice for both of them in nearly every situation, and she had seemed to be accepting of her role as mother, housekeeper, and silent partner in marriage, though Walt seemed to value her input at times. On the few occasions when Bill had encountered Carrie alone, either in a department store or at home before Walt's arrival, she had exhibited a frailty that was alarming in its magnitude. It was a wonder she had managed to survive this long without Walt, the shield that deflected life's assaults. Hers had been a passive existence, utterly dependent on her husband for support and guidance in the most simple of circumstances.

The Carrie that had evolved before his eyes was a complete opposite of the whisper of a woman he had known for so many years. No longer melting into the shadows of those more aggressively attacking life, Carrie was independent, single-minded, and outspoken. The verbal bashing Bill had taken recently at dinner was a perfect example of Carrie's metamorphosis. She had been bitter and sarcastic, intimidating in her assault. Caught off guard, Bill could only sit under the hail of charges. He had sought some answers to his growing concerns about her condition, her state of mind, in a way he thought lacking in accusation. The parry to his thrust was swift and undeniable. The progress of their relationship was on indefinite hold, and there was little he could do to free it from its anchored position and set it afloat again.

Carrie was working through something he didn't understand, had tried to relate to but had failed. It had been best to back away from things for a while, to allow her the space to adjust to her new surroundings. She was showing homes at a staggering rate, still dealing with a home and children, and now entering into what Bill hoped was an emotional bond with him. It was enough to set the strongest of women back, to make them examine their growing list of responsibilities and prioritize for the time being until they were better able to juggle more than a few balls at once. Bill was willing to be one of those set aside temporarily as she managed her job and home.

What bothered Bill though and made it difficult to await her acclimation process to reach its end was the bizarre manner in which she had defended her management of Raven properties. Granted, Raven was rich in affordable homes, reasonable to the point of ridiculous. A realtor could enjoy sales success and make a modest income, but the fervor she demonstrated, the protective nature of her actions and statements, made it suspiciously wrong. It was understandable to wish to see a small hometown survive the migration of its residents to larger, suburban communities, and even big cities. In some cases these same types of towns were growing at remarkable rates as developers and investors realized their potential and sought to appeal to those yearning for the way things used to be - simple. That growth was not the case in Raven. Nothing new was under construction, no investment for expansion. Downsizing had been the name of the game in Raven for years, and even the public works and administrative buildings were shrinking in their output and productivity. It was a cancerous action, a town once booming with youth and newness, succumbing to the mass exodus of its members as it failed to keep up with the changes sweeping the country. What was innovative before was obsolete today, and some city planners had missed the mark when it came to future endeavor. Raven had had a good run, had been an important player in the game, but was now an also-ran, left behind and put to pasture.

Carrie stoutly defended the continued push of Raven as a thriving town, when in all reality that was not the case. A quick examination of its administrative capabilities would reveal a shrinking of major proportions in the last two years. An elected town council was a thing of the past. Little more than a part-time mayor and a staff of three oversaw the functioning of the community. Public works were nearly extinct as larger entities were quickly absorbing the remaining residents in need of services. Small local business were closing at an alarming rate as demand decreased rapidly in favor of the larger and diversified chains popping up in outlying, growing suburbs. Even public education had met its match, as Raven was unable to provide a daily attendance viable enough to keep classrooms operating. This too had been incorporated.

The good ship Raven was taking in water at an incredible rate, and Carrie had presumably declared herself captain. Before the last mast passed below the surface, though, she would fight to keep it afloat. The key factor in her equation apparently was residents. As long as people resided in Raven, it was for all intents and purposes a town. Forget that it would soon lose its postal address. Forget that downtown was an empty shell of boarded windows and forgotten glories. People gave towns their existence, and Carrie would strive to keep that dream alive.

Bill knew he had to do something to alter the direction Carrie was taking. He cared for her a great deal, more than he thought he would be able to find in himself after his disheartening past. If it was medical attention, counseling, a new job, whatever, he was willing to provide the means for her to escape this runaway train of living. Nothing good could come out of her spiraling descent, and when she hit bottom, Bill could only imagine the effects it would have on her self-worth and dignity. A flower pressed to the wall of life before, she was guaranteed to recede into a cavernous lifestyle of disappointment and regret, a place from where he feared he could never rescue her.

He would tap some resources, talk to the right people, and eventually save her from herself. Why be a lawyer if he couldn't use the system every now and then to his advantage? There were the right people out there with the ability to help, and he would call in some tabs if it meant bringing resolution to the problem. Knowing he was doing this for himself as much as for her didn't matter. A well-adjusted, vital Carrie was what he valued in his life, and he was determined to have it and bring peace to her as well.

■

Bobby Rollson was tired of it. He was the one that had to get up at 4:30 every morning to make sure Raven was up on the news of the day. Whether he was throwing the local paper or The Paul's Valley Gazette, Bobby was reliable. What he asked in return was little more than the folks on his route to gather their papers in a reasonable amount of time, let him know when they were canceling their subscriptions, and pay at the end of the month. Nothing more. He would be sure the paper was right where it needed to be, whether it was the driveway, on the front porch, or, in the extreme case of Mrs. Sanderson, inside the storm door.

Rain? Count on the papers to be bagged. The big Sunday edition? Mark it down. The paper was not strewn all over the yard in response to its sheer weight hitting the ground on the run. Tips were not a requirement, but he appreciated it when he received them. Bobby was, without question, good at what he did. Never late, never off duty. At the young age of thirteen, it was remarkable to see a boy so responsible, willing to give up late nights and lazy mornings to perform his job. Remarkable.

Pedaling down the streets of Raven like clockwork, Bobby would make his rounds, get back home in time for breakfast before catching his school bus, and then repeat the whole process the next day. He had settled into a personal system of retrieval and dispersal that had become second nature over the past year and a half. The only hitches he ever encountered were the rare additions of subscribers and the now more frequent cancellations. He had always been able to take these in stride, learning a new series of houses within a few short days.

The recent problem he was facing, though, left him perplexed and unsure what recourse to take. Over the past week he had noticed that two of his regulars had failed to pick up their papers from their various delivery locations. The occasional paper from the previous morning often greeted him as he returned to continue the never-ending cycle, but in these cases the papers were piling up at an odd rate. Mr. Garrett's driveway looked like an archeological site, the papers scattered about like the bones of prehistoric beasts. He had watched the piles increase at both homes, and each day he told himself to give it another before inquiring. Surely they would gather them at some point. None of those in question had informed him of vacations that put a stop to his deliveries until they returned. It was summer now, though, and maybe they had forgotten to let him know. But *two* subscribers! He couldn't figure it out. He concluded on the eighth day of witnessing paper hills becoming paper mountains that he would call each home to ask. It was the responsible thing to do, and no one had ever denied that Bobby was just that.

On the morning of the day he was to search out answers to his paper pick-up dilemma, Bobby started out on his route at 4:30 as always, down Wister Road, across the Highway 74 intersection, and through to First Street south. The summer heat was an obstacle to a biker at even this time of morning, and Bobby had finished each route over the past month dripping with perspiration. But he was in condition good enough to deal with what Mother Nature threw at him, whether it was extreme cold or, in this case, stifling heat. And like a postal worker clinging to his creed, Bobby would never let the weather conditions stand in the way of his appointed rounds.

Too many people depended on him to start their day, to not only be the messenger of all the news fit to print, but also to provide the addiction to their habit. In lives built on routine, newspapers were often the starter's gun to the daily race. Coffee, a bite to eat, maybe a smoke, and the newspaper. Familiar. A comforting need. Starting out under any other circumstances could possibly throw the whole day off. Bobby had recognized the importance of his job early on, benefiting from his own father's dependence on the paper's timely arrival.

It normally took him an hour to complete the circuit, unless, as was the case now, he had to distribute the Sunday Gazette, a massive roll in comparison to the flick-of-a-wrist Raven editions. This morning called for him to leave the street at times and ascend driveways, and since some customers only received the Sunday paper, the number of throws he made increased dramatically. Bobby considered it a good day if he was back home from the route before a quarter after six.

As Bobby stood on the pedals and pumped the familiar, easy burn into his thighs, he noted that the forgotten papers still lay strewn about in their increasingly bothersome places. He was going to wait until people had a chance to get back from church and settle into their day of rest and then begin the process of bringing to their attention the paper wasteland forming in front of their homes. He planned on radiating a genuine concern, while at the same time forcing folks to clean up their driveways. If by chance he got no answer, Bobby had considered checking with neighbors in an inquisitive manner as to their whereabouts. His fear, one he pushed beneath the surface and refused to accept, was that a large number of his customers had skipped town without notifying him or the news offices. Where the lost revenue would be excised he dared not guess.

Turning conclusively onto Anderson Drive, a dead end road that represented the last of his obligations, Bobby wiped the sweat from his upper lip and steered into the morning sun that tipped the horizon. Red and defined, the half oval promised another full day of penetrating heat. To his right on the short stretch of road were three homes needing his services, and he deftly completed his deliveries to these locations without pause. He negotiated the left-hand turn at the end of the block, avoiding an old truck that had sat on blocks for as long as Bobby could remember in front of a guardrail, and started up Anderson with two final papers in tow occupying his front basket. The two side baskets at the rear wheel had been empty for a while as Bobby worked back to front. This final stretch was the part of the route he enjoyed the most, a light bicycle and the end in sight. He was one of the few young boys he knew that could take satisfaction in a job well done. Again, he had his father to thank for that one.

Dawn had brought a mixture of soft colors to the landscape, penetrating the shadows that usually protected their secrets as he completed his work. Light pushed and spread its way into every recess, creating a pleasing view that Bobby rarely experienced except on Sundays, and particularly in the summer when the days grew longer. He negotiated a perfect throw to the Sanders, the paper sliding to a stop at the steps leading to the long walk ascending to their front door. Having coasted to complete the toss, Bobby pumped the pedals a few times and smiled at the prospects of a final delivery.

To his left he noticed Mr. Peler, robe clad and headed down his driveway to retrieve Bobby's first delivery on Anderson. Peler was a nice man, short and stocky with little hair remaining on a head he fought dramatically with a comb to cover, and always with a kind word when Bobby came around for monthly subscription collections.

Bobby divided his customers in three groups: the Good, the Bad, and the Ugly, from a western he had seen on television with Clint Eastwood. He loved the old westerns, featuring real actors like Kirk Douglas and Robert Mitchum. They were the true artists, and he appreciated the effort these men put into their craft, not relying on special effects and million dollar stage sets to make their movies go. The performance was the thing, not what a computer could generate to wow an audience.

The Good were subscribers like Mr. Peler who paid on time and added a little gratuity to show Bobby they recognized the effort he was putting into their service. He never turned down a tip, viewing it as a reward for his diligence. The Bad, on the other hand, failed to honor him with any monetary recognition, simply paying their bill as requested. The only negative thing he dealt with in his job was the Ugly, a small group of, well, desperadoes, who avoided Bobby and their obligations, rarely paying on time or without some minor complaint. It was the Ugly that Bobby envisioned riding down like John Wayne, capturing them on his Schwinn turned palomino as they fled, a month behind on their payment, and hog-tying them until authorities could assess the proper punishment.

Mr. Peler was not a tremendous tipper in comparison to most of the Good, but Bobby was grateful for any pat on the back. As he pedaled toward the Peler driveway, Bobby raised his hand in greeting, hoping to catch the attention of his prized customer who was beginning to bend to his paper. Peler responded in kind, adding a smile that told Bobby he valued the work ethic of one such as young as he, while others his age were still in bed, earning nothing but expecting everything.

Bobby was still two houses from his final objective, and after glancing up the street to confirm the target, he swiveled his head to Peler for a final look at the man and maybe a hello. A kind word went a long way with people. His father had taught him that as well.

Peler had gained possession of his paper, and with the smile still occupying his face; he watched his paperboy's approach with expectation. He appeared to have something to say, and in the split second before life would forever change for Bobby Rollson, the paperboy prepared for a pleasant exchange with his thankful neighbor.

The rays of the sun that were already promising another uncomfortable day caught Bobby on the back as they progressively clarified the world that lay before him. Images slightly diluted in the murky transition of night to day were sharpening with each additional measure of light. Peler stood rigidly in his blue bathrobe and house shoes, his lips slightly open in anticipation of the words ready to be expelled in honor of the passing cyclist. His reading glasses rested high on his forehead in preparation for the morning's news ahead. Bobby imagined him seated in an ancient but infinitely comfortable recliner, his pajama-covered legs crossed, intently studying every page. If there was anyone that Bobby figured got their money's worth when it came to newspapers, it had to be Mr. Peler.

Bobby began to coast as he neared Peler and decided he would allow him to speak first. It was the respectful thing to do, and among the many positive things adults said about him, respect was an often-used word. The progressing light allowed for near objects to be seen clearly; farther back, night tried to maintain its hold for another few minutes. Bobby could see the relaxed, peaceful expression on the old man's face as he approached, a look that took a drastic change with the blink of an eye.

In one swift rendering of an artist's brush, the picture before him dramatically changed. Peler dropped his paper as both hands shot immediately to his head, the once-pleasant face gathering in on itself in a mass of wrinkles and distortion. His eyes were tightly shut, and in the instant that he began to bend over in what Bobby registered as incredible pain, he emitted a long, terrifying howl.

Startled, Bobby hit his foot brake and let his other foot down as he came to a stop. The man not seconds ago standing easily in his driveway, looking happy and at peace, was now doubled over in agony. Bobby was frozen, fearful to say or do anything as he sat wide-eyed on his banana seat, the thrill of throwing his final paper long gone.

Peler continued to clutch his head, his knuckles showing a stark whiteness as they tensed their grip. He bent slightly at his knees, his elbows pressed firmly to his stomach, as he appeared to be fighting to remain standing. The howl had become a throaty groan, and it was losing intensity rapidly.

Bobby swung his leg over his bike and let it fall to the pavement, his obligation to assist someone in distress finally registering itself.

"Mr. Peler? What's wrong? Mr. Peler?" he asked as he walked to the edge of the drive and stood helpless.

Peler did not respond but sank to his knees roughly, still maintaining the viselike grip on his head. Bobby took a few more steps toward him, unsure of what was happening or what he should do. He had taken a few life-saving courses as part of his swimming lessons over the past few summers, an attempt to eventually earn some lifeguarding money when he was old enough, but he didn't think this was a situation that called for CPR. Peler was conscious. He was breathing as far as Bobby could tell, and a heart attack victim didn't hold their head that way. He would have to get help, but he didn't think he should leave him alone at the same time.

Bobby looked up and down the street, hoping some others had risen early to get their morning news. There was no one in sight. Peler lived alone, Bobby knew, so he couldn't expect to find help in the house. He came within an arm's length of the fallen member of the Good, and putting an arm on his shoulder and bending down to look at him, asked Mr. Peler what he could do.

What Bobby was answered with sent him backpedaling. Mr. Peler's face was a study in complete pain. His eyes, no longer clenched, glared wide with whites infused by heavy, blood red tendrils. Sweat was pouring from his face, and his entire head vibrated rapidly within the grip of his hands. Blood was gathering at the corners of his lips, and his nose had already begun to run in a heavy crimson flow.

The entire look was of vast horror. He seemed to be struggling to regain his original position, but instead he was becoming more and more cocoon-like in his appearance. Bobby continued backward, his own mouth standing open in shock as he slowly shook his head side to side. He stumbled over his bike, falling down in a heap of tires, baskets, and confused terror. Sitting frozen with his hands thrown back for support, Bobby watched the picture before him continue to change.

The air surrounding Mr. Peler began to distort, getting heavy as if it were slowly liquefying. It moved in waves over and around the crumpled man, defeating the clarity the sun had so recently offered. Bobby watched spellbound as a diameter of roughly ten feet created a circle of movement, and Peler, closing more upon himself, quickly began to fade within its area.

As Bobby sat in horror and watched the spectacle unfold, he was reminded of his favorite western, High Plains Drifter. Clint Eastwood, supposedly back to avenge his own death in a small town riddled with cowards, had made a remarkable entrance and exit in the film that could be construed as either a trick of the eye or some supernatural event. While the camera focused on a stark plain, heat radiated from its surface and created a watery distortion. Sitting ever tall in his saddle, Eastwood had materialized from this ribbon of convolution, riding toward the audience, and had galloped away into its same murky depths at the end of the movie following the vanquishing of the bad guys.

And now, like that same cinematic jewel that had captivated Bobby on television, the terrifying ordeal on Anderson commanded his attention. Mr. Peler was almost invisible now behind the waves of heavy air, and Bobby could feel that weight reaching out to affect the space in which he lay helpless. The distortion was at its greatest point, appearing as a huge pearl of varying earthen colors and undulating shapes as Peler was lost in its movement. For a few more seconds the orb stood, mesmerizing the young paperboy who had only a minute ago looked forward to the end of his route and the start of a new day, and then, with what Bobby sensed as a suction, it was gone, leaving behind Peler's paper but nothing more.

He's gone, Bobby thought, distrustful of the images his eyes had presented him up to this point and now even more doubtful. He sat a moment longer, his expression in permanent awe, and attempted to collect what little courage remained in his youthful bones. After a minute he scrambled to his feet, lifted his bike, and raced home, the delivery of the last paper on his route long forgotten.

15

Even The Circle honored the Lord's Day, and in a town where every day looked like a Sunday morning, the desolation was slightly more evident. Churchgoers and shoppers sought refuge in their desired places of worship outside Raven, most making a day of the trip. Those that remained behind burrowed in cool, shuttered homes, escaping the heat that continued to plague that part of the country.

The sheriff's office was uncharacteristically active in the dead city, abuzz with life as a handful of state detectives relinquished their day of rest under the ever-vigilant eye of Steve Edwards. Never one to forego work when it was the right thing to do, Edwards had made this like any other, a time to chase answers. His assumption of the Raven investigation was evident in the changes that had occurred in the law enforcement offices. Sam Butler's former domain had taken on a major transformation as every wall and bulletin board was covered with time lines, victim bios, and street maps. For each case, Edwards had ordered a detailed breakdown, ultimately hoping to find a common thread that would tie the many disappearances together. Interviews were duplicated, last known locations of the missing were revisited, and lab tests were ordered, in most instances over the same materials.

The police work prior to the Edwards' team had been superficial at best, yet expected under the circumstances. Sam Butler had few resources, no manpower, and little experience in dealing with missing persons. Yet the findings of the state department had uncovered little more worthwhile, a fact frustrating to the man heading the investigation. The amount of time and money devoted to the cases paled in comparison to the embarrassment Edwards and his men were feeling. Having marched into town with the bells of salvation ringing loudly, proclaiming to be bearers of justice, efficiency where none existed, they had failed to make a dent in the mystery. Butler, though he had every right to gloat and take personal satisfaction in his old friend Steve Edward's poor showing, was actually upset that nothing more had been found. It was this concern and care for his hometown that brought him to his own offices that Sunday morning after letting his wife go to church and pray for both of them.

With his pupils forced to pinpricks in the bright summer sun, Sam entered the building and paused to let his eyes adjust and at the same time observe the metamorphosis his place of employment for eighteen years had undertaken. What caught his attention first were not the additions of paperwork tacked to every free space, but the constant motion that flowed throughout. Detectives were hard at work in a variety of activities: checking files against larger charts, answering phones, commanding computers, sifting through cardboard file boxes, making Sam think of worker bees molding and shaping their hive. In his time in the department, no more than three employees were in the offices at the same time, creating a peaceful, somber atmosphere. This was the investigative process in high gear, a finely tuned machine of various mechanical parts functioning in synchronized order, a ballet of movement and grace. Sam felt a pang of jealousy and desire to join the hunt as he closed the door and sought Edwards.

Bent over the desk once the domain of Sheriff Butler, Steve Edwards looked frustrated and helpless. Standing next to him and intently surveying the same littered desk was one of his team, a younger detective with a determined scowl on his face. Edwards looked harried, his trademark suit and tie abandoned for a more relaxed informal look. Sam felt a little awkward awaiting admittance into an office he had spent the better part of two decades occupying, but he paused to give Edwards the opportunity to complete his work with the other investigator before asking him in.

Edwards glanced up from the desk, a weary glaze spread across his entire face.

"Oh, Sam. Come on in and have a seat. I'll be with you in just a second," he said, immediately returning his attention to the paperwork before him. Sam shuffled to the nearest chair, feeling a little obtrusive under the circumstances. Everything remained relatively the same in his old office, though the addition of an extra table and easel gave the room a cluttered look. The vacating had come quickly, probably too quickly for Sam, who had had little time to organize his personal effects and turn control over to the state department. During the interval of SBI occupation, Sam had spent more time at home than was his nature, and the anxiety of being back in the game had drawn him to the investigative headquarters. He knew in his heart that his work up to the point of his removal had been detailed and proper, and he needed to know what new information had been revealed with a more sophisticated approach.

Edwards and his associate summed up their discussion with a few meaningless conclusions before Sam was finally left alone in the office with the man in charge.

"Well, Sam, what brings you by today?" Edwards said in a tone of voice that offered little reception. "Stop in to see what we've done with the place?"

Sam looked around the office with a cautious smile. "I love what you've done. I didn't recognize it." The comment fell from his mouth like a lead weight, failing to lighten the mood in the now claustrophobic office.

"Actually, I just thought I would see what progress you've made on the cases and if I could offer any assistance. I hadn't heard from you and wondered whether there were some town-related questions I could help with."

In reality, Sam wanted little to do with helping his old friend and his band of robots. What he truly wanted to know was whether any ground had been gained on the investigation since his abdication.

"Well, Sam, I appreciate your offer, but at this point in the investigation, there is very little that you could provide that would help. Don't get me wrong. A local officer could be vital to our research into the cases at some future date, but right now we are at a preliminary stage, simply trying to piece together what facts we do have."

His demeanor, as always, was condescending, and Sam wondered for the first time since knowing Edwards if this wasn't just who he was, the way he talked to everyone.

Angry more at himself than his old friend, Sam fell into his customary submissive mode, expressing his concern that he had left the state investigators starting at square one.

Edwards was quick to point out the error in Sam's thinking.

"No, you did some important initial work, and for that we are thankful. It's just that we have had to follow up on so many things to guarantee thoroughness."

For Sam the answer to his question was thanks for nothing. It really didn't matter what Sam's investigation had uncovered, the state boys would somehow find its faults and declare their presence the salvation of a dead end piece of police work.

"What new information have you found?" Sam asked, hoping for a small morsel of news to satisfy his inquisitive appetite.

"I'm not at liberty to say at this time, Sam. You know, legal limits on disclosure of an ongoing investigation. What I will tell you is we have a working list of suspects, both here and outside of Raven, and we plan on narrowing that to a short list in a matter of days."

"Really? A suspect here in Raven? Hard to believe being how we're such a close-knit community. Everyone knows everyone else's business."

Edwards leaned back in his chair, Sam's chair, and smiled.

"Sometimes you can't see the forest for the trees. It just took a fresh pair of outsider eyes to make some connections."

Sam had heard enough. Another shot like that and his next statement may permanently ban him from the investigation, at which point he would never learn of their progress. One thing was for sure - Edwards had no "suspect." Sam could see it in the man's eyes, knew him well enough to know that he was treading water with little hope of a flotation device being thrown his way anytime soon. It was Edward's way of staying on top, presenting the aura of progress. Patting his lap and standing with a feigned look of contentment, Sam met Edwards' eyes.

"Well, I guess you have things well in hand here. I'll get out of your hair. It looks way too busy around here for me. I'm kind of enjoying my little sabbatical."

Sam turned to go.

"Don't worry, Sam," Edwards offered. "We'll get to the bottom of this. It's what we do best."

"I know you will," Sam said, emptying his last drop of patience. "I know you will."

The two men shook hands and Sam walked the obstacle course of busy detectives to the front door and outside, welcoming the oppressive heat for the first time since its arrival, glad to be free of the domination he had felt inside.

Sam walked down the sidewalk toward his car, wondering what leads if any Edwards and his men had come across. He feared nothing new had been discovered. Feared it for Raven, his family, and himself.

■

Bobby pumped his bicycle at a rate far surpassing anything the little bike had withstood before. Two miles separated his house from the end of his paper route, but Bobby completed the distance in record time, ignoring the deep pain in his thighs and thinking only of Mr. Peler. *Mr.*

Peler! He was there and then he was gone! It couldn't, didn't, happen. Bobby stood tall on the pedals, sweat pouring from his face and down his back as his mouth took in the humid air of the morning. He was frantic and confused, unsure what to do or who to tell. He just knew he had to get home, where it was safe. Nobody disappearing in thin air at home, that was for sure. *God, what happened?* For Bobby this was not an interjection. Only God could have the answer to what he had witnessed, could be the only one responsible for such a vision. He, or the Devil.

The only thing that accompanied Bobby home was the sound of his tires on the macadam and his normally rational thoughts gone haywire. Every bit of his father in thoughts and actions, Bobby sought some logical explanation for what had launched him homeward bound. It hadn't been a trick of the sunlight or shadows. Mr. Peler was the last guy to come up with some kind of magic trick to frighten his paperboy. He wracked his brain. *What was it? Terrestrial?* Bobby couldn't see how, unless someone had gone to a huge financial extent to scare the life out of him. A Hollywood miracle it could have been, a computerized product of virtual reality, but was that logical, here, in Raven? No way. *But supernatural? Extraterrestrial?* Was that reasonable either? No way again.

Bobby recalled reading a dramatic offering from Rod Serling's *Twilight Zone* during English class one day, something about monsters and a street. The title eluded him. In that story, a neighborhood street becomes the site of some unexplainable events. As the weird occurrences continue, the town folk, having exhausted all rational thought, begin to propose and believe illogical answers to their predicament. Serling understood that it was human nature to need answers, to the point of believing the ridiculous to provide explanation.

Though Bobby enjoyed tales of the supernatural, he was the last to accept their place in anything other than a fictional setting. Mr. Peler had not been beamed aboard a flying saucer (besides, Bobby had not seen any signs of that). He had not been teleported into another dimension. There was a better, safer conclusion. His mature approach to living struggled with his childlike imagination to bring resolve to his dilemma. He found none. All Bobby knew was that he had to get home and explain to his father what he had seen. If anybody could determine the cause of something, it was Bobby's dad. The other force driving him at such an accelerated pace was the need to close himself behind the security of his own front door.

■

Calling in every marker at his disposal, Bill was unable to find the information he needed to steer Carrie in a more healthy direction. An examination of Shephard Realty and its owners found the company to be a sound business, well respected in land and property management. It was growing rapidly, having diversified its representation to include corporate clients, while at the same time abandoning those real estate ventures that were proving to be unproductive - like Raven. Bill discovered that while Shephard was expanding his business with the additions of new housing developments and city strip centers, rich in profit margins and more attractive to members of a recovering economy, he was pulling out of low income, aged housing and mom-and-pop operations in small towns. Pulling out in all except Raven, where properties continued to buy and sell at a crisp pace, all a result of the efforts of one Carrie Hammons. In the past three weeks, Carrie had placed five families in homes in Raven to the surprise of her employer, fellow realtors, and the real estate market in general. Her persuasive approach and easy manner with clients was the understood tool of her trade and secret to her success, but the results were still viewed as uncanny by those close to the real estate scene.

How was Carrie accomplishing the impossible? Bill had no answers after his initial probe, and felt that there was little information available from an outsider's perspective to be had. Whatever success Carrie was experiencing was a Midas touch, and if Bill was going to determine the reason for her uncanny performance in realty and extract her from the clutches of what held her psychologically, he had to look elsewhere.

He determined he had to go to the source, step onto the playing field and find out what the allure was, ask those close to the action what they knew. He had to go to Shephard Realty and start asking questions, hopefully identifying the truth. Lord knew he had seen the effect. Maybe then he could approach Carrie armed with a cure, a means of resurrecting her from this self-destructive course and salvage what he could of their future.

If anybody were to draw back the curtain on his motivation, they would see a selfish purpose. He couldn't deny the feelings he had for Carrie and was fearful her sudden transformation was jeopardizing his happiness, his vision of what could be. Telling Carrie at this point would be a lost cause as wrapped up in her professional life as she was. He could see her staring long and hard at him following his profession of love, looking him up and down as if he were a neighborhood eyesore in need of renovation or a small child experimenting with adult feelings. Rocked back on her heels, arms crossed, a look of utter disgust on her face, in Bill's daydream Carrie would let him know in terms best suited coming from the mouth of a hardened sailor that she had no time, interest, or desire to be in a relationship with him.

"Now if you'll excuse me," she would say, lifting a For Sale sign and turning in defiance, "I have some houses to sell."

His subconscious had battered him relentlessly following Carrie's transformation, that part of everyone that imagines the worst and does a fairly reliable job of administering the poison of worry and doubt under the skin, where it greedily festers and takes root. Bill hurt for himself, that was true, but it pained him to think the old Carrie was gone, a woman now absorbed not by family and friends, but of all things, by the inexplicable desire to populate a dying old town, one that couldn't hold too many good memories for her to begin with.

Why, Carrie, why? He would find out. One way or another, he would make sense of it and save her from herself. Save them both.

16

The sun at day's end finally made its inevitable contact with the horizon, promising an explosive joining of heat and earth that would render the latter unlivable. But the encounter was uneventful, bringing a welcome respite from the day's ruthless barrage of glare and humidity. The summer was shaping up to be the very vision of The Circle, a literal spawn of nature's evil ways. Raven was the epitome of the oppressed, as the entire town browned and shriveled under the combined weight of a thousand desert summers. Plant life suffered, paint peeled, and residents continued to vanish - some legitimately, others not so explicably.

Carrie made her way home, preoccupied as usual not only with her successes of the day but also the promise of more of the same tomorrow. She had sold yet another home in town, a three-bedroom steal on the south side of town. The owners had left months ago, and the lack of interest from prospective buyers had driven their asking price way down. So was the situation for everyone in Raven, and Carrie found a low price coupled with her sales pitch to be the remedy for a needy homebuyer.

She had been selling at a rate unheard of in the cubicles of Shephard Realty. What Carrie was losing in commission she was more than making up for in sheer volume. No other salesperson dared to venture into Carrie's claim on Raven real estate, even those of other agencies. It was her territory. Signs in dozens of yards proclaimed her dominance and exclusivity. She was Raven Realty, and no one challenged her claim.

Since the realization that her job and life were uniquely intertwined in a special purpose, what she had grown to consider a divine calling, Carrie had given little else thought. Her children continued to suffer from her lack of presence, and when she was home, her absence of attentiveness. With all her interest in other homes, her house had taken a major blow to its appearance of order and care. Sara and Tim did what they could for themselves, now home all day with school out for the summer, but a sense of organization is rarely inherent in a young child, so the house was in a constant state of chaos. Anyone who knew Carrie would take one look at her home and realize something was very wrong.

For years, while Walt was around, she kept an immaculate home, free of clutter, capable of passing the strictest white glove test the military could administer. But now, well, the transformation would worry those who knew her well. Friends like Bill, who already recognized reasons for concern but felt helpless to fix. Carrie was a different person, and among the many changes in her life and personality that people noticed, her intensity toward her job was the most evident. The soft-spoken housewife, forced to take a job after the disappearance of her domineering husband, had evolved into a competitive, driven, working machine. Few doubted her future prosperity; most remained baffled at her behavior.

Going home, dealing with the kids, going to bed, it was all a pause in the action to Carrie, timeouts she regretted taking. Staying at the office until the last possible minute or scheduling showings late into the evening, Carrie pushed the envelope of career success.

She stepped through her front door at 7:30 to a quiet welcoming. Putting her purse on the kitchen counter and making her way down the hall, she found her children mulling over a jigsaw puzzle in Sara's room.

"Okay, I'm home. What's been going on here this afternoon?" Carrie asked.

The kids hardly looked up from their shared table, mumbling a "Hi" and "Nothing." The cohesion that held the family together was slowly failing, and the kids held on to each other as the unit began to disintegrate. They had begun to expect little from their mother - even dinner was not always a given. Too young to understand the magnitude of their mother's changes but old enough to register the complete alteration in her behavior, the siblings found solace in themselves.

"Well, after a hard day of work, is that all the greeting I get?"

The kids remained passive, having withdrawn many weeks ago to this catatonic state when in contact with her.

"Hello? What's going on here? Remember me? Mom. The mighty hunter, the provider?" Carrie said.

"Yeah, Mom. Hi. How was work?" Tim offered in a tone lacking in the slightest interest. Carrie failed to pick up on the mood that presented itself now as she had in past conversations.

"Sold another family residence in the best little town going. Give me enough time and I could sell every empty house around here. Raven's growing, thanks to your dear old mom," Carrie boasted. The children remained disinterested.

"Well?" she asked.

"Uh,...great Mom. Great. Another house," Tim said, never looking up from the table as he continued to try puzzle pieces without fail.

"Boy, you guys are a barrel of laughs. I'm telling you. I have a good day, and you manage to ruin it every time. Well, I'm going to fix some dinner for us and act like my kids like their mom."

Carrie turned to march out of the room and head back down the hall in her self-righteousness when Sara said, "We already ate."

"Ate? What did you eat?"

"I fixed some macaroni and cheese and hot dogs," Tim said.

"And it was pretty good," Sara answered.

"Fine, I'll fend for myself. I'm sure you didn't save any for me."

Her children wearing faces of hurt and confusion, Carrie turned a second time and headed to the kitchen where she found nothing that interested her empty stomach. Instead, she grabbed the paper and sat on the sofa to read, a ritual of the Old Carrie yet to be destroyed.

The newspaper failed to tell any stories that could hold Carrie's attention, and after flipping through channels on television for a while, she decided to head to bed so she could get an early start at work. The kids had retired at some point in the evening as Carrie sat in the living room, failing to bring her a goodnight yet again. Ungrateful beggars! She worked her tail off for them, making sure they had everything they needed, and she got nothing but a cold shoulder for her efforts. No one, not even her own children, respected the monumental task that had been given to her, the duty that she was bound to perform. If anybody had the slightest idea of her role in the future of Raven, she would be receiving their praises, not their coldness. She understood that even the most famous of leaders and pioneers, when their calling and purpose was revealed, were unappreciated, often seen as crazy by their contemporaries. No one at the office could appreciate her commitment, nor could her friends and family. She would have to continue on the path laid before her, and in the end, after she had fulfilled the goal of her assignment, they would realize their errors in perception. Everyone would come to her in penitent homage, seeking her forgiveness. This she would give grudgingly, until she had been given a heartfelt apology. Until then, those who questioned her actions would be treated the same way she was being treated now - as if they had the plague.

Carrie readied for bed, debating whether to try a little television from the comfort of her bed or just welcome sleep as a quick path to tomorrow and the promises it held. As she combed her hair out and stared hard at the face in the mirror, one hardened with lines of stress and exhaustion, she felt her equilibrium give way. Carrie blinked, grasping the counter to maintain her balance, but she felt a blackness descending on her.

It was another visit, another encounter with whatever needed her. This time she advanced willingly, allowing herself to be swept away on the waves of entrancement. She was not afraid, and here, now safely lying on her bathroom floor, Carrie opened up to her new benefactor.

As before, Carrie felt a dizzying, lifting sensation, and a euphoric transportation from the quiet solitude of her bathroom to another place, another dimension of experience. It was hard for Carrie to categorize the feeling, and it was even more difficult to determine whether she was traveling in her mind, in her body, or both. The entire event was naturally foreign to her, but she felt that if what she heard was true about out-of-body experiences, the ability for certain people, usually those in some sort of meditative state, to leave their physical selves in a spiritual/mental journey, then this must be very similar.

Carrie did not necessarily believe she was being physically conveyed elsewhere; more closely, she strangely understood her physical self endured behind as her conscious self was escorted. The means, the destination, all were beyond her grasp, but it was as real as getting up and walking out the door.

Only Carrie wasn't walking. She would not be the least bit surprised if she were informed that Clark Kent had made his telephone booth wardrobe change and had whisked her away. She felt aerial, projected forward on a comfortable wave of motion, perceiving her surroundings visually, but there was something more, almost emotional.

Her movement appeared to be at a high rate of velocity, the ground, the heavens, now flashing by her in a panorama of liquefied color. But the air stayed still, failing to divulge the true nature of her conveyance. And the sensation! She felt alive, free of the pressures and stress her daily life had built around her like a hardened fortress. Here, she was released, almost giddy with delight and the anticipation of what was to come.

Underlying Carrie's experience was an unheeded voice at the back of her mind, not bothersome, but definitely unyielding. It was the voice her mother had described to her so many years ago. The one that analyzed, evaluated, past judgment, and ultimately reminded Carrie of the moral and ethical choice she may be making. It was the voice that caused her to miss out on many things in her adolescence, but she knew at the same time it had spared her from a few difficult situations as well.

"Carrie, that other you, the one with patience, common sense, the realist," her mother had told her one evening over hot chocolate following a heated debate over curfew. "It will keep you safe a lot of times when you think you are making the right decisions. Listen to that voice, Carrie. Listen hard. That's the part of you that recognizes danger and keeps you from harm."

She listened to that voice now, and gave it the attention her mother had begged her to give it. What Carrie heard was clear and rational, a side yet unspoken during the previous journeys she had taken. Why the voice spoke up now was not clear, but for the first time since her visitation on Vandalia and the subsequent calling for her assistance, Carrie had not questioned her own actions or the bizarre mental treks she was involved in. It had all seemed so...right. She still believed in her purpose, the goals that had been laid before her, and her undying commitment to carry them through, but here she recognized the unnaturalness of it, the potential for danger, though she felt very secure. For now, the voice offered suggestion, subtle warning, and Carrie promised herself to be on guard.

Mothers. They make their marks permanent. Well, Mom, this is for a good. The salvation of a town, its long history, depends on me. I'm doing a good thing here. What can be wrong in that?

■

A kaleidoscope of blurred images and bright, mesmerizing colors passed all around Carrie. She continued to enjoy the experience, casting her eyes about her. She became sure that her physical self was not present, as if she were watching a movie of immense proportions played before her. The sensation was similar to viewing a huge theater screen, as if she were a part of the action of the camera, the rise and fall of the landscape, while relaxing comfortably in her seat. It was motion without physical movement, and Carrie realized that her body probably lay slumped on the floor of her bathroom, lifeless yet very much alive. It was her mind that traveled, and the result was breathtaking.

The texture of her visions began to change after a while, and Carrie was able to distinguish shapes, define lines and create clear images. Never before had her travels been so lengthy, both in time and distance, in her estimation. She could now make out a horizon, a separation of light and dark, blue sky and rich, dark earth.

Her attention was fixed on the deep blueness that domed the ground, though she was closing in on the shapes that dotted the horizon. At an elevation equal to a midday sun, Carrie saw a strange, elongated tube of what appeared to be a gray liquid flowing in random currents. It stretched outside her vision at both ends, and her impression was that the animated substance was confined, though it didn't have any discernable borders. A mixture of large and small waves curled among and upon themselves, and, unlike a river, the flow gave no commitment to a definite direction. It meant nothing to Carrie.

Turning her gaze away from the odd aerial display, she saw along the horizon buildings of various structure and make. There stood a water tower, and intersecting it all, earthen roads, and in some cases, paved. Here and there this established town teemed with life. Children played with dogs. Men worked in fields, plowing and gathering crops, and all the while Carrie closed in on the scene, circling it widely as the entire picture was presented to her.

Carrie's progression had slowed considerably, and as she took in the sights, a feeling of déjà vu overcame her. What was it that she recognized? The whole image seemed rustic, from a time long ago, yet the town appeared familiar at the same glance. What looked to be the heart of town boasted fresh brick construction, skillfully inlaid with ornate architectural design and handcrafted molding. She could see it all quite clearly and understood it to be of a time long ago, a stop along history's highway, something that pre-dated her. And yet...a friendly acquaintance.

Her gradual descent took her closer to the community, and the feeling of recognition grew stronger. *Where was this?* Carrie quizzed herself. *I've been here, but how?*

She glided effortlessly over the main part of town again, low enough to see businesses and shops that lined the recently tarred streets. Here was a general store; there, a five-and-dime. A supply store looked especially busy, men in overalls and various modes of headwear shuffling in and out. Carrie was impressed with the activity the town was experiencing, wishing her own Raven could be inundated with the same supply of residents and patronage.

Coming to the end of the road, leaving behind the last building on the corner, Carrie readied herself for a soft banking to the left or right, to once again traverse the town, when her eyes fell upon a sign at the side of the road. Carrie stared for as long as her progress would allow. Had she been conscious of a physical self, she would have hung her mouth in amazement. The sign, sturdily planted in the ground and colorfully painted in bright hues, proclaimed its disappointment in Carrie's exit.

"Come Back to Raven Again. You're Always Welcome"

Carrie's shock slowly graduated to understanding.

■

The locked door of his room was not enough to take the edge off the panic that Bobby felt as he sat on his bed deciding what to do. Involuntary shutters coursed sporadically through his body, and he wrung his hands in a mindless search for direction. Whether his parents would understand, would listen to any of his story, was doubtful. He had been raised in a levelheaded environment, and rational thought was of prime emphasis. No way his folks would for a minute buy into his tale of a neighbor vanishing before his eyes in a supernatural display.

Bobby stood and paced back and forth, the expectant father of an untold secret, unable to come up with an answer to his problem. He knew he had to tell somebody. Maybe Sheriff Butler down at the police department would listen. No, no, not a chance. What adult would give this the time of day, especially coming from a kid? It would be a matter of pubescent imagination, nothing more. Sure, they would soon discover that Mr. Peler was missing, but it wouldn't make them accept his explanation. It would have to be his parents. At least with them he may be spared a little embarrassment. He would tell them now, and possibly, they would listen.

Making his way into the house earlier, Bobby had raced upstairs to his room without a simple hello to anyone there. His parents had probably been in the kitchen - Dad reading the paper, his mother preparing breakfast for his return. For him to come through the door without a proclamation of his arrival was not odd. He usually liked to shower after pedaling his bicycle over the many streets of Raven, so they would not think anything wrong right now.

Bobby, his mind made up, went down the stairs to tell his tale, torn between the need to report what he witnessed to an adult and the fear of how it would be received. Either way, he was doubtful he would want to throw his route for quite a while.

His parents were at the tasks he had envisioned, his father hidden behind the paper, legs crossed, a cup of coffee awaiting him on the table. Bobby's mother was ladling the last of a pan of scrambled eggs into a bowl as Bobby stood over his regular chair at the table.

"Morning, Bobby. Ready for some breakfast?" his mother chimed, always the bright centerpiece of his family's setting.

"Yeah, sure," Bobby uttered, commanding the courage that still failed him in this moment.

"Route finished?" Dan Rollson said. The paper was his morning's singular pursuit, and Bobby rarely got much in the way of conversation from his father until he came home from work in the evenings.

"Yeah, all done," said Bobby.

He paused, looked for the best way to breach his subject, and then just went straight to the point.

"Dad, do you know Mr. Peler? He lives over on Anderson. The older man with the lawn you always comment on?"

"Sure, Ramsey Peler. I know of him, though I really haven't ever had the pleasure."

Bobby was always impressed with his father's grammar, what his English teacher Mrs. Morris would call impeccable.

"Well," began Bobby, "I always finish my route with him, and something strange...something I've never seen before...happened, and I don't know what to think of it or even do."

Bobby's mother dropped in her chair in a gradual, crumbling descent. "What do you mean...happened?"

Dan looked up from his paper.

"What did you see, Bobby? Are you all right?"

The words didn't make any sense to him no matter how many different ways Bobby had thought through the telling of his tale, and so he stumbled through the story, leaving behind all his rational maturity and letting his need to be a child, in the face of his parents, come spilling over.

"He just vanished...Mr. Peler. One minute he was there, the next minute he was gone. I was going to bring him his paper, but he disappeared right in front of me..."

"Bobby..." His mother came to him, a note of concern in her voice and on her face.

"Disappeared? Come on, Bobby." Dan was his usual doubting self, logical to the end.

"I know, Dad, it sounds crazy, but he got, I don't know, wrapped up in something, and then he wasn't there anymore."

Bobby's shaky voice was obvious to both parents, his look of legitimate fear, and for the time being, they seemed willing to allow their son the benefit of the doubt. His eyes filled with tears as he began to lose control of himself. Bobby realized it wasn't going the way he had intended, and he was angry at the childish way he was dealing with it. The story certainly wasn't going to carry any credibility if he stood there boohooing his way through.

"Dan?"

Ann Rollson, for all her intelligence and independent ways, usually acquiesced to her husband in difficult situations such as this.

"Bobby, I want you to start from the beginning and tell us everything. Sit down and relax. We're here to listen."

Though he fought with the memories as his incredible adventure unfolded, the words flowed from a distraught yet remarkably composed Bobby. With his eyes downcast in unwavering study of his hands that had taken up their ritual of movement, he became the kitchen's focus. Now that his parents were committed to giving him a chance, Bobby was able to recount everything he had seen that morning, ending his recollections only to be met with a sustained, empty silence.

He looked up after a time and sought reaction in the expressions of his parents. There was little in his father's countenance to divulge his feelings, but his mother sat with the patented look of maternal concern. They both gazed on him with puzzled regard, as if he were a creature that, though they didn't fear him, were unsure of what they had encountered.

Dan finally broke the silence.

"Well, that's quite a story, Bobby. Are you sure of what you saw?"

Bobby's hopes, what little he had, vanished like Peler.

"I knew you'd think that. Dad, I'm not making this up. He disappeared in front of me. He was in a lot of pain and then he was gone." The tears were welling up again, and Bobby fought for control.

"It's all right, dear," Ann offered.

"Okay, okay, I'm not saying I don't believe you. I believe you think you saw what you claim, but Bobby, come on, this sounds like something out of a science fiction novel."

Bobby pressed on.

"I know, Dad. I've been asking myself this whole time if what I saw really happened. But it did, Dad. It really did."

Ann sat quietly as her husband worked through their options, wanting to comfort her son, but aware Dan was working Bobby through it and her mothering would be a distraction at this point.

"Well, I guess the first thing to do is go see Mr. Peler..."

"He's gone, Dad!"

"... *and*...if he is not home, then we go to the sheriff's office and let them know we have some concerns about his whereabouts," finished Dan.

"Sheriff Butler won't believe me. You don't even believe me," Bobby said in desperation.

The atmosphere of his home was heading in a direction he disliked, so Dan took immediate steps to squelch the fire.

"We will go to Peler's, then the sheriff's office. Period."

The finality in his father's voice, a familiar tone to Bobby, ended the discussion. He headed back upstairs to shower and get ready. He and his father would be leaving shortly, to drive to Peler's and then the sheriff's office. The thought sent chills up his spine. He couldn't convince them the trip would turn up nothing, but he would do as he was told. He always had. It was the very genetic nature within him steering Dan Rollson to Peler's for answers. Bobby, unlike his father, knew what answer awaited them.

17

It was a Raven of decades ago, probably as far back as the mid-30s from what an uninformed Carrie was able to deduce. The general appearance of the store fronts, the dress of the town's inhabitants, the feel of the picture laid before her, spoke of at least sixty to seventy years ago, a time of post-Depression recovery, New Deal economics, and the sense of a common bond in communities throughout the nation. Industrial cities, growing suburban sectors, and farming regions were licking their wounds and moving forward to a better existence, a proud refusal to fully bow to years of unemployment, welfare, and big-business takeovers. Towns like Raven were renewed, rekindled with the fire of promise for a better tomorrow, and began to prosper with this newfound agenda.

Carrie had never researched the history of Raven, though she had lived through its gradual decline during her thirty-two years of residence. Always a farming town, Raven had progressively changed over time, the result of a second world war and two police actions that forever altered the course of history. Those sons that returned home pursued careers far different from the lives led by their fathers and those before them. A desire to leave behind the trappings of the past, to seek out dreams long imagined, was the cornerstone of rural disintegration, no better displayed than in the historical course of Raven.

Not a hub of agricultural endeavor, Raven had been a productive ranching and wheat farming community, strong in its output and outlook for many years. The change had been subtle, a steady decline in population and new business until, in the 80s, little was recognizable of the busy town of half a century previous.

Today, Raven was scrambling to hold on to the last few retail shops and farms that continued, and their future seemed a grim and ultimately short one in truth. Carrie had been called to help stop the trend, the slide into extinction, and here, hanging perilously yet safely a few stories above a once-thriving Raven, she was reminded of what was.

Carrie had not received any communication from her visionary as she had in past visits, but it was now that the familiar, tranquil voice spoke to her mind in its soothing, comforting tone.

"Carrie, behold what was, what must be again. See, and remember."

Its statements were non-threatening, yet as before, Carrie felt an insistence underlying the requests.

Her past attempts to respond, to ask questions, had gone for naught, in a large part due to her natural desire to speak. But now, in a moment of revelation, Carrie calmly thought through a response, projected a mental question toward whatever was the source of the voice she was receiving.

"Why? Why do you need me to help? Who are you?"

She focused her thoughts, pushing them out of her forehead in what she imagined a mental casting of her inquiries.

After a long moment in which Carrie figured her communication must have gone unheard (*unthought?*), she got an answer, and now, at a telepathic level, dialogue was primitively established.

"As it was, it must remain. The end draws too near. The process must be reversed. Together we can restore the order, the life, again."

Appealing, slightly demanding, the owner of the thoughts caressing Carrie's mind was vague, speaking in circles she couldn't comprehend.

"I understand that Raven is coming to an end. I have been working to keep the town thriving, but there is only so much I can do to..."

"No," the other said, this time with a hint of impatience, *"it must be done. Complete and total. There is only this to be done."*

"But I don't understand. Raven will always be Raven, no matter how many people live here. I'm staying. Some others will. Can't that be enough?"

Carrie was beginning to hear another voice in her head, one at a different frequency, the one her mother spoke of. She began to feel uneasy.

But the other was insistent.

"No, it must be as it was. Alive. Full of life. Only then can I survive."

Only then can I survive, thought Carrie. Who, or what, was she in contact with, and what would Raven's population have to do with its survival? She felt as unclear on things as before she was shown this living stretch in time.

"Why do you need Raven to be so? What is it to you?" she propelled, still puzzled as to the driving force behind the events over the last few months.

There was an interminable pause, and just when Carrie thought the conversation was over, *"Because I am Raven."*

Carrie was puzzled. "*You* are Raven? The name? Was the town named after you?"

"I am Raven, that which is the life. My existence is the result of the lives that have and will be here. I am a creation of the forces of human life, the energy that is emitted in their daily lives. I must continue to be provided for."

It was beginning to come together for Carrie. She was seeing a connection.

"And so as long as Raven...and so long as *you* are inhabited, as long as families live within you, you will remain...alive?" She wasn't sure of the direction this was going, but she tried to make sense of it all.

"Yes, I need them to stay, to live their lives, and for their children to live their lives as well, so that I may continue. From nothing I came. I grew. I was vital. And now I know of the end. The time of no more your kind fears."

Carrie struggled to understand.

"There is little to maintain me. You and others have fed me for my eternity, and the taking of energies has proven only a temporary cure to my situation. Your vitality, your essence, *is what I need."*

"Wh - what? *Taking* of energies? What does that mean?"

A rush of utter fear and panic swept over Carrie, and the fog of bewilderment began to lift.

The other spoke matter-of-factly. *"It has been necessary to...absorb...the physical shell to draw the full potential of energies from it. This has been moderately effective. The sustenance I require is the release of energies in all their forms."*

Carrie was beginning to understand the terrifying truth, and the drawing back of the curtain of ignorance shed light on a horrific image. It was terrifying and fascinating, a blend of spine-tingling reactions.

"You live on the emotions of us, the expended feelings of what makes us who we are?" Carrie asked.

"You have no further use for the energy. It is expelled and in turn fortifies me."

It was like a parasite, Carrie saw, feeding off its host without any detriment to the provider. Nature had many examples of parasitic relationships, but none as far-fetched and supernatural as this one.

"Yes, but now you are...what...*absorbing* people? What, cracking them open like eggs to reveal the energy inside? You're killing to survive?"

Carrie felt a flush of anger coarse through her, and pictured her physical self tensed and shaking.

"It has been a necessary result, but I must live. I am not the creator, you are. You and those like you. I will continue to draw the life forces as I need them until you have provided me with enough emitted energies. Your work thus far has been helpful, but there is so much more to be done. I am here because of you, because of your kind, and I will not be denied continuation."

Carrie was a mixture of fear, anger, betrayal, and helplessness. The very emotions this thing relished, she thought. It was crazy, unbelievable, the ravings of mad men, but it was also quite logical, quite possible, to Carrie. A town formed and grew. Its residents multiplied and went about their daily routines, along the way experiencing a wide range of emotions, feelings with variety and frequency. Was it possible that a life form could evolve from this, separate from humans but forever bound to them? It was like a vampire, created through the shared emotions of countless Raven dwellers, feeding off its unwary hosts. And here she was, an unwitting Renfield, playing the role of provider for her master. It sickened her. Why these revelations were exposing themselves now, she couldn't say. And why she had been an unquestioning participant in the events was beyond her. But that would all change.

"You will continue your work, filling the homes, replenishing the borders."

"And if I refuse?" Carrie asked.

The voice changed to a dark menace. *"Then I shall absorb all that remains, including your precious children."*

Carrie reacted with a mother's protectiveness. "You touch them and so help me I will..."

"You will what, Carrie? Good Carrie, don't stray from your chosen path. You will provide for me. You will ensure the return of this Raven before you."

Carrie looked upon the scenery so recently forgotten to her by the divulgence of the last few minutes.

"And I will know of your treachery. I see into your heart, Carrie. Your mind. I know what you feel. It is from where I feed."

Carrie was not through with her telepathic encounter, but the other, that which embodied the supernatural side of Raven, had had its word. Before she could retaliate to the threats thrown her way, the vision before her melted away into a blur of color and shape.

She came to conscious thought on her bathroom floor, smartly nestled between the toilet and the cabinet sink. She spent a brief time orienting herself, and then stood unsteadily, grasping for the counter for support.

In the mirror she saw a beaten expression, very similar to the feeling she carried with her from her experience.

She shut off the bathroom light and shuffled to her bed, not taking the time to fold back the covers but lying prone on the comforter. Staring at her bedroom ceiling, blindly noting the spider-like shadows cast there by the moonlight and branches outside her sheer draped window, Carrie remembered. It all came back to her, as if she had never really gone away, and maybe she hadn't. It was quite possible that the journey had been a mental projection, one with dream qualities, but this dream came back fully intact, every word, every emotion.

Carrie wondered if her apprehensions were being consumed at that very minute.

18

The summer heat was in full swing as Steve Edwards made his way back to the Sheriff's Department, now his bureau headquarters, to start yet another day searching for answers. In his years of law enforcement, nine of those with the state bureau, he had never come across a situation as frustrating as the disappearances in Raven. What was even more distressing (and an embarrassment to his lead position in the investigation) was that two more residents of the community had vanished since his arrival.

The town remained the stagnant dwelling it had been when his team swept in, marshalling command of Sam Butler's jurisdiction and promising swift action. As he maneuvered his way down 74 onto Main, Edwards realized he was really no further in the matter of missing persons. Nine residents' names had initially covered his master board in the sheriff's offices. In his team's initial search, they discovered that two had taken leave of Raven without announcement, but now two others had gone unseen for days. He had hoped that his further involvement would uncover their whereabouts, but minor leads had proven worthless.

He stepped from his car and let the morning sun wash over his failing confidence, but the sense of foreboding remained with him. Standing alone, Edwards acknowledged that few townspeople occupied the streets anymore, especially in the evenings as a mass hysteria was beginning to rear its ugly head. He had had Jimmy Trathor run numerous articles assuring the community that the state bureau was on the case, that there was little to fear, to allow his men to do their work and find an answer to the problem. But locals are not usually trustworthy of outsiders, and they saw their situation as a terminal illness that was best left to those familiar with the area. The growing panic was not lending itself to a mad exodus of those that stayed, but many were giving serious consideration to removing themselves and loved ones from harm's way until the mystery was solved.

The office was a hive of motion as Edwards entered, heading immediately to his desk to look for any updates. He knew he would find none since he had instructed his lead assistant, Charlie Knowles, to contact him should anything break. It would be a matter of days before his authority would be relinquished to the feds, who were already making inquires as to his progress. Since there was no proof of kidnapping across state lines or the involvement of federal suspects, the case had remained his. But the lack of solid evidence and the additional disappearances left him and his subordinates on thin ice.

As Edwards sat in the overused chair behind the desk and pondered the day's direction, Knowles approached, his arms laden with paperwork.

"So how was your night?" Knowles inquired.

"The same. I never relax in these country settings. What have you got for me?"

Knowles collapsed in the chair across the desk. "Nothing really. We got a report of a stranger seen driving the back roads northeast of town, but he turned out to be a reporter with the Cedar Hills paper looking for a story."

"Why do these guys think they can find an article on their own when we can't even make a move on this? Did you send him packing?"

"Told him to grab his steno pad and head on. Started quoting free press rights and all that crap. He forgot who he was dealing with," Knowles said.

"Yeah, we're the high-ranking incompetents. A lot of nerve."

Edwards' self-assuredness had faltered in the last few days, and it was becoming a shared attitude among all his men. Their frustration was beginning to show, as more and more reporters and denizens were boldly inquiring as to when the "state boys" would have an answer for them.

"Get me the grid and the MP list. Did we get the last of the recent interviews completed?"

"All done. Nothing worth following. It's as if these people are sneaking off, trying to avoid detection."

Steve felt he was having a reoccurring conversation, which he was in all respects.

"Yeah, but they're leaving behind families, homes, jobs, everything. You know as well as I do that there is some individual or group doing this. We just have to keep plugging away. Something will turn."

His attempt to bolster his underling's confidence was ineffective.

"One lead, just one. It's looking pretty grim. I'll get the stuff you need," Knowles said.

While Edwards waited for his map and list of missing persons, he checked the duty roster and his messages. It was simply uncanny. A small town, with no more than four hundred residents, has nine people vanish without a trace. No one sees a thing. No ransom demands, no information to provide the slightest reason for their unannounced departure. Maybe the feds did need to intervene. He had tired of slamming himself into the roadblock.

Mulling over the combined efforts of his six-man team, Edwards looked for anything that would lend itself to a pattern. The town map plotted the locations of missing person's homes, or in the case of individuals like Ed Stevens, their last known location. There was not a significant concentration of cases in any one place, and nothing indicated the residents were in similar environments or activities. Some were last seen at their place of employment. Others, at home or nearby. Arthur Towers had been seen walking his dog moments before failing to return home. The collie was found on its master's front porch later the next day, cowering when approached. In every case, though, the person in question was apparently alone, in pursuit of what was apparently normal activity.

The list of names offered little as well. It was comprised of both genders and a wide range of ages. Detailed studies of their backgrounds produced no common bonds, and the possibility that everyone had a single person, organization, or quality that tied them together was considered and analyzed from a thousand different angles by some of the best in the business, and all for not. A half hour of study provided Edwards with no earth-shattering revelations.

He would have sat their longer in frustration had Knowles not interrupted him.

"Steve, I've got a couple out here with their son. They claim that on his paper route he witnessed a man vanish in thin air. This isn't the normal thing coming through here from locals, so I thought I would let you know. I can take a statement if you'd rather not deal with it, though."

Edwards looked up from the papers, his eyes struggling to focus after staring at the stark white paper for most of the morning.

"The kid saw the guy vanish?" His interest was coupled with a tired note of sarcasm.

"That's what they say."

Edwards weighed the time he would be spending with the couple versus further analysis of the charts before him, and decided to welcome in the diversion. Besides, this was the first eyewitness claim they had had, regardless of how farfetched the story may sound from a child.

Maybe he could piece together something usable from it.

"No, Charlie, that's all right, I'll take their statement. Why are you still here anyway? I figured you were gone half an hour ago."

"Nothing to do but sleep as it is, and I'm too frustrated to relax. Figured I could be more productive here."

Edwards stood and stepped around the desk.

"No, go back to the hotel and get some rest. I'll handle things here and see you back around, say, five, for a bite to eat?"

"Whatever you say, boss. Let me bring the Rollsons in first. Are you sure I can't stay around to hear this one?" Knowles asked.

The lead investigator knew what Charlie was implying with his comment. The office had received phone calls and personal appearances from people having the definitive answers to their situation here in Raven. Everything from space aliens to the mafia had been blamed for the disappearances, and in every case the storyteller was one hundred percent sure of the information. Of course, none of the tales ever led to anything worthwhile, but no one was turned away no matter how outlandish their story. The standard jokes in the office centered on things like Elvis riding the Loch Ness Monster or the discovery of the remote burial location of Jimmy Hoffa. Edwards allowed the less than professional dialogue as a means to keep his men bonded, relaxed, and, most importantly, in the game. For ultimately it was a game they were all playing, one of cat and mouse.

One thing that Edwards had gained from his investigative career was a very realistic understanding of what his basic function was, whether it was a murder or missing person's case. Put aside the high-tech equipment, the authoritative demeanor, the sharp suit and expensive sunglasses. He was capable of shedding the layers of bureaucratic accessories, peeling back the image that came with the title, and seeing himself for what he really was - a hunter. No different from the fatigue-clad weekend warrior who slung a shotgun over his shoulder, hopped into his '85 Chevy pickup, and spent the day hoping to bag a winner. Like the stereotypical, blue-collar, trailer trash planted throughout mid-America, he went to the hunting grounds, followed the signs, used his instincts, and more often than not, came home triumphant. Simple seek-and-find. That was all the police business really was. Raven, though, was proving to be a challenge, not the happiest hunting ground. Like a hunter, he knew his game was near, but he had not been able to find a way to flush it out. Right now these Rollsons were a track on the path, a broken limb on the trail - maybe something, maybe nothing at all. But everything had to be looked into, because the mighty hunter never knew for sure what might lie just over the next rise, beneath the next outcropping, right under his nose.

"Send them in and go home," Edwards instructed.

A few seconds later a tall, dignified man, his petite-pretty wife, and their ghostly-looking son preceded Charlie as they joined Edwards in the office, giving him the impression that the walls had converged upon themselves a few more feet. The space was inadequate for the functions of one man. It certainly did not double well as a parlor for receiving guests.

Charlie introduced the Rollsons before heading out to fight the battle with The Sandman that most of the task force lost daily. "Mr. and Mrs. Rollson, this is Special Detective Edwards. He'll handle things from here."

After the formality of handshakes and pleasantries had been completed and everyone had managed to sit, Edwards settled into his listening posture and allowed Dan Rollson to tell the story. Though it was the child who had apparently witnessed the event, Mr. Rollson was obviously the voice for the family, and the other two members sat silently in deference to him, the mother holding her son's hand and stroking it in a worrisome manner.

Rollson was a well-spoken man who Steve was able to determine felt a great deal of embarrassment for having to bring himself to the sheriff's office and admit the ravings of his offspring. The story was thorough and concise, with Bobby nodding his head in confirmation as his father spoke for him.

Having listened to the testimonies of thousands of witnesses, victims, and suspects over the years, Edwards had learned with time the nuances of vocal patterns and body language. He had learned to pick up on the subtleties of inflection, tone, and pitch, along with physical demonstrations that pointed to lying and fraud to draw further information from his subjects. No matter what Rollson might say, his voice and facial expressions showed his dislike of his predicament, yet he was definitely not there to make a false report. Apparently the very fact that the son believed in what he saw and Rollson's inability to immediately discount its truth were what had brought him in.

"I assured my son that the authorities were the best people to handle his situation, as I have tried to be a responsible parent and come to some resolution of the problem," Rollson said, glancing from Steve to his son in a rhythmic beat. "After determining that Mr. Peler was not home though his car was in the driveway, I felt the logical step was to this office."

"And I appreciate your responsible delivery of this information, Mr. Rollson," Edwards said. "Let me first say that whatever information you have will be taken seriously and given every minute of investigation it deserves."

He often thought of himself as a salesman supplemental to his hunter status.

"Now, Bobby claims he saw Mr. Peler vanish while bringing him the Sunday paper. You have checked for yourself and Peler is gone. I'll have a man follow up on him right away." *So much for the father*, thought Edwards.

"Now, I'd like to hear Bobby's version of what happened, if he could. Bobby, can you tell me exactly what you saw this morning?"

"But I just told you everything, Detective. He can't add anymore," Mr. Rollson said in defiance, obviously angered that his version of the events would be questioned.

"Let Bobby tell him, Dan. Maybe he will remember something else," Mrs. Rollson said, opening her mouth for the first time since her hello.

Edwards seized the opening. "That's true, Mr. Rollson. Bobby may recall a useful piece of information in telling his story again."

Rollson acted surrounded, put against the wall. "Fine, let him tell it again. I just think it is undo stress on the boy, considering the nature of what he...what he says he saw."

Edwards could tell that the father was just being protective, guarding his son against the evils of the world, which sometimes meant the criticisms of others. Turning to Bobby, who sat complacently as his mother doted on him, Edwards said, "Bobby, can I get you a Coke or something? No? Well, I just want you to relax and try to remember everything that happened this morning, from the beginning. Have you had your route a long time?"

"A few years," Bobby said, his head down.

"I used to throw a route when I was about your age. Great source of responsibility and not a bad day's pay, if I remember."

He was trying to loosen the boy, make him feel more comfortable, but he kept rigid and sullen.

"Now, you got up at the regular time and started your route. Was there anything out of the ordinary this morning before you got to Mr. Peler's? Did you get plenty of sleep last night? Was anything bothering you when you left your house? Anything at all?"

Bobby seemed to gather himself before looking up at the detective. He spoke lucidly and direct, very much like his father. "It was like any other morning on my route. I wasn't sick or angry or seeing things because I was tired. I saw Mr. Peler standing in his driveway as I came toward him on my bicycle, and then he was gone."

"What was the visibility like, Bobby? Was the sun up yet? Were there still shadows on the lawns near the houses?" Edwards asked.

"I saw him clearly. I saw him smile. I saw him bend over in pain, then everything around him got fuzzy, and then he vanished," Bobby said, a note of defiance beginning to make its way in his voice. If the kid was dealing with a traumatic experience, he was doing it very well. "He didn't run behind a tree or step into a shadow or raise a blanket over himself and give me a David Blaine magic show. I looked right at him as he faded away. No tricks, no illusions. He is gone, and your officers better look somewhere other than his house for him because he won't be there. If everyone else in Raven is missing for the same reason Mr. Peler disappeared, I don't think you're going to have much luck."

"Why do you think that, Bobby?"

The boy gave his answer some thought. "Because I think where Mr. Peler went you won't want to go."

Spooky, the boy demonstrated a pride and intelligence that Edwards had to take seriously as a chill ran up his back and tickled his hairline. He was very believable in his convictions, and Edwards figured it was harder for the boy to divulge his story than the father. Bobby had evidently measured the merit to his tale, realized the absurdity of it, but decided he had to reveal its facts as he witnessed them or consider himself crazy. The boy *needed* the event to be real, for his own peace of mind. That, or he was telling quite a lie.

Edwards was impressed with the young boy, willing to accept that there was something viable here, something worth looking into. The only problem, as he saw it, was how to follow up on a tip like this. He would have someone check Peler's home, ask the neighbors what they might know, and go from there. It was the same direction his team had gone countless times since its arrival. If for a minute Steve was to believe the story, and he had to admit it sounded so incredible he was at a loss to find value in it, where was he to go from there? Ask a psychic, a member of SETI? If he went to the outer office and told his men that they were now on a witch hunt, a supernatural safari, they would think he was sharing the joke of the day, much better than the popular Elvis sighting.

The story of Bobby Rollson would require careful consideration. The boy may be an attention seeker, spinning his yarn in an attempt to get noticed at home since school let out. Edwards would look into the boy's background, at the same time hoping Peler showed up. There was no reason to believe that there was foul play involving the Rollsons, and for now he would treat Peler as another missing person.

He thanked the Rollsons for their time and interest in doing "the right thing" and showed them to the door. As they were leaving, Bobby turned back.

"What I told you is true. He vanished."

Mrs. Rollson put an arm around her son and led him slowly toward the outer door as he put his head back down.

Edwards went back to his office and sat down heavily. His problems had just multiplied.

19

Bill waited impatiently outside Ross Shephard's office, having arrived without an appointment and predictably cast to the purgatorial waiting area. The realtor's offices were smartly furnished, and it appeared as if employees had their own cubicle space for the private manipulation of potential buyers. The décor was earthy and comforting, designed to relax homebuyers and keep them unaware, Bill speculated. His attitude toward Carrie's employer had digressed to contempt, in a large part due to his belief that her preoccupation with selling was a strong directive being enforced within these very walls. Talking with Carrie had become impossible since her last blowup, and Bill was determined to find out what was going on. Responsible for her job in the first place and now regretting ever hooking her up here, he had wanted to speak with Shephard earlier in the week but had failed to catch him in his office until today. The thought of scheduling a time with him never crossed Bill's mind. A businessman himself for many years, Bill realized he was being consumed by the events surrounding Carrie and was beginning to show signs of abnormal behavior himself.

Since mustering the resolve to free Carrie from whatever was driving her, Bill had had to accept some things about his feelings toward her. First and without hesitation, he admitted he had cared deeply for Carrie for many years, reaching back to a time before Walt's disappearing act. His desire to help the whole family early on had been an underlying need to see her happy. If it was a deep affection, a strong attraction then, it was a formidable love now, one that reached to his very soul. Carrie had filled the void within him completely, a cavernous hole in his heart that he feared would remain with him forever.

Bill had to also come to grips with the idea that his future depended heavily on Carrie's desire to be with him. To have her pulling away, removing her blossoming emotional attachment to him now, when everything was going so well, was devastating. She had been able to blanket him with a happiness that was being ripped away. He didn't want to imagine what it would be like without her, to have that hole reopened, only this time he knew it would be so large that there was little hope of ever finding meaning to life again.

Without Carrie there to help him solve her problem, Bill thumbed distractedly through a Better Homes & Gardens to take the first step in finding a remedy. Ross Shephard had been an acquaintance of his for many years. The two had shared the recreational interests of the local wealthy many times - golf, club dinners, fundraising events - and though they weren't necessarily close friends, they each had done for the other various things along the way as a mutual favor. Bill had helped Shephard in a few legal matters involving properties, and Sam in turn had given a few of Bill's clients choice deals on real estate purchases. The agreement to give Carrie an opportunity was an example of those favors, and now Bill regretted ever sending her to the company. He knew the owner well enough to surmise that Carrie could be running herself ragged in the job, and Shephard would only see the bottom line. It was money and its pursuit, wealth running in the same circles, which had brought the two men together. He looked around himself again, at the homey atmosphere, the lure of comfort and security, and was disgusted.

About fifteen minutes into his exile, Bill heard Ross coming out of his office, ushering two well-dressed men through the door and across the main floor toward the entrance. Shephard reminded Bill of a used car salesman, boisterous, animated, and with a toothy smile and in-your-face manner that was inherent to the sales industry. *Remember me*, that approach said, *and what I can do for you. Because that is why I am here. To help you. Help yourself, you mean*, thought Bill.

Shephard gave his pigeons a final farewell as he whooshed them out the door and then turned back to Bill, who had already stood as if he were next, definitely next on the hit parade.

"Bill Curtis. How are you, sir? Long time, no see. When are we getting back out on the course so I can get some of my money back?"

Bill took the extended handshake and allowed Shephard to pump his hand unmercifully, a trademark that he must have thought made people remember him. Bill always recalled it as obnoxious.

"Hello, Ross. Sorry to bother you at this time of the day. Hope I didn't catch you in the middle of something," Bill forced with a smile, determined to play the part until he could evaluate Shephard's role in Carrie's sudden change.

"No, no. Just touting another commercial property. You know, Paul's Valley is exploding with new industry. I see this area really expanding in the next decade, in residential and commercial growth," said Shephard, always the salesman. "Let's go in the office and have a sit, and you can tell me what brings you here. Hot enough for you?"

Bill countered with some standard observation about the heat as they headed into Shephard's office, the only one with permanent walls in the building. It was richly decorated with a Southwestern motif, and Bill couldn't help but laugh to himself at the lengths people would go to surround themselves in luxury, at the same time wanting everyone to notice their opulence. Bill realized his occupation was historically just as poorly received, if not more so, but he had always considered himself an exception to the standard rule of thumb that lawyers were money-hungry and narcissistic. As he sank into one of two leather chairs facing Shephard's overdone, massive oak desk, he could only wonder what expense had been taken to create this illusion.

"So, what can I do for you, Bill? Not interested in selling that nice place of yours, are you, because I can get you above appraisal."

Bill shook his head. "No, nothing like that. I just wanted to talk with you about Carrie Hammons, see how things were going. I've been checking in on her since her husband left, and I just wanted to make sure things are going all right. I recommended her, you know."

"Oh, I remember you bringing her to me, and I can't tell you enough how pleased I am with her performance. She's a natural - a real wildcat," Shephard said.

Bill hated the way Shephard was a salesman to the bitter end, even in casual conversation that didn't mean a commission, but he had helped Carrie, given her a leg up when she was in tough straits, so for that Bill was grateful, enough to listen to Shephard's incessant pitch.

Bill went on. "I've noticed she has really pushed herself lately, especially in Raven, and I was getting a little concerned that her work habits were putting a strain on her health, possibly her family. You know she has two young children at home."

He had planned on feeling Shephard out, find out if Carrie's schedule was self-inflicted or a demand put on her to keep her job.

"Well, no one ever got anywhere in sales waiting for the phone to ring. She's out there moving properties at an impressive pace, and far be it from me to tell one of my employees to stop making me money," he laughed, leaning back and pointing his egotistical nose at the ceiling. "Really, Bill, I can't be happier with her work ethic and desire."

"But why are you giving her a Raven portfolio? She can't be making you much money in that dying town?"

"On the contrary. I'm turning a good few dollars with residential sales in Raven. Owners are willing to take a huge cut in property value to move elsewhere, and those that are buying are realizing great deals through Carrie. True, her commission is marginal, would be a lot better out here and in some of our surrounding areas of interest, but it's where she wants to be. I'm as puzzled as you are by her commitment to Raven, but, hey, she's getting the job done," Shephard said.

Bill shook his head. "I don't get it. If she is so good, why not get her out here where she can better help you and herself? Seems to me you're not taking full advantage of your resources, Ross."

Shephard intertwined his fingers and smiled, "I see Raven as a proving ground for bigger and better things for Carrie. Before long she will tire of average returns on her investment, and when she does, I will be ready to set her loose on some big time properties. A girl like Carrie has to be aged, like fine wine, until she is ready to be uncorked." He chuckled at his own analogy, at the same time making Bill angry and sickened. "I really don't think there is anything to be concerned about, Bill. Carrie is a big girl. She knows what she is doing."

"It does sound like she is making her own decisions."

"I can assure you, Bill, she is charting her own path. Quite successfully, I might add."

Bill realized that his suspicions regarding Shephard were unfounded, that though he was not discouraging Carrie's single-minded effort to sell off Raven, Ross was not forcing the issue. He considered whether further discussion would convince Shephard that Carrie might not be benefiting from the experience, but Bill figured the owner of Shephard Realty would never compromise income for human compassion. He decided to let it drop. The answer was not here. Carrie was behaving erratically for personal, not professional, reasons, and Bill would have to turn elsewhere for assistance.

After thanking Shephard and being led out the door in a manner very similar to the two men before him, Bill made his way to his car and back to his own office. He wasn't sure what direction to go next, but his love and concern for Carrie would not be denied. He had only begun.

■

Carrie slept little before finally getting out of bed long before the summer sun had broken the horizon for another full frontal assault on the Midwest. After starting the coffee pot and sitting down to watch some morning news, she let the night's encounter wash over her troubled thoughts once again, and whether she could face a day at work from this point on was questionable. There wasn't a time while she lay in bed harboring resentment for having subjected her children, clients, and Bill to her single-minded craziness that Carrie had considered how she would carry out her realty responsibilities. The thought of bringing another family into Raven as the unwitting fueling station for the voice that revealed its purpose to her last night was no longer desirable. All along Carrie had believed in her cause, an effort to revitalize a dying town, re-establish the community to its former glory. She had lived in Raven all her life - gone to school, married, raised children - it was natural that her willingness to revamp the town could be misdirected. She felt used and cheated at the same time, a pawn in a game that really had only one player - the soul of Raven.

Most of the night she had considered this possibility. Having had similar supernatural experiences prior to this one, she believed that what was happening to her was real, real in the sense that she was not dreaming or delusional. She had never had an encounter while sleeping or in the process of falling asleep. There was no single location or time of day when the visits occurred. She believed, though the prospects of revealing the nature of her beliefs did not appear likely for now. Opting for a visit to the doctor lasted a few seconds. This wasn't a physical problem, one that was affecting her ability to think and reason. What would she complain of anyway? That the spirit of her hometown had visited her in the bathroom demanding she steadily increase its population or else? She didn't think a psychiatrist would even find merit in the story. But she was confident that it wasn't hallucinations, set upon her by some mental illness. How she could reason things, how she could justify the validity of it all, she couldn't say. It would take her some time to determine the best course of action, but if she trusted what she had been told, her very thoughts were not private any longer, or ever were.

Carrie toyed with the idea that a being, an intelligence, could be manifested from the emotions of a population of human beings. Raven had been around many years. Was it possible that a steady flow of expended emotions could create a life form, one born, grown, and now demanding continued sustenance from a history of concentrated human endeavor? And were other long-established towns under the same spell? Were cities an even greater threat to creating such a force? She had always left her imaginative door open to the idea that the universe held secrets yet revealed, but this, this was a stretch. Religion, science, common sense - they all told her no. But she couldn't deny the last few weeks, her behavior, and the realness of her experiences. Raven was alive. She felt it to the very core of her being.

The biggest concern that Carrie had, and intentionally tried to ignore because of the fear that accompanied it, was the mention of her children. She had been told that non-compliance would result in their *absorption*. Whether the thing could take them from her in this ghastly way was not debatable. Its mere presence was enough to keep her attention. Though she had not witnessed what had been described, she couldn't take the chance that it was an empty threat. A change in her performance up to now could spell trouble for Tim and Sara. Taking them out of town seemed risky. Who knew what it was capable of? For all she knew the moment she packed a suitcase and hurried her children to the car, her intentions would be known, and the three of them would become permanent members of Raven. For now she would leave them at home. There was no other option except to continue showing homes, selling property, and filling the bowl that was Raven.

After a few cups of coffee, Carrie returned to her bedroom with a little foreboding. She stopped outside her bathroom door, hesitant initially to re-enter, yet something told her there would be no more unearthly visits for a while. She had been charged with a task, and whether she chose to follow the will of her oppressor or revolt remained to be seen. For now she figured she would ready for work and hopefully some options would make themselves apparent to her once she got out of town.

What she couldn't do and yet must bounced about her head like a pinball. Could she tell anyone? Bill, for example? Would the entity read her thoughts and bring an end to her and her family, or did it only tap into emotions? Was it limited to its borders, only able to manipulate those contained within its perimeter? She didn't know, hadn't the slightest idea how to answer her questions, but at some point she would have to make a move. Like a waiter bringing food to the table, Carrie would eventually be consumed herself by the guilt of what she knew. True, no harm would come to those whose abandoned emotional discharges were consumed. They would know nothing. But what of those who may be at a physical risk? To believe in this thing, this entity, was to know that it had already consumed, *killed*, and could again. Its next victim could be someone who had signed on the dotted line at the encouragement and recommendation of Ms. Carrie Hammons herself. She couldn't live with that.

An hour later, a new, though hardly improved, Carrie made her way out the door and out of Raven. She had looked in on the kids and left a long note filled with promises of fun upon her return (they had suffered during her sabbatical from reality and she had some apologizing to do), yet she was filled with self-doubt about leaving them behind. As long as she did as ordered, she concluded, they would be fine until she could solve their predicament. She drove faster than normal out of her beloved hometown, inundated by a feeling of cleanliness as she passed the dilapidated sign that signaled she was exiting town, the same smartly painted one in her visions from the night before. Carrie hoped to return that evening with an answer while remaining under the guise of compliance. Her best chance of revelation would mean administering another apology. Though her kids were likely to welcome her back with open arms, Carrie couldn't be sure how receptive Bill would be.

20

Knowing that Raven's inhabitants were in the grips of a supernatural power capable of ending all their lives would have been of little concern to Phil Jenson. Not only would he have scoffed at the very idea, throwing back his head with wide-eyed amusement at such a story, but he would also dismiss it as being secondary to the problem he was facing. Out of work for six weeks now and not a sniff of prospects on the horizon, Phil knew it was a matter of time before creditors, especially the bank holding his mortgage, would be demanding their money. Until now he had managed to get the family by on savings and the miserly two weeks of severance Huggins had handed him, accompanied by a worn out apology.

"I hate to have to do this, Phil, but the way things are going around here, I don't know how much longer before I have to shut the whole assembly area down," he'd said. The small local plant had made air exchangers for multi-engine aircraft for years, only feeling the crunch of competition recently as larger companies began diversifying and providing faster, larger quantities of product. Phil knew Huggins was faced with trying to compete, a no-win situation for his small manufacturing company, or make his own changes to survive in the ever-changing marketplace. Assembly was the most obvious cutback. The company would probably be able to continue by providing service on special orders that would not be cost-effective for large assembly plants.

It seemed the bite was being felt all over Raven, not just in the home of the Jensons. AirXchange, Inc. was one of the few businesses still operating in town, and Phil figured it would not be long before everything shut down. Without a school, major industry, or even a local attraction, he could understand why most were opting to sell everything and head to Davenport or Hermitage. Hell, even Sommerset in Coal County was a far sight more promising situation than Raven, and they had only a few ranches and a couple of residential streets to speak of. He had to do something, and quickly. Mary and the kids would be feeling the effects of his unemployment soon, and if there was anything that made Phil Jenson shudder more than the thought of moving was the idea that he could not provide for his family.

Angry, ashamed of his inability to provide, and with little in the way of leads, Phil had set out every day since his dismissal to outlying towns in search of work. His timing could not have been any worse. What few jobs that had existed were swallowed up during the gradual Raven exodus, jobs that met Phil's needs anyway. Sure, he could go flip a burger or sweep a school hallway, but the money would not be near enough to salvage his home and family needs. Mary working was not a possibility, since daycare would consume most of her paycheck. He had to have something comparable; not the same, just enough to get by. The hours, the time shifts, he wasn't averse to any conditions, but there was just nothing out there. Slowly resigning himself to the reality of moving the whole family, out of state if necessary, Phil had decided to spend a few more days trying to find something that would allow his family to stay rooted before having to tell Mary he'd tried, but they had to go.

A reassuring "Good luck" and a kiss for double measure from Mary sent him out the door that morning hoping his fortune would change for the better. He had heard of some new factory underway in Paul's Valley and hoped to land something there, even if it meant being a part of the big city atmosphere every day. The Valley was expanding geometrically it seemed, and Phil and Mary frequented the heavy traffic and interchanges only on occasion to shop or enjoy a nice dinner. They were small town folks, and nothing could replace living in a quiet, scantly populated place like Raven. Who wanted the noise, crime, and rush of the big city? For people like himself, rural life was an escape to solitude and uninterrupted pleasures. Phil preferred the pace.

Now finished checking the job board at the post office and scanning the morning Valley paper he picked up religiously at Noah Carpenter's grocery, Phil completed his morning ritual by crossing Main to Cleeger's for a cup of coffee. He wasn't part of The Circle, had never really had any desire to sit and talk with the old men of Raven, but he did enjoy dropping his quarter in Fred's Folgers can near the coffee maker and shooting the bull with the owner. Phil's dad and Cleeger had known each other for years prior to his death, and Phil had found some unspoken bond resulted from that tragedy. What started as casual reminiscence had become a friendship unlikely between men of such diverse age. But Fred was always ready with a good story and sound advice for Phil, who had found himself needing a little of both lately.

"How's the job search, Phil-my-boy?"

Fred had always called Phil that, and privately it made the younger man feel like his father had never really left him.

"Not so good, Fred. I'm afraid if something doesn't happen soon, we may have to pack it in."

Fred studied his young friend, saw the disappointment in his face, and tried to rally him. "Ah, stop that nonsense. Something's bound to open up. Your dad used to say the most unexpected pleasure is the one that..."

"Blows in on the wind," Phil completed the oft-used sentence. "I know. I know. But it's been six weeks and I haven't had nearly a sniff. We can't go on forever without me working, Fred."

"Oh, I know that, and I know you've been busting your tail to find work. Just try to hang a while longer. You know if you need a little bit to get along, I'd be more than happy to..."

Phil interrupted for the second time. "No way, Fred. You know I couldn't accept money from you. It's not that I don't appreciate the offer. It's the principle."

Fred grinned and looked down at his half-empty cup of coffee. "I'm not offering out of pity or to shame you, Phil. I want to help you and Mary if you need it."

Phil was determined not to fall upon the gratuity of anyone, especially relatives, and in the time he had know Fred, their tie had become like blood.

"No, Fred, but thank you. We'll manage just the same. Who knows? Today may be the day I land something big," Phil said, draining his cup. His growing pessimism would not allow him to believe what he told Fred, and he wasn't sure if he had sounded believable, but pride was a mighty deterrent in the face of a hand out.

Fred wished him luck as Phil made his way to the front of the store. Along the way he noticed The Circle gathering for their daily ritual of world evaluation. He had overheard on a few occasions the conversations that drove The Circle's existence, and in his opinion the group was comprised of old men too set in their ways to accept a changing society. They had chosen to alienate themselves, refusing to adapt, and in so doing had found this stagnant existence. Phil realized that every generation holds to the belief that it knows better and suffered more than any group that succeeds it. He appreciated their wisdom, respected their elder status, but refused to give credence to their pity parties.

Out the door and into a curtain of heavy humidity, Phil was sweating by the time he got the air conditioner blowing in his car and himself down the road toward the Valley. The only plus in his unemployment was imagining just how hot the processing wing of AirXchange would have been this summer. Big industrial fans rotated warm air through the sheet metal encased area, but there were few ways to combat Mother Nature and the machinery chugging away inside. He knew the work he was inquiring about today probably operated under the same conditions, but it would take more than heat to discourage him from a fair paying job. For the right money he would dance barefoot on the asphalt.

He didn't know why he happened to glance to his right as he cleared the last commercial property on Highway 74. With his family's future on the line and surrounded by sights he had seen thousands of times before, there was little reason to look down the north side of the old Flair's Clothier, empty these past six years, a huge For Lease sign plastered to the dusty store front. Beyond the dirty windows lay empty shelving and the skeletal remains of clothing racks. No longer maintained and desolate, the dilapidated structure symbolized the decay of Raven, a proverbial House of Usher. Bent over and obviously in a great deal of distress, Tom Brayton stood rigidly along the path leading behind the business. A few homes lay farther on, and Phil, who was already negotiating a U-turn and coming back around, figured Tom had probably been heading home along side Flair's.

As he pulled to a stop ten or so yards from Tom, Phil squinted through his windshield and tried to cut the glare that was clouding his vision. Tom had not registered Phil's arrival, and as Phil exited the car and stood behind the open door, he was somewhat shocked that Tom's appearance remained unchanged - cloudy, out of focus.

"Tom? You all right?" Phil called, closing the door and stepping a few feet toward the distressed young man. Tom was a fixture in town, often seen wandering the streets of Raven dawn to dusk in his purposeful stride. Mildly retarded and dependent on his parents since birth, the thirty-seven year old Tom was a harmless landmark, policing the main thoroughfare and neighborhoods of Raven with his ever-accompanying black lawn bag for trash. His parents kept him uniformed in a bright orange vest, contribution of Sheriff Butler, and he did little else but fill his day and bag with Raven's discards. Right now, though, soda cans and store fliers were the least of his concerns. Tom grasped his head in what was apparent pain, his bag at his feet, empty and unmoving in the still, heavy air.

Struck by a rush of concern and compassion for the man he had always thought his younger when he was actually three years older, Phil walked, half ran over to Tom, who continued to not register the presence of the other. The air around the stricken man was distorted, seemingly swimming before Phil's eyes. Tom bent farther still, knees slowly buckling, his elbows tucked to his ribs as his fingers tensed under the pressure they applied to his temples and forehead. Phil forgot all about his job search and the financial burden his family was under as he closed the gap between himself and Tom, finally close enough to extend his arm to the hunching figure.

If the odd turbulence of the air immediately surrounding Tom had puzzled Phil's perception, the look of his own hand convoluted on Tom's shoulder instilled panic. What was even more terrifying was the realization in that split-second that his hand refused to leave the confines of the murkiness. Yank and strain as he might, Phil was tied to Tom's cocoon of suffering, a shell that had reduced its victim to a fetal ball.

Phil looked over his shoulder, hoping to see and flag down anyone passing. He began to register tightness in his hand, radiating gradually up his arm and he instinctively cried out for help. His screams bounced back to him off the brick of the deserted building, failing to fall on anyone's ears but his own. He continued to try to pull away from Tom, leaning backward over his feet in a desperate attempt to create separation, a former savior now bailing out in self-preservation, but it was no use.

It was then that his own head began to throb, a quickly developing stabbing sensation that was commandeering his entire skull. The world around him was now completely out of focus, and he could vaguely make out the continued presence of Tom Brayton, a circular mass of yielding flesh. The pain was excruciating, beyond anything Phil had ever experienced in his life, and at that moment he realized that this must be what it was like to die. He tried to yell in anguish and fear and frustration. His head felt like it would explode, the pressure advancing to his chest and legs, and he found that he was falling to his knees with little resistance. Was it an aneurysm, a vessel in his brain having burst in some unfair genetic twist of fate? Wasn't he just on his way to find a new job, having stopped here to help someone? Who would help him?

These and other questions flashed across Phil's riddled mind as he and Tom were finally consumed in the supernatural feeding process. Nothing would be found of the two except Phil's idling car, strangely abandoned at the edge of town. Mary Jenson would grieve the disappearance of her husband, fighting back the subconscious thought that he had brought harm upon himself in a desperate moment of displaced anger and responsibility. Phil's children would ask where their father had gone and when he would be back.

A few days later, a distraught Mary packed her kids and a few suitcases and said good-bye to a couple of friends, explaining she was headed to her mother's home in Indiana, though the grandmother she referred to never saw her daughter again.

Tom's parents, older now but still dedicated to the raising of their son, drove all over town in search of their orange-vested adult child, soon resigning themselves to the idea that he may have wandered beyond their ability to return him.

The two men became missing persons ten and eleven, added to a list that Steve Edwards had been unable to explain.

Raven appeared capable of totally cannibalizing itself if necessary.

21

The phone call to Bill was a stilted one, both of them very uncomfortable in the short conversation. Carrie was thankful that Bill hadn't hung up the moment she identified herself, and was surprised at how receptive he had been to the suggestion that they meet that afternoon. He had sounded cautious though, and preferred their discussion to take place privately at his office. The embarrassing public displays she had created in the past probably precipitated his request, but Carrie had wanted the meeting away from prying eyes anyway. What she had to tell him was going to be hard for him to swallow, and the process of convincing him may make the dialogue loud and animated at the least. Bill was sure to have a lot of questions, a lot of doubts, and she had to accept the possibility he may not ever believe her wild tale, let alone forgive her past behavior. Carrie worked through lunch, met and confirmed appointments with three separate buyers, then headed to Bill's office in the northwest portion of Paul's Valley.

The fifteen-minute drive gave Carrie a final opportunity to gather her thoughts and prepare for what would probably be one of the hardest things she had ever done in her life. The road before her was relatively clear, bordered on both sides by dying vegetation. Brown, spotty grass and wilting oak and willow trees bowed to the dry, resistant sky. The area had not seen rain in six weeks, and the soaring temperatures held little respite for the dry, humid conditions. Cars and trucks, their cooling systems buckling under the heat, littered the shoulders everywhere. The oppressive weather, having staked its claim on the land, sat heavily, sapping the very life from the earth. Carrie was consciously aware of the similarity between the climate and the perilous state of Raven. In both cases the essence of life was being gradually drawn unabated. If relief did not come soon, and the prospects seemed remote, Death would be a busy visitor everywhere.

Across town, Bill paced in front of his desk, the anticipation of

Carrie's arrival causing his stomach to do cartwheels. Her call had caught him off guard, as had her demeanor. Sounding level headed and what he hoped he had not misconstrued as regretful, Carrie had requested they meet. She had something very important to talk to him about, and it couldn't wait. Fearing another spectacle, Bill had suggested she come to his office. He could clear his schedule for the late afternoon and she could have her say. Cautiously optimistic, Bill was nonetheless excited to see her again. He hoped in the course of conversation he could convey his feelings and justify their continued relationship. On the other hand, if Carrie's path of destruction continued, he would have to emphasize his concern and extend his support. Either way, he wasn't letting go. Carrie meant the world to him, and he would carry its weight on his shoulders if it made a difference.

Before either of them had fully settled on their approach, Carrie had arrived and now sat comfortably on a Victorian sofa in Bill's massive office, tastefully adorned in turn-of-the-century décor. She had been to the office a couple of times, especially during her difficult months following Walt's disappearance, and had always found the place warm and inviting. A diffused shaft of light from the afternoon sun penetrated a window and fell subtly on the thick crème carpet, offering a soft natural glow to the room. Bill was well known, a prominent legal mind in the state, and his surroundings spoke of his importance and success.

After the initial awkwardness had worn off, Bill having played the proper host in ensuring Carrie's comfort, he sat patiently nearby in a deep mahogany chair, his eyes busily moving from his hands to the floor to her. She hated herself for what she had done to him, this caring, warm man who had extended his friendship beyond the norm. It would be difficult, but Carrie was determined to make it right by him.

"Bill, I want to first apologize for the way I've acted lately. No, no, let me finish," Carrie said, raising her hand as an obstacle to Bill's move to counter her statement.

"This needs to be said. I know I have been out of control, behaving irrationally. My intentions were misguided and the way I treated you, I...I, can't say sorry enough. There is a reason for everything, though I don't expect you to accept my excuses, especially as farfetched as they will sound. Please forgive me and know that I'd like things to go back to the way they were, if that is possible, but I'll understand if you say no."

It was halting and she could have rambled further, but the need to tell him of her other concern was pushing her to conclude this part of her visit. Bill could give it some thought if he had to. The mending of their relationship seemed inconsequential to the plight that awaited Raven and lay yet unspoken on her lips.

Bill did not answer immediately, as she had expected. His rational side, that part that made him an accomplished attorney, pondered her words, and she could see the wheels of logic working overtime in his head. Bill would never place himself at a disadvantage. He of all people was familiar with word play, the complexity of language, and would always engage in discussion when he felt properly armed.

Having mulled her words over briefly, he said, "Carrie, I have thought of nothing else but you, wanting to fix this situation. My problem has been that I don't know how things got broken. I'm confused, a little scared, but I can't deny how I feel about you. I want to do whatever we can to make this work."

Carrie was relieved, and Bill's expression spoke volumes about his frame of mind. They would be able to put this behind them and move forward, given time.

"I'm so happy to hear you say that. I have been agonizing over how I was going to convince you, to make you see that I never intended to mess up the..."

Bill, ever comforting, stopped her. "It's okay now, Carrie. It will be all right."

It may be all right between them, but Carrie, having cleared this emotional hurdle, had to now tell him what was going on in Raven, and she feared that he would not be so understanding this time.

"I appreciate your standing by me, not counting us out through all this. I've learned to lean on your strength, your judgment, and I've needed those things, but there's more to this than just my behavior lately, an unbelievable amount more. I can't believe it myself, but I will need you more than ever after you hear what I am about to tell you."

He could see the distress she was experiencing and wanted to take her in his arms and tell her it would be okay, but he let her continue with what she obviously needed to say.

"You first have to believe that I never meant for any of this to happen, what happened with us, what's going on in Raven," she said.

"Raven?"

"Raven, and the people that live there." *My kids, Bill. My kids.* "It's got to stop. We have to try to stop it."

She was becoming very agitated, and he worried that she may get crazy on him again, but she stopped and caught her breath.

Bill leaned forward, as if getting closer to her would allow him to figure out what she was saying, at the same time letting her know he was there to listen.

"Stop what, Carrie? What's happened to Tim and Sara? I don't know what you're trying to tell me."

She shook her head. "I know I'm not making any sense. Let me just start from the beginning."

Over the next thirty minutes, Carrie told Bill everything as she remembered it, from the first encounter she had at the Vandalia property to her H. G. Wells journey the night before. All the while Bill sat passively, not asking questions and not revealing whether he was accepting her story at face value or thinking she was a candidate for a padded room. When she was finished she looked at him expectantly, feeling the ornately covered walls closing in on her as she waited for a response. Bill sat a moment in silence, then stood up and looked out the window, the light enveloping him in its soft glow. With his back to her, he said, "Wow. That's quite a story."

He turned back to face her, walking over to the sofa to sit by her, where he took her hand. "Carrie, it's not that I don't believe you. I believe you think what happened was real, whether it was a nightmare or whatever. But after everything that has been going on with you lately, your fits of rage, your obsession with Raven and the job, are you sure you couldn't just be hallucinating, hearing and seeing things because of all the stress you've been under?"

Carrie looked away and sighed. She knew he would be skeptical, but hallucinations?

"No, Bill. It all happened. Just as I told you."

She was going to have to convince him of her sanity at the time of her encounters as he appeared accepting of it now. Her problem was proof. There was nothing in her story that could be supported with hard evidence. It was her word, and that would be all she could provide. She changed her tactics.

"I know it is hard to swallow. I doubted myself in the beginning, but then I started to put some things together. They may just be coincidence, but it may explain what's been going on in Raven."

Carrie laid out her theory. "We have to first accept the possibility, the supernatural likelihood, of Raven, the town of Raven, being possessed of an intelligence as I described."

"Right. The hardest part to believe. It sounds like something you would find in a Stephen King novel. Pure fiction," Bill said.

"But remember that space travel, transplanted organs, and cloning were all fiction not too long ago. We are discovering things and inventing ways of doing things that were laughable fifty years ago."

"Yes, but a town that has evolved into a supernatural vampire, living on the emotions of its citizens and sucking the life out of them when food is scarce?" he said, his face riddled with doubt. "That's a giant leap from men on the moon."

His pun hung unappreciated in the air.

"There is evidence throughout history of cultures believing in a spiritual world, parallel to their own, that sometimes overlaps into the here and now. Ghosts, the soul in most religions. And don't forget the scientifically proven auras that encompass our bodies. These all could point to the existence of a spirit existing within the town. People claim to have had encounters with ghosts, claim to be in tune with the other side. Our feelings, both good and bad, released and then bonding to create some alien form, not physical, but surviving in a separate dimension. Can't it be possible that I have that ability, that I have communicated with something beyond our reality?"

Bill leaned back and put his hand to his chin, pondering everything Carrie had told him.

"For the sake of argument, let's say this...thing...is real," he said. "Why doesn't it just absorb everyone and move on to a more populated area, here for instance?"

He was referring to Paul's Valley, with a population far exceeding anything Raven had ever accomplished.

"It may be confined to a sort of physical border, just as we are as individuals. Our hopes, dreams, attitudes, goals, our souls, are limited to this shell we call a body," Carrie countered. "Since it has needed me to bring it dinner, so to speak, I don't think it has influence on anything outside itself."

"And you think it is using you, now threatening you, to provide for it?"

"Yes, I do. Since it operates at a supernatural level, maybe it is able to read the thoughts of its inhabitants, and it chose me, because of what I do, to populate it."

Bill was not going to give in easily. "And since its intake has decreased, it is now picking people off one by one to temporarily satisfy itself. If it isn't of our physical world, how can it manipulate our bodies, take the emotion, the soul, and the shell?"

"That's the one thing I am still not sure of. Maybe by thoroughly draining the body of everything that makes us human, makes us who we are, there is nothing left. As if the people it has taken are imploding. Look, when the essence of a grape is removed, you have a shriveled raisin. When the human body is exposed to the elements, over time it wastes away. Maybe this thing can rapidly empty us until the vessel is of no consequence, until all that remains is a trace of our ever existing. Dust to dust, Bill. Remember?"

"But you are suggesting an intelligence here. If it uses up all its food sources, doesn't it realize that it will die of attrition? Killing people off will be a short-lived solution to its problem," Bill said. It was his turn to speculate.

Carrie shook her head. "The taking of bodies seems to be temporary. It's like us coming up for air momentarily and then going back underwater to complete our objective. It believes it will be repopulated. Showing me the past was not just a history lesson – the thing expects to return to an existence it has always known. I don't think it knows a town can die out."

Bill stood again, battling with the love he felt for Carrie and the logical part of him that was having trouble accepting the unfathomable. If she had come to him saying she was having personal problems, issues that were affecting her ability to think rationally, he could have dealt with that, gotten her to a specialist to treat her. But this? This needed a witch doctor, a priest, the damn Ghostbusters. He was lost as to what to do.

"Carrie, I want to believe you, really I do, but a power this bizarre, manipulating an entire town and killing people on some spiritual buffet line? I just can't go there. I'm sorry."

Had Bill been a God-fearing man, the jump from reality to fantasy may have been more plausible, but his upbringing had never led him to regard life at a religious level.

Carrie was not completely disheartened, but she felt as if she may be facing this battle alone. If Bill, who claimed he cared for her deeply, and she had no reason to think otherwise, was not jumping to her side of the fence, who else would? The police? Not a chance. She knew one thing for sure - more people would die before Raven was satisfied, if it could be. Something had to be done, and soon.

She got up to leave, gathering her purse and smoothing her skirt, not angry with Bill but feeling anxious about spending any more time trying to sell her story when things could be getting worse back home.

"Well, I have to do something. People are dying and I have to try to help them. I didn't totally expect you to believe my story. Hell, it's hard for me to accept it, and I have seen the proof. I guess I was counting on your open-mindedness, your willingness to explore new ideas."

Carrie started for the door.

"Wait," said Bill.

He came to her, putting his hands on her shoulders and looking down at her with his sharp blue eyes. She had gazed through those windows many times, finding a safety she had never known before.

"Look, I'm worried about you, Carrie. I don't know what to make of this, and I'm scared that it is going to in some way put you in danger."

"We're all in danger, Bill. All of us in Raven, that is."

"Then pack some things, get the kids, and come to my house until everything blows over. You don't have to be the leader of this crusade," he implored.

"Haven't you heard a word I've said? I *can't* leave. It will know and then it will take my children. And I do have to do something. Aside from you, I'm the only one who knows what's going on in Raven. I can't walk away from this."

Carrie was to the point of tears, not because she was scared or angry but frustrated. She had come to him to apologize and open herself up to his understanding. He recognized two things at that moment - she needed him but she was determined to beat whatever had a hold on Raven, with or without his help.

He let his head fall backward, his shoulders heaving upward in a sustained sigh.

"All right, what do you want to do?" His chin descending as those trance-inducing eyes gazed into Carrie's. "Hey, maybe it's time I give my open mind free reign, don't you think? I'll explore the possibility."

He would stand by her, the rock she so desperately needed.

"I'm not saying I believe all this, but who knows, before it's all over, I may have discovered my spiritual side."

He hugged her, long and fiercely, needing to not only reassure her, but also let himself feel something physical, something real.

"I hope we don't live to regret this," Bill said.

Carrie whispered prophetically, "I hope we live."

22

Raven was beginning to take on the appearance of a graveyard, its silence and desolation interrupted sporadically by a lone vehicle cruising unnoticed down empty streets or a solitary figure making his way over the uneven, cracked sidewalks that had served pedestrians for too many years. The vitality of the town had ebbed away over the years, giving way to a stark and shadowy existence, a dim reminder of its once vibrant past. Homes previously filled with the laughter of children, the woes of familial interaction, and the dreams of a productive, meaningful future had been replaced by a predatory stillness that crept throughout the town, a pestilence that slowly invaded everything, leaving behind a lifeless vacuum.

Residents had recognized the gradual slide over the years, a result of societal and economic factors, and many had left ahead of the tide that now trapped those that remained. With those fortunate emigrants went their collective emotional outpourings, signaling a change in the passivity of that which was the spirit of Raven. Born of the consistent flood of human feelings, the spirit of Raven evolved, thrived, and ultimately depended on its creators for its continued survival. As the nourishing mixture of positive and negative human interaction lessened, as the communal activity dissolved, the need became a craving, a demand that had to be fulfilled. Years of vibrancy, decades of bustling life, and now the supply was being cut off. That which had been conceived of human emotion was now in a life and death struggle. When the flow of sustenance reached a trickle, a barely useable amount, Raven was forced to take what it needed. A human host, it found, could be tapped and drained like a well, releasing the life-giving force that it stored. The result was satisfying, but the vehicle that carried the rich store was rendered useless in the process.

It knew that this could not go on, the sapping of the vessels, but it was necessary to relieve the pain, the emptiness that had overtaken Raven a few years ago. The slow but steady gnawing that had signaled change was now a debilitating roadblock in the fulfilling pace it had come to know. Raven would return to its rich store of human emotion; it had assured this with the use of the vessel Carrie. In time the scarce supply would rekindle itself into a bountiful harvest. Until then, an occasional body must be destroyed.

The end of other lives did not affect it. It was only trying to survive.

■

Steve Edwards' deadline for substantial progress if not summation of the case in Raven was nearing, and he was nowhere closer to solving things than he had been on his arrival weeks ago. His superiors were jumping through rings keeping the media at bay so that he could properly carry out his investigation, but their patience had worn measurably thin. He was to turn over all the information gathered during the course of his team's presence in Raven, at which time there would be federal intervention.

Edwards couldn't help but feel a personal sense of failure for his poor showing on this one. Regardless of the lack of evidence, witness testimony, and usable leads, he thought he could get to the bottom of anything in his business. His bullheaded nature was what had shot him to the upper level of the bureau, and he had envisioned new doors opening soon. The Raven embarrassment would taint an otherwise stellar record of achievement. Once the youngest field operative to ever carry the SBI shield, he had been instrumental in the capture of over thirteen Most Wanted fugitives, led the much publicized exposure of drug dealing within the state senate, and had most recently received endorsements for federal service. And to have it all come crashing down now because he couldn't find the psycho playing hide-and-seek with the yokels of some dead end field in the sticks. *Damn, I've got to catch a break on this.* But there was nothing to go on.

To illustrate his predicament, the best lead he had received in a week was the fantastic account of hocus pocus involving a teenage paperboy and his elderly client. The man, sixty-three-year-old Ramsey Peler, was reported to have disappeared in thin air as the boy brought him his paper last Sunday morning. A subsequent check of the home turned up no Mr. Peler. Neighbors were unaware of his location or if there had been a planned departure. He was simply gone. Like the homes of other victims, there appeared to be no preparation to go on an extended trip. Vehicles remained, mail was not stopped, and clothes were not packed. In some instances the home looked instantaneously abandoned - coffee pot on, television broadcasting, water running. It was indeed odd, but Edwards had dismissed the boy's story. As if he didn't have enough trouble, pursuing the tale of some supernatural body snatcher would be the death of his investigation and probably his career. Resigned to the inevitability of his forthcoming departure, he had decided to at least spend the last days shoring up the team's paperwork, guaranteeing at the least that a clean, orderly stack of records would be turned over. From there he could only pray in his selfish assault on the ladder of success that the feds had the same luck he had - none.

Sam Butler stood at the door of his former office, waiting for Edwards to acknowledge his presence. It was nearly a month ago that the bureau had descended on Raven and minimized his importance to little more than a security guard. In that time he had frequented the department's former dwelling to try to stay abreast of the progress being made. More than a feeling of duty, Sam was brought back time and again by pride and a civic concern for the well being of his fellow residents. Each visit was unremarkable as Sam was given little if any respect for his position. One thing he had gained during that period of time was recognition. None of Edwards' detectives felt inclined to make his arrival announced. They usually gave his appearance a cursory glance, if any, and had begun nodding toward the office before getting back to their work. Though Edwards had not asked him to forego any future drop-ins, Sam believed his presence was nonetheless unnerving to the team for whatever reason.

Special Detective Edwards, his hands on his hips while he stared intently at a gigantic map of Raven pinned to the wall, finally looked over his shoulder to the door.

"Sheriff Butler, how's it going? Just looking over your town here. Perfect grid layout, I'd say."

Sam crossed over to the wall where the detective remained. "Yes, eight square miles. Makes it easy to patrol."

Raven's fathers, for a reason even The Circle was not privy to, had intersected roads and designated property boundaries at true right angles, equidistant and simply designed. The town had a perfectly square topography, blocked off in uniform sections, both residential and commercial. There was no denying the limits of the town, its borders precisely parallel and shared with county jurisdiction.

"I would think so. Have a seat," Edwards said, pointing to a chair across from his, Sam's, desk. "I can't say that I have anything important to tell you. Everything's about the same since the last time we spoke."

The detective appreciated the interest Sam had in the investigation on his town, though he knew he would not have been quite so cordial had a team outside his responsibility stepped in and taken everything over. Raven's police department had been relegated to setting up a temporary location in an empty office south of their former location. The SBI had indicated to Sheriff Butler that his offices would be utilized because of their suitability to its investigation. Phone lines, computers, bulletin boards, and the general makeup of the offices were ideal for the SBI's needs. It was argued that Sheriff Butler's department could more easily improvise until their work was complete. Edwards saw the way Butler relinquished everything with little resistance as a weakness, especially for a member of law enforcement, but the sheriff's hands were tied, and there was little he could do but continue his policing of the community while Edwards' team did their job.

But now, with the feds breathing down his neck and subsequent disappearances marking his unproductive stay, the SBI's star detective felt more inclined to elicit the help of the sheriff. There was little else for him to try.

"So what your telling me again is that there is little I can do for you right now," Sam said, the sarcasm evident but not overdone.

"Look, Sheriff...Sam. I understand your dislike of the situation. We coming in here and taking over your investigation, but you have to realize I am just doing my job. The truth is, we aren't going to be in charge of things much longer," Edwards said, his hands folded on the desk.

"What do you mean?"

"I mean that in a few days control is being turned over to the big boys."

"FBI?"

Edwards pinched the bridge of his nose, the lines on his forehead drawing weeks of exhaustion on his face.

"Yeah, the feds. Seems we aren't moving fast enough for them, and with the additional disappearances since our arrival, it is felt that a swifter remedy is called for. The national media is starting to get wind of this, and before long, your little town here is going to be crawling with television trucks and reporters."

Sam was aware that the number of missing persons in Raven was well above average, even if it were a major metropolitan area, but he had not thought the problem of national concern. He let his momentary satisfaction at Edwards' failure wash over him as he concentrated on the implications of what he was being revealed.

"But your efforts, they have produced nothing?"

"Little to nothing. We have swept every crime scene clean, interviewed countless people, and submitted hundreds of materials for lab analysis. Nothing. I don't know what more can be done here, even by the FBI, but the ball is in their court now. I can only minimize the pertinent info we have compiled and submit it upon their arrival."

For the first time since he showed up, Edwards appeared lacking in any confidence.

"What do you think is happening here?" Sam asked.

"Given the complete, and I mean complete, lack of physical or witness evidence and the inability of either of us, and I include your department because of its intimate knowledge of the victims, to find anything that ties these people together, I haven't the slightest idea."

Sam already knew the efforts of the state bureau were turning up little if any new information. He hadn't needed Steve to tell him to know, but he had failed to consider that with the tools and manpower they had at their disposal that they would still draw a goose egg.

"And there have been no eyewitnesses?"

"Nothing credible. We get a dozen calls a day from people claiming to have seen one of the missing walking the street or driving around in another town, but they always come up empty," Edwards said. "Had a paperboy in here a few days ago with his parents claiming to have witnessed a guy dissolve into thin air right in front of him. Can you believe that mystical crap? That's the kind of stuff we're getting."

Sam perked up. "Bobby Rollson said he saw a man disappear?"

"Yeah, just vanished from where he stood. We checked out his story, verified the guy is missing, but I can't spend valuable time on the fantasies of a twelve-year-old kid," he whined, showing a little of the sore loser he was in the face of adversity.

"Did he describe the disappearance?" Sam asked.

Edwards acted perturbed, as if this was not something they needed to spend time evaluating.

"Yeah, he said he was standing there one minute and then he was gone. Faded away."

"The Rollsons are good people. Bobby is highly intelligent for his age, a very mature young man. I can't believe he would make up something like that," Sam said.

As sheriff, Sam had worked closely with the Raven school district before it eventually fell to budget crunches. While providing various demonstrations and lectures, often in conjunction with the volunteer fire department, he had become familiar with many of the children. He especially recalled Bobby, whose parents were highly involved in their son's education, and his penchant for asking remarkably bright questions.

"As a police officer, you know as well as I do that investigative procedures call for sorting through the ridiculous, the absurd, and following the facts."

"I attended the same enforcement classes you did, Steve," Sam said. "I'm speaking from that intimate knowledge you mentioned earlier. That boy is not the make-believe type. He is two grades ahead of his age, a great student, and I just think there is something to what he said that refutes a quick dismissal."

Edwards had considered soliciting the help of the local sheriff a last option and a peaceful gesture as the outgoing authority in Raven, but now he regretted the move. Butler was asking him to give serious consideration to a fairy tale.

"I think verifying Mr. Peler's disappearance, examining his home and the surrounding area, and talking with a few neighbors was credit enough for the whopper he laid on us. Even his parents acted embarrassed about the boy's story."

Sam looked unsatisfied.

"It could have been a trick of the light, an overactive imagination, any of a number of things. No, no, no way. I refuse to believe that our situation here is the result of some supernatural event," Edwards shook his head. "A man vanishing like in a magic act? Come on, Sam."

Edwards got up and looked out the window, sorry he had toyed with the thought that Butler could help him, hoping the conversation was near an end. The sheriff was persistent though.

"It would explain the lack of any solid evidence, the fact no one, alive or dead, has been found. Steve, what are the odds that eleven people in the same small town disappear without a trace, leaving behind family, possessions, and no reason for their exit? We're not talking about one or two flighty individuals. We're talking about respected members of the community, loving husbands, wives, sons."

"But what your espousing is straight from Asimov or Bradbury."

Sam was pleased to learn that Steve was well read. *There may be hope for this guy yet*, he thought.

"Science is probably a big part of it, especially if people are being teleported, their molecules scrambled, transferred, and reconstructed elsewhere. Or for some ghastly reason, they are simply being eliminated in some secret biological event. Who knows what advancements have occurred, what technology exists? This is a small, remote community. Testing done here would be looked over, ignored."

What the sheriff was proposing went against everything Edwards understood police work to be. Like Bill Curtis, rational thought was what had elevated him to his present position, what would continue fueling his career objectives. The obscure, unproven theory that Sam was suggesting was beyond his ability to consider. He needed more, so much more before he could pursue such a possibility.

Detective Knowles popped his head in the door as Edwards was preparing his counter attack on Sam's explanation for Raven's admittedly unique situation.

"I've got a couple out here asking to see someone in charge. They claim to know what is happening to everyone in Raven," Knowles said.

Edwards sighed, "Tell them to wait a few days and then come back with their problem."

Sam could see how the ineffectiveness of the investigation, now coupled with his appeal for giving credence to Bobby Rollson's story, had worn Edwards ragged. But he was able to smile measurably and instruct Knowles to show them in.

Sam stood to address the new arrivals, but Edwards was under the impression he was intending to leave.

"Oh, no, you stay right here. I want you to hear first hand some of the stuff we've been getting."

Shown through the door came a woman and a man unfamiliar to the detective. The woman, an attractive brunette in her thirties, saw Sheriff Butler and exhibited immediate recognition.

"Sheriff," she nodded.

"Hello, good to see you again," Sam said as he held out his hand in welcome to her.

The man was older, well dressed and dignified, walking with the air of authority and respect. Edwards figured him as a politician or government type. He also shook the sheriff's hand.

"Long time, no see, Sheriff."

Sam's smile grew during the hardy handshake that followed. "Don't see much of you around here lately, Bill. Where have you been hiding yourself?"

"I'm afraid you're going to be seeing a lot more of me in the future," the man said in an ominous tone.

Sam turned to Edwards, who stood idly by during this short reunion.

"Special Detective Steve Edwards, I'd like you to meet Carrie

Hammons and Bill Curtis. I'll vouch for their reputations," he said with a wink, recalling that Knowles had announced them as having information on the case.

"Won't you sit down, please," Edwards instructed, letting Sam maneuver a few chairs in a semi-circle around the desk. "Sheriff Butler and I were just discussing some theories of his on the events occurring in Raven. I understand from Detective Knowles that you may have some information for us?"

Ms. Hammons was the first to speak. Her self-assured posture and pleasant yet forceful voice immediately captured Edwards' attention.

"Thank you for seeing us, Detective. Mr. Curtis and I have discussed this from a thousand different directions, and I think it is best if I just come to the point and save you the trouble of a long explanation, at least for now. Here, anyway."

"Well, we want to help you, Ms. Hammons. You and all of Raven. We want to figure out who is behind these missing person cases," Edwards said.

Carrie remained stalwart.

"That's just it, Detective. *Raven* is responsible - the town. There is an entity, a spirit if you will, that claims to be Raven, and it is slowly consuming the people that live here."

Edwards quickly looked at Sam, who could only shrug his shoulders in vindication.

23

While Carrie was holding her audience spellbound in the sheriff's office, Bill sat and studied her in captivated silence. The sun was penetrating the office, diffusing itself to every corner of the room as it denied the cover of shadow. Bill studied her face, mesmerizing himself with its beauty and expressive lines, only half listening to the soliloquy she voiced. There was no denying the power she now possessed to demand attention. Her independent, self-assured design was a far cry from the meekness that constituted her personality as wife and mother when he had met her years ago. He stood amazed at Carrie's confidence and determination, born in the aftermath of the challenge of going it alone. Those qualities, presently on display in the sheriff's office, had stolen his heart. At a time when his own career and daily routine had left him unsatisfied, sure that life had dealt him all the cards he would ever be allowed to play, he had found new purpose in Carrie.

He knew he would do anything for this woman, one who had given him a new start, offering him a second chance. She had been able to convince him to accept her story, crazy as it sounded, and that it needed to be presented to the authorities, though he had strongly recommended that she think through that decision. The police department was overrun with their own problems, he had said. State authorities had descended on Raven to quell the townspeople's concern and handle the ever-growing criminal investigation. The last thing they needed was someone disturbing them, spouting tales of the macabre. She was hurt by his comment, and having realized he was failing to demonstrate the support he had promised, he apologized repeatedly.

"Carrie, shouldn't we think this through, though? Try to come up with a better solution other than involving the police?" he'd said.

"And let them continue to look for people they'll never find, while those that stay are sitting ducks? I can't let that happen," she had said.

Bill knew she was right, that the police were probably their best bet, but he was actually trying to protect her from the embarrassment her story would surely bring. He could only imagine the good-hearted laughter that would well unchecked from the state's investigators when they heard it. What she was suggesting was alive and prowling the dark shadows of Raven was better suited for a screenwriter's interpretation or an occultist's intervention.

Without being able to offer an alternative, he pointed out that the thing had warned her about not helping it. Going to the police might be detrimental to her safety and that of her family. Even she had mentioned her own fear that packing up Sara and Tim and trying to leave was dangerous. Changing her mind and refusing to bring new homeowners to Raven would bring a heavy price, one her children, she was warned, would pay. If Carrie valued her family, she would wait and give it more consideration, go about her daily routine as if nothing had happened. In the mean time, they could consider their options.

That had stopped her abruptly. Considering what the entity had told her, Carrie had to accept the idea that any further exodus from Raven would not be tolerated. The police may call for a mass evacuation of Raven in order to spare more lives, but she was convinced that would surely bring deadly retribution. They would have to understand that fleeing was not a choice. The thing had to be dealt with on its own terms, within its borders. They just had to understand. She gathered her resolve.

"It's a chance I have to take, Bill. Everybody is in danger as it is. We don't know what it is capable of, what it knows. This thing has lived in our midst since, well, since the town began, feeding and growing stronger. Its power may be limited or it may be beyond our understanding. But do I continue to bring residents to Raven like lambs to the slaughter, hoping that I get enough people there to satisfy its thirst for human feelings? No, thank you. You know as well as I do that Raven will never be the town it once was. It would be a miracle for it to have five hundred residents again, let alone the thousands that it once held. We can't sit it out, hoping this little problem passes over, because all the while, everyone, including my kids, is in danger. I see no other way."

It had been enough for him. By accepting her story, he had also come to terms with its implications. Over a short period of time, Raven would eventually consume itself, and the personification of a "dead" town would hold truer than it had ever held before.

The one concern Carrie continued to voice during their debate was how much discussion of their plans could take place within Raven. If the entity possessed the ability to make a psychic connection with humans, communicate with them as it had done during Carrie's visit to the Raven of old, then it made sense it could comprehend human interaction.

"If we march in there and tell them what we know and start planning a way to defeat this, it may retaliate, or it could foil our plans before we can act on them," she had said. "We're taking a risk right now, talking about this, but I am convinced it is confined to Raven. If it could reach outside its borders, it could draw people in by itself, using some mental trickery. It wouldn't need me."

They agreed that the information they brought to the authorities must be convincing but limited, especially any talk of taking action. Further discussion would have to take place outside of Raven, possibly here in Bill's offices. Bill, though disappointed in himself for dismissing Carrie's story as unbelievable, still had to point out that believing her had taken him hearing the whole story.

"And *I'm* in love with you. If these guys believe you, am I to assume you have a special relationship with them too," Bill had kidded, hoping to break the tension that had stood as a sentinel over their meeting.

"Well, of course. You don't think I'm limiting myself to some middle-aged attorney when I can have the thrill of law enforcement in my life, too, do you?" she had smiled, poking him playfully.

He kissed her then, tenderly and long, as they found a moment of comfort in each other, holding on to the one reality they were sure of. He thought about that kiss now, the passion it had stirred within them both, and the promise it held of things to come. In time Bill had stood to gather his things to leave, but Carrie wasn't ready for the trip to Raven just yet. The entity had impressed her with its formidability, and she refused to leave anything to chance.

"My greatest fear is that it knows what we are thinking," she said. "It's one thing to scheme and plan here in what we believe is private, but our thoughts, together with the emotions that accompany them, will be there for the tapping if it does have a psychic ability, which we have decided is probable. How can we possibly hide what is in our minds?"

Bill considered her comment, impressed with her insight. It was something obvious he hadn't considered.

"I don't know. Think of something else maybe? Carrie, there's no guarantee we will be able to get out of Raven once we get there, but if nothing else, we have to get to your children, regardless of what we're thinking. Like you said, it's a chance we have to take."

They had first gone by her house to check on the kids, who received her apologies with open arms. Carrie recognized the nature of children to quickly forgive and forget to be a quality sadly left behind in the climb to adulthood. After a half hour of reassurances and the shedding of guilt,

Carrie was able to leave the children once more to join Bill downtown.

And now, gathered at the headquarters of the investigation fast approaching national attention, Carrie finished her story, and both men sat in stunned silence, though not for the reasons that Bill could imagine. She had been careful to only describe her three encounters, leaving out her ideas discussed earlier with Bill. Detective Edwards and Sam Butler had been exchanging glances during her entire oratory, their faces displaying a genuine concern. Though Bill knew these men were professionals and had probably heard countless stories that required a major stretch of the imagination, he was surprised at their demeanor. He was beginning to wonder whether the two were being considerate of Carrie or were actually giving her story credit. In the next second he expected either or both men to burst out in uncontrollable laughter, apologizing for their mirth through watery eyes.

Edwards was the first to speak.

"Ms. Hammons, that's quite a story you told, one that asks for a lot of irrational thinking. Thirty minutes ago I would have humored you briefly while arranging for a mental hospital to come take you away. That was, of course, before your Sheriff Butler arrived. Now I'm not so sure what to think."

"What do you mean?" Carrie asked.

Sam said, "Ms. Hammons, the Rollson family was in here earlier claiming that their son Bobby had seen a customer on his paper route vanish in a way very similar to this absorption thing that you described."

"You're kidding," Bill said. "You mean someone saw what Carrie said is happening to the people of Raven?"

"Well, I'm still not sure what we are dealing with. The two stories do seem to support each other," said Edwards, "but how do I know you didn't set this up, all of you, to get us out of here? You have to admit this is pretty out there, talk of town spirits consuming residents in a desperate attempt to exist. Maybe you want us to look bad, chasing this ghost of yours, because you resent our being here."

"I'm not even going to dignify that with an answer," Sam said.

Carrie spoke up. "Detective Edwards, this isn't some joke or fantasy, some make believe game we're playing. Your suspect is supernatural. Whether you accept that or not, it's what is causing the problems in Raven."

Edwards seemed unsure, or unwilling, to jump on the bandwagon, possibly by doing so would jeopardize his career.

"But come on, a supernatural being? What am I supposed to do, stand in the middle of the street and exorcise it, invoke the apostles and saints to intervene? This is crazy."

He shook his head and appeared ready to withdraw from entertaining the chances further.

"Detective, I can sympathize with you," Bill tried. " I really can. Carrie came to me with this today, and I immediately dismissed it as mental exhaustion, fatigue from working too hard. I tried to come up with a thousand different reasons to justify rationally why she was telling me this. I couldn't. If you knew Ms. Hammons at all, and I know the sheriff will back me on this, you would realize that it is totally out of her character to create some wild science fiction story. What would she have to gain? Nothing. What does she have to lose? Well, that's what did it for me. I realized she was risking public ridicule, not only for herself but her children, her job, her personal relationships, all for the people of Raven.

"I'm convinced, and whether you want to believe it or not, Raven's problem is not in the form of a kidnapper or international hit man. It is an entity, that exists like the town's soul, and if we don't do something soon, it and every other soul in town may be damned to an eternal hell."

Carrie looked at Bill with loving regard. He had fought against the illogical and the woman he cared about more than anything else long enough. The ball was now totally in the court of Steve Edwards.

The detective fiddled with the pen on his desk, drumming it in deep thought. Finally, he looked up at all three.

"Okay, what do you suggest we do?"

"Well, that's where this meeting needs to end," said Carrie. "For lack of a better description right now, I think this room, and any place in Raven, is bugged. Whatever we say here may work against us. I think we should just go about our business and reconvene out of town later, for reasons I'll explain then. We may already be cooked. I don't know, but Bill and I agree that it is the safest way. If everyone is in agreement, we will continue at Bill's offices in Paul's Valley at eight o'clock tomorrow morning."

"Are you sure that is absolutely necessary?" Edwards said.

"I don't know anything for sure, but I do know that it communicated with me. It understood me. I think it is worth the inconvenience," said Carrie.

Sam, who had remained relatively silent since Carrie and Bill's arrival, said, "I'll give the detective directions, and we can pick up from here."

He looked at Edwards who nodded his approval.

"Very well, then. Tomorrow," Carrie said as the four of them stood in unison. "And I might suggest that as you leave town in the morning, mask your intentions if possible. This thing spoke to me telepathically, so it is very likely it can read thoughts, especially those accompanied by strong emotion, like deceit or fear. Think of a movie you saw, sing a song with your car radio. Anything. It is not totally clear what we are dealing with, but one thing is for sure – it's dying, and like a wounded animal, its strike may be deadly."

24

For the first time in weeks a light breeze penetrated the heavy stillness in the air. The slumping, dry shoulders of the trees were crudely lifted as their leaves caught the welcome wind that meandered down the empty streets. Faded and frayed, store front awnings danced lazily with the midnight stranger. Trash tumbled along the sidewalks, settling in already littered corners and wrapping around the poles of flickering sodium-vapor lights. A visitor happening upon this scene would have noted the sense of desolation, of abandonment, that refused to relinquish its hold to the moving, though thick and sultry, air. Raven appeared the picture of death, like a fallen soldier left behind on the battlefield as the war moved on, though there was no visible indication this warrior had struggled to survive. Dark, empty windows, staring out from long deserted shops like dead eyes, extinguished any hope of finding some signs of vigorous living.

Members of the Raven community showed an unexplainable passive interest in the events unfolding around them. Local news and the gossip in public places like Cleeger's did little to instill a sense of dread or even mild worry in them as they met each day with a perpetual lethargy. The majority were retired, satisfied to complete their twilight days in the formerly tranquil area, and too old to seek a new life elsewhere. Sharing with the elderly were the low-income families, embedded like ticks in the steadily appearing cheap, affordable housing around town. Moving for them was a financial risk. The chance of finding a comparable situation was next to impossible, so for now the disabled, unskilled laborers and welfare mothers clung fiercely to what little they had. Life for everyone in Raven was simple, lacking excitement and the fast-paced nature of the big cities, but comfortable. It would take more than a few disappearances to drag them away.

Beneath this funereal setting pulsed a faint but steady force, an underlying presence that existed within, yet on a plane parallel to, the town's dismal reality. The spirit of Raven, molded over decades with the emotional clay of thousands of its residents, found itself in unfamiliar surroundings. A relatively inactive creature, the entity had never needed to play the role of predator, content to cast its tendrils upon the river of ever-moving human emotion and drinking deeply from its depths. Its non-aggressive existence was second nature, as it fed without competition.

A shapeless, undulating mass, amoeba-like in its structure, the entity had been forced to explore its capabilities, to test the extent of its unique creation. Before the food source had begun to diminish and no longer fill its ravenous need, the entity had floated effortlessly across a stark, simplistic landscape. In a desperate effort of self-survival, it found in time that it could make contact with the sources of its previously rich harvest of sustenance, feeling out the human vessels across the void that separated them, and bond in a pseudo-psychic manner. By tracking the latent wisps of emotion that left a discernable trail back to their source, the entity was able to establish a link with humans. With this discovery it found that each vessel had identifiable patterns of emotion that separated it from the others. These fingerprints allowed the entity to single out an individual and use the vessel for its particular needs, whether absorption or contact at a sub-conscious level. The creature had learned that it could tap the very conscious of a human and even communicate, as it had done with the Carrie vessel. Humans possessed various depths of consciousness, and at their deepest, which the entity could invoke by rendering the upper levels incapacitated, the entity was able to carry on dialogue, a telepathic give-and-take.

It had also evolved over time an awareness of self, a primitive response to its needs and environment, a result of absorbing the by-products of earth's most specialized inhabitants. This facilitated the unions it formed during its advanced bonding. Through years of consuming the essence of humanity, its positive and negative emissions, the creature had gained an understanding of its benefactors, their knowledge, interactions, even their sense of right and wrong. They were a diverse group, though not wholly different from it, their offspring. Mankind was driven to survive, seeming to base its entire existence on perpetuation. Intensive labor, medical advancement, the importance placed on sexual coupling, the production of food, and long-term education were aimed at extending the lifespan. The entity's rudimentary grasp of death, enough to realize its own mortality, had also come from its close association with man.

As it began to more fully comprehend that aspect of life during

Raven's dark decline, the will to live became more pronounced. Now, with the possibility of Death's shadow being cast even here, in this otherworldly abode, the child of Raven had found the need to reach across the boundaries that separated it from its unknowing parents and, like them, fight to continue.

■

Carrie spent that evening devoting every second to her children, tearing down the fences of neglect built during her possession of the thing that called itself Raven. The children, as she expected, let the past few weeks dissolve in the layers of affection she showered on them. It had not been easy for them, dealing with the loss of their father and the confusing behavior of their mother, but they were strong kids and would be fine in time. Carrie promised them as well as herself to make the most of their time together in the future, not allowing her job or even her blossoming relationship with Bill to stand in the way.

"Can we go to the pool in Davenport like we said?" Tim asked, his eyes searching Carrie's for recognition of plans made long ago.

"You bet we can, and I even think you're big enough to try the slide this year," she said. Tim had begged them every summer to make the trip up the twelve-foot ladder to the twisting ride that awaited each adventurer at the top. She and Walt had feared the obvious - Tim losing his footing on the ladder or skidding over the edge of the rounded sides to the pavement below - and had always delayed the event to the next summer. Carrie's change of heart in a large part had to do with the rather mature way both children had dealt with home life minus one self-involved mother. Their rooms and the house in general had remained clutter free. They had bathed regularly, fixed many of their own meals, and had complained little. Most of this was due to Tim's protective qualities, but Carrie knew that Sara had fallen in line with her brother's responsible behavior without complaint after spending most of the evening reacquainting herself with the children.

The most difficult subject she had to breach with them though was her personal battle with the entity that threatened their very lives. Of course she couldn't tell them the complete truth about her involvement, starting with the meeting to be held the following morning at Bill's, but she was able to convince them that she had a few more important things to do at the realty office. It shouldn't take long, she had told them, and then they could get back to the way things used to be. Their disappointment was short-lived, and they were eventually off to bed arguing over who could hold their breath the longest underwater.

Carrie spent the rest of the evening checking her ignored pile of mail and putting a coat of cleanliness on all the exposed surfaces of the kitchen and living room. She vowed to give the home a major scouring when things had returned to normal, but for now she couldn't gather the positive outlook necessary to do more. In less than ten hours, Carrie and the three men privy to the most outlandish yet potentially terrifying truth about Raven's disappearances would be discussing a plan of action. Their choices could result in the renewed safety of the town or, realistically, the utter annihilation of everything and everyone. It was a sobering thought.

Restless and unable to wind down, Carrie called Bill to see if he was suffering the same anxieties.

"Did I wake you?" she said.

"No, no. I was just sitting here."

He sounded tired and less than positive. Carrie regretted having dragged him into this supernatural nightmare, but she was glad he had come aboard.

"Still asking yourself what your doing hooked up in this mess with some crazy woman?"

He chuckled, "Yeah, I was thinking I must be crazy myself to be preparing to confront the spiritual significant of a tapeworm, but then I remembered how much I love you and wouldn't let anything happen to you, so here I am."

Carrie was touched by his devotion.

"I love you, and I promise to make it well worth your time to protect me against the powers that be," she said.

"I'm holding you to that."

They talked at length in sporadic bursts of subject about the children, her job, and their plans for the future, all the time avoiding their impending date with the unknown. Sleep would not provide the comfort and security they found in each other's voices, so it was the late hours of the night before they relented to the need for rest.

"We're going to come through this," he said.

"I keep telling myself that," Carrie responded, though her confidence was precariously balanced on the edge of surrender. "I want to believe that, but we're not dealing with a normal situation. There is no precedent out there in the elimination of a spirit that has invaded a town to my knowledge."

Her tone was flippant, her words full of defeat, but it was hard to feel otherwise.

"We'll think of something. We have to."

She hung up the phone with difficulty, needing to hear more of Bill's confirmation of their eventual success, desperately craving the strength she had just recently found in his enveloping arms. On the other side of the dark terror that awaited them, she envisioned a beautiful peace with Bill and the kids by her side, full of love and happiness as far as she could see. The entity's lurking presence was casting a dismal shadow over that bright tomorrow, and Carrie feared that if they failed, that monstrous darkness would swallow everything, the now as well as the future.

■

Carrie's attempts to close her eyes and briefly escape the worries that lay like a rock hard mass in the pit of her stomach were fitful, her mind racing with the wild imaginings of an upcoming adventure into the macabre. Prior to coming to bed and after talking with Bill, she had made a final check on Sara and Tim. As she peered in at their undisturbed sleep, Carrie was struck with a flush of anger, hot and intense. Her life, the lives of those that meant everything to her, was being disrupted by this evil, this devil incarnate. A longing to confront the beast, to berate it in a verbal tirade of hatred and accusation, stayed with her until she finally settled to bed. Once there, her light sleep was broken often, her skin beading with sweat in the cool bedroom whose walls appeared to compress as she tossed in claustrophobic panic. Night invaded every corner of the room, a shield of impenetrable darkness.

On one occasion she flew awake with a jump, sitting up in bed breathing heavily, the residue of a violent scream burning her throat and punctuating the air audibly. She got out of bed, checked on the kids to be sure her nightmare had not disturbed them, and then returned to her room. The sheets on the king size bed were disheveled and dampened during her restlessness.

Having changed her wrinkled nightshirt that clung to her uncomfortably, Carrie returned to bed and tried to relax, breathing slowly, rhythmically, attempting to push the inevitability of the next day's fears aside. She knew she would be of no help to anyone in the morning if she couldn't think clearly, be able to provide ideas or variations to suggestions made that might ultimately spare the group's lives as well as others. She had to sleep.

As Carrie washed her mind of everything, sheer mental exhaustion allowed her to climb down, down into the realms of unconsciousness. Once there, her dreams began uneventful, nondescript replays of the day's most mundane activities. Had she awakened early from her deep alpha stage, Carrie would have been hard pressed to explain the nature of her nocturnal make-believe, but instead she continued to skip from scenario to scenario like a rock on water. The images were non-threatening, pleasant in their construction and subject matter. The ebb and flow of sleep-filled clips of her recent past joined with hazy segues of bland color and unidentifiable shapes, eventually leading her subconscious to a markedly different landscape.

Before her sleeping mind's eye lay an empty field of infinite dimension, marked here and there with scraggly brown tufts of grass and short, windblown dunes of earth and sand. A deep azure sky lay like a blanket over the wasteland. Spanning the breadth of the cloudless cover was the familiar tubular gray flow, moving without direction in its continuous swirl above the horizon. Carrie noted that its width had diminished greatly, though, and large gaps of emptiness pocked the entire structure. She also registered a loss of intensity, both in color and motion, which defined the strange form. She was struck with a feeling of hollow regret by the sight as well, a sense of responsibility pelting her like hail from a rushing tempest. But she registered this scene as the result of the entity's doing, so she fought the urge to shower pity on the creation.

Nothing stirred in the forgotten barrenness. Carrie walked without purpose across the wilderness, casting her gaze side to side to the distant horizon in hopes of finding something significant, a landmark, anything, in the dreamy place. Though odors are not usually associated with dreamscapes, she was aware of a sulfuric tinge to the condensed air, a quality that burned her eyes and throat. Clouds of red dust billowed at her shuffling feet. She noticed shards of glass and chips of mortar scattered randomly over the uneven ground.

The sense of desolation was evident, but Carrie felt watched nonetheless, a cold dagger of observance penetrating the back of her neck, watching her every move. She looked behind her in hopes of catching a glimpse of her yet unseen companion, but the terrain she had covered had been swallowed up in a darkness like no other. Carrie felt like she was looking into a bottomless well, the joining of earth and sky undetectable in the void. Whatever distance she had covered, whatever perception she had had of wandering aimlessly in this vast field, was seemingly negated with each step. She was standing on an edge of existence; one step backward could mean a fall into eternity.

Carrie continued moving, a little faster now, intent on coming across something, anything, which might give purpose to her journey. Her legs were beginning to weary, her breathing laborious, and all the while the sense of being watched hung with her.

In time she noted an object on the ground ahead and to the right, roughly fifty yards away and indistinguishable. As she neared this derelict form in her constant environment, Carrie perceived it to be a pile of broken timbers, lengths of wood splintered and piled as if in haphazard preparation for a bonfire. Other than the pieces of debris she had come across earlier, this was the only proof of a human presence she had seen. The wood was old, its shattered ends marred after seasons of climatic and insect abuse. Carrie stood over the remains, hands on hips in an exhausted pose. A measure of script caught her eye, just below the top layer of discarded lumber. She nudged aside a few half sticks, and what she saw froze her in place. Here, on a foot wide surface, was an R, which flowed perfectly into an A, and then into what appeared to be the start of a V before ending in multiple points of destruction.

Carrie's heart stopped, a lump of anxiety pushed its way to her throat, and only a familiarity with the sign and her apparent location allowed her to avoid uncontrollable panic. This was Raven, or what once was Raven, and Carrie now sensed her companion more than ever, its stare discomforting and penetrating. She had been ushered here to be shown this empty plane. A sudden flash of understanding hit her like a well-thrown stone, giving credence to her presence and terminal wanderings. *The entity*. It had shown her the Raven of the past - young, populated, the circumstances that surrounded its conception. This forgotten world must represent the future, what would become of Raven if the present course of events played out to their final, deserted end. Carrie's thoughts, calculated and active, signaled that her conscious mind was becoming a participant in the play that was unfolding in the theater of her subconscious. What had started as a deep-seated dream found renewed life in her wakeful brain, elevating the entire experience to nothing more than a daydream, an animated catnap. She was aware of her physical self, prone in her bedroom, while at the same time an actor on this bizarre stage of psychic contact.

The sky made an abrupt change, becoming bright and revealing, mimicking the clarity that had swept Carrie's mind. Behind her, the cavernous void she left with each step was now whole again, as if a dark curtain had been pulled away to reveal the total picture. Carrie sensed an impending event, could feel, even in her dream-state, the air changing, molecules condensing in preparation for the arrival of what must be the entity. It was coming, she could feel it hurtling toward her in the nothingness she found herself in, launched from whatever world it was akin to. The intensity of the light grew stronger, and Carrie shaded her eyes against the searing brightness. Her skin crawled with the effect, the hairs on her arms standing on end.

She became aware of sound for the first time in her dreamscape - a rolling, monotonous rumble like thunder from miles away. Carrie thought of her grandfather, leaning back in his leather recliner while she was propped precariously on his knee, telling her not to fear the thunder. *It's only God doing a little bowling to relax*, he'd said. She believed it then, and so wanted to believe it now, but she knew it wasn't as comforting as that. It was ironic that she recalled the spiritual explanation her grandfather had given her so many years ago, here, in the supernatural world of the entity.

The sound drew nearer, its volume increasing as the very ground shook in reaction to its location. Carrie continued to look about her like a bull in the ring, unsure of where her persecutor would materialize. Eventually she noted another irregularity in the sky, though she was so disoriented by this time that it wasn't clear whether the spot lay in her former path. An area as large as a sun was out of place just above the horizon, inconsistent with the whiteness around it. It was turbulent, a waving mixture of movement on the boundary of focus. Carrie watched it grow gradually, at the same time appearing to close around her, until it looked as if it may swallow her in its convulsive form. The thunder reached a fever pitch in conjunction with the obscure hole in the sky, and just when Carrie thought her eardrums would burst in response to the growing pressure of terminal sound, there was a huge, suctioning pop that brought the noise to its end.

Carrie looked to the spot where the translucent shape had evolved and saw a uniform sky. But what was different was the sinuous mass that floated twenty yards from her. A soft red hue defined the entirety of the form, which immediately reminded Carrie of the single cell organisms she had studied in her physical science class in high school. There was no consistency to its edges as amoeba feet extended and withdrew in a variety of lengths and thickness. The terrain that lay behind the entity's position was visible to Carrie, though its murkiness resembled a foggy car window in the rain.

The entity, which Carrie understood this to be in its physical form, continued its unearthly levitation for some time, making no threatening advances while it floated unattended. Translucent appendages worked their way sporadically along its borders, stretching and bending in a fluidity free of skeletal restriction. Occasionally one of these extensions would reach up to the highway of gray matter that occupied the skies of Carrie's vision and touch the tubular flow. The swirling substance within gathered and appeared to drain from its invisible pipe into the amoebic foot, lasting only a few moments.

Carrie was hit with revelation as she stood in observance. The flow was, had to be, the discharge of residential emotion, a culmination of the anger and joy and everything in between of those living in Raven. This was the food source, a buffet line that was dissolving at a rapid pace. Carrie remembered how it looked over the city of Raven past and realized how desperate the entity's situation must be. Was it a matter of months, weeks, or even days before the flow ran dry? And what then for the creature? What then?

Soon one of the feet reached out to Carrie, and though she had stood in shock since the entity's arrival, she was unable to move her own feet that felt heavy and cumbersome. The liquid shape neared, its opaque design rolling and gyrating in a seductive dance. Carrie was frozen, willing herself to run but no longer master of her own body.

Soon that part of the entity enveloped her like a cloud, not restraining but simply surrounding her body. Carrie was hit with the familiar relaxation that had marked her previous encounters, a draining of surface tension and a soothing caress across every inch of her skin. Her mind was opened (*invaded?*) after she reached a general calm, and the entity began its alien communication, one that Carrie knew quite well.

"My sweet Carrie."

She resented the owner/pet relationship that pervaded these dialogues, and Carrie was determined to demonstrate a combative attitude, though she feared pushing the situation too far.

"I'm not your Carrie, and why have you brought me to this...this desert?"

She winced. Thinking, projecting her speech was unnatural, but she noticed the turnaround time to be remarkably shorter. Her biggest dread was the inability to think through what she wanted to say. Juggling her thoughts for the best response was impossible in this venue. She had to concentrate, settle her mind before replying. Nonetheless, her challenge was graciously received.

"I wanted to show you what would come of your home if you failed me."

Carrie realized the entity had played on her nostalgic love of home from the beginning, using her attachment to Raven as a means to further itself. The insinuation angered her, though she practiced a calm frame of mind.

"If this is what Raven becomes, it will not be my responsibility. I have done everything in my power to bring people here. I can only do so much."

"It's not enough," the entity screamed in her head. The reverberation of the emotional outcry hurt Carrie's temples, initiating a dull pain behind her eyes.

"It's not enough, Carrie." Composed this time. *"Carrie, don't you see, feel, what is happening to me? Don't you care? I will die without you. Raven will die. They must come back to me. They must. I need you to help me. Help me stop the pain. Carrie, please."*

"Why should I help you? You threatened my children, you've absorbed people I call neighbors, people I call friends." In that instantaneous moment Carrie knew, knew without a doubt, what had happened to Walt. He hadn't run off, leaving her and the children alone. Her husband, who in her new outlook on life she saw for what he had really been in their marriage - controlling, overbearing, petty - had not abandoned them. Time and responsibility had provided her this vision. But even with all that, he had not deserved the end this murderous creature had brought him. The damn thing that was disrupting her life, putting everyone she cared the most about in grave danger.

"I refuse to help you. I'd rather watch you die!"

Her mind raced with vicious hatred like a runaway horse, and she would have been unable to tie it down, tame it, had she even wanted to. Her loathing was undeniable, and welled and spewed forth in volcanic intensity. It may have been her undoing, but in that brief period of emotional upheaval, she believed the contrary to be true. The logical side of Carrie's brain knew she was all the thing had, the only human it couldn't destroy to be able to count on a tomorrow. No, it could rage and promise swift, gruesome punishment, but it was all a ploy, a way to motivate her. She was the entity's one link with living, at least for now, until it found a better way to fortify itself.

There was an infinite period of emptiness following Carrie's outburst, her mind receiving the equivalent of psychic static. She knew that every thought that ricocheted off her cranial wall was there for the entity's taking. If she had harmed herself and the rest of Raven's surviving population, she would know soon enough.

It didn't take long.

"Ah, what a welcome taste that was. I thank you for that nourishing response," the entity said in genuine satisfaction.

Carrie felt violated, sickened.

"You will do as I say, Carrie, because if I die, I will take you and Bill and your precious kids with me. What would I have to lose?" Its tone had decidedly changed, and the thoughts were clearer than any sent to her previously. She paid an attention that seemed vital to her future existence.

"Don't fail me, Carrie. You and I will always be together - in life...or death."

Though she had perceived a childlike quality in the entity's initial thoughts, the last were an indication that she was dealing with a ruthless, intelligent being. It was true that it needed her, wouldn't risk destroying her, but that was if survival were still an option. Carrie and her friends were getting ready to devise a way to destroy the entity, but in so doing, were they planning their own demise?

She awakened to the morning sun penetrating her bedroom chamber. Its promised heat did little to dissolve the gooseflesh that covered her body.

25

Sam Butler chauffeured Steve Edwards and Detective Knowles into Paul's Valley for their morning meeting at the law offices of Bill Curtis, picking them up at Raven's lone hotel, a one-story stretch of twenty rooms at the west end of town. Its designation, The Fortune Hills Hotel, spoke of a time long past, when the place was frequently flashing a no vacancy sign over its often-renovated accommodations. Now it sat like a forgotten dinosaur, overgrown with weeds, the parking lot potholed. It was all Raven had to offer, and visitors to its carpet-worn, musty roach traps left with weary eyes, thankful their stay was over.

When Knowles shuffled down the sidewalk and joined them in the squad car, Sam greeted him with a demonstrative nod, not surprised that Edwards would bring along his lackey for the questionable gathering. Presumably, if the decisions made that morning had a negative result, the bureau's number one mover and shaker could fall back on the observations of his second in command. Even in the world of law enforcement, there was safety in numbers. The three men were silent as they negotiated Eighth to Main, unconsciously abiding by the warning Carrie Hammons had issued the night before. Each was a study in deep concentration, pushing away any thoughts of their intended destination until they were safely outside Raven's border.

While Knowles continued to sit stolid in the rear seat, the other two men discussed the ramifications of their involvement in what was becoming, in Edward's words, "a witch hunt."

"One thing I'm not doing is entertaining any talk of involving parapsychologists or ghost hunters. When word hit the streets that the SBI has hired some spiritualist to rid Raven of a killer poltergeist, my butt would be dragged over the coals. Any support I could still count on in these last few days would be out the window. They'd rather see the media chew me up and spit me out than stand behind this."

Edwards had looked defeated the day before, his efficient, reasonable approach to investigative work failing him in the face of the allegations of Carrie and Bobby Rollson. A night's sleep had apparently renewed his vigor as he rediscovered his detective's demeanor. Sam was not surprised.

"Steve, you've, *we've,* got zilch to show for the time we have put into these cases. I would think you would be a little more receptive to another approach, no matter how out there it may be."

"Damn right, out there. Come on, Sam. How can you be so quick to jump on this supernatural bandwagon? I've known you for years. Hell, we roomed together, were rookies together, back when a simple patrol duty seemed like heaven's gate."

Sam couldn't help but register that his present law status was little more than a patrol duty. Edwards seemed unaware of his own observation.

"Are you willing to sacrifice everything on the overactive imaginations of a kid and a depressed single mother?"

The quick glance of confusion on Sam's face was evident.

"Yeah, I checked on your Ms. Hammons. Husband left her a year ago. Struggling to keep a roof over her two kid's heads. I've seen it before. Classic attention-seeker. Her story could bring her quite the recognition."

"Whatever you think you know about Carrie Hammons, you're wrong," Sam said. "She has faced a tough time lately, true, but she is the last person I would figure a publicity hound. Carrie is an unassuming, dedicated mother just trying to make a life for her family. I think the big city has diluted you a little, Steve. Not everyone is out to make a buck on the pain of others. Besides, she's not the author of this unbelievable tale. Remember, Bobby Rollson's family graced your door days before Carrie showed up."

Edwards was adamant. "Could be working together. These small town people love the limelight. What better way to cause the national media to descend on Raven than a good old alien abduction?"

"If you believed what you were saying for one second, I'd be taking this drive solo. You can play holier-than-thou, but you know as well as I do that the disappearances in Raven are beyond any of our experiences."

Sam was driven by his own belief and Edwards' pompous attitude.

"Multiple missing persons in the same small community, offering no evidence, no leads, nothing to go on. Even the toughest of cases reveals some shred of usable information, but we have zero! My familiarity with the town, your high-tech involvement. Nothing. What are the chances we would be without any discovery? I don't care how wacky their stories are - they fit, they provide explanation, and they are all we have!"

Sam had wanted to tear into Edwards since he had first taken over the investigation, flaunting his title, belittling the efforts of the local authorities while he used his administrative muscle. But now Sam was just trying to get him down from his self-imposed pedestal and give it some open-minded consideration. If what Carrie said proved to be as threatening as she believed, they would need the expertise of the state department, at least its access to manpower and federal support.

Edwards sat slumped in the passenger's seat, his countenance sullen. It was a hard pill for the career man to swallow. Something other than basic detective skill was needed, and he was without gifts for this party. He was between the proverbial rock and hard place - days away from being relieved of his duties and the potential shame it could carry and this spectral foraging in the dark. Out of his league, losing control while treading on ground meant for Hollywood, the wonder boy of the SBI was being relegated to the unbecoming art of grasping at straws, a behavior beneath him until now.

"Okay, okay. I'm here, aren't I? I agreed to attend this séance, didn't I? But let me promise you this, the first mention of my participation in some voodoo exorcism to rid the town of its supernatural inhabitant, I am out of there!"

Sam chuckled, "Let's hope it's as simple as that, Detective. I'm afraid before this is all over, we may all be in the need of some religious intervention."

■

Carrie arrived early at Bill's office to find him already there, making coffee and pacing around the spacious rooms like an expectant father. He looked tired, his normally pressed attire bearing creases that shadowed the lines gathered around his eyes and forehead. She surmised he had come to the office not long after their phone conversation in an attempt to psychologically hurry the anticipated meeting. They hugged briefly, re-establishing the bond so cruelly broken only hours ago.

"Did you manage some sleep?" he said, pouring her a cup of the aromatic brew.

Carrie took the drink gratefully, eager to stimulate some clarity in her still dream-fogged mind.

"A little. You, on the other hand, look dreadful."

Bill sipped from his own cup. "Well, good morning to you, too. I guess those dark circles under your eyes are meant to match your shoes?"

"Ha, ha, ha. I guess I deserved that one," she smiled sheepishly. "Did you stay here all night?"

"Most of the night. I'd rather get some work done here than stare at the ceiling at home." Years of legal counsel had among other things made Bill an efficient user of time.

"You just don't have a finer appreciation for insomnia," she joked.

"Oh, I agree. Sleep is over-rated. There is nothing better than the weariness and burning eyes associated with consciousness," he volleyed.

Carrie's guilt over Bill's involvement was undeniable, though she knew he was joking.

"I'm sorry for all this, this mess," she said. "I hope that some day you can forgive me." She collapsed in a leather chair near the receptionist's desk, looking like she bore the troubles of the world.

"Did it come again?" he said, her worrisome manner more obvious than yesterday, and Bill suspected that more than a sleepless night was responsible for her behavior. It was part of the growing connection they were making.

She nodded, "In a dream, but it was so real, so vivid. Frightening."

Carrie stared with her memory's eye, recalling visions Bill could only imagine.

"What happened? Did it hurt you in any way?"

"No, just reaffirmed its commitment to wiping out the town if I don't cooperate. What I did discover, though, was the nature of the bond it creates with us, the implications of it anyway. I thought I would just share everything when the rest of us got here."

They sat in silence for a time, talking occasionally, happy to be together while drawing strength from one another. They recognized privately the importance of the next few hours, the effect the conversations to come would have on the future of so many. The fate of an entire town and its inhabitants rested on the shoulders of a meek and lonely few. They questioned their worthiness. It was a terrible burden to bear.

■

The arrival of Sheriff Butler and Detectives Edwards and Knowles marked the beginning of an uphill run toward a common goal: the deliverance of Raven from the mysterious disappearances plaguing its borders, whether real or of supernatural design. They were at a fork in their lives, a moment of supreme decision, and they had a choice to make. Allowing federal authorities to inherit the cases was the simple, easy road to traverse. That had been the result of thousands of other investigations leading to a dead end in this country. Federal intervention was the logical, safe direction with their widely proven resources when local and state authorities had exhausted their capabilities. Pushing the plate of problems down the table was common, even expected, as crimes increased at an alarming rate.

The other option, a risky, career-threatening plunge into the unknown, meant leaving comfortable surroundings, summoning up a load of courage, and abandoning reason. With only one of them an actual witness to their enemy, and others carrying heavy bags of doubt, the direction they would tread was a toss up.

After Bill had assured himself that everyone was taken care of, the group gathered in a small conference room just off the main reception area. Housing a long table and six chairs, the room served primarily for depositions, when a stenographer or videotaping was required. The table spoke volumes of Bill's successful practice. Deep intricate molding covered the heavy oak's perimeter, supported by wide, hand-tooled legs. The chairs accented the table's command of the room, and the five settled in these to begin their much-anticipated discussion.

No one seemed willing to breach the subject, letting small talk mask the purpose of his or her presence. Finally, Bill got them on track in his lawyerly assertiveness.

"I think the first thing that we need to do is listen to what happened to Carrie last night. It could have a bearing on the conclusions we draw."

Everyone looked at Carrie, who was noticeably uncomfortable as the center of attention. She shifted in her chair, cut Bill a sharp but playful glance, and began.

"I don't know if anything that I say will change what has to be done. The fact remains that this thing is dangerous. It will stop at nothing, even its own destruction, to bring Raven back from the brink of death, and that was reinforced to me last night. The one thing I am sure of is that we have to do something right away, or officers, your number of missing is going to skyrocket."

Her speech cast a heavy blanket of foreboding over the assembly, and over the next half hour, while Carrie described her desire turned dream turned reality, the feeling intensified. Surrounded by legal professionals whose job it was to question, she fielded various requests for clarification and detail when finished. Sam Butler showed particular interest in the creature itself, its make up and characteristics. Following a brief retelling of Bobby's eyewitness account with help from Steve Edwards, he asked Carrie to tell them more.

"You said it was transparent, yet had distinct color and definition. Did you get the sense, especially when it made physical contact with you, that it was solid, like a liquid, or more gaseous?"

"I can't say. Remember, this started with my strong wish that I could confront it, tell it the pain and misery it was causing us, and it carried over as a dream. I don't know when I was wakeful. The things I'm telling you began in my sleep, and evolved to a conscious level. My environment, my subconscious, limited my sensual experience in the beginning.

"When it touched me, I was thoroughly relaxed. I had the sensation of a soft caress, a gentle soothing of the skin. I was aware of my physical self, but I think that was part of the mental event. I guess what I'm trying to tell you is it touched my mind and my body, though I'm not sure how or at what stage. Even a gentle wind can create a sense of touch, of contact. I had the definite sense that it exists in or attained a physical state. It stands to reason that since it is having contact with people in our conscious reality, your missing persons, Detective, it definitely has substance."

Edwards looked up distractedly.

Carrie continued with this line of narrative. "As it materialized, I had the distinct impression that the entity had to cross over, had to, I don't know, *transport* itself from its own world to ours. I'm convinced it lives in another dimension and has learned how to invade our physical plane, driven by its primitive hunger."

"You mean like some hibernating bear that has to feed in the spring?" said Bill.

"No, not hibernating," Carrie said, sitting up in her chair, animated and totally involved in her theory. "I don't think it ever sleeps. The lack of human hosts filling its dinner plate has forced it to find a way to provide for itself. Like any creature struggling to survive, it has had to adapt."

"Wow," Knowles chirped, and immediately reddened in his embarrassment. Edwards looked at him in frustration.

"You sound like you admire it," he said, speaking for the first time since they had entered the windowless chamber. "If what you say is true, this thing of yours is killing indiscriminately. Killing your neighbors. I wouldn't be preaching its grandeur so proudly."

If Carrie was hurt by his personal attack, she didn't show it.

"Yes, I admire it. Its uniqueness. Its creation. But I want it stopped, probably more than you, Detective. This is my town we're talking about here. I don't need you judging my intentions."

It was an uncomfortable moment, one that illustrated the stress and anxiety that filtered through the room. Sam made a quick intercept.

"All right, we have a common problem here that needs addressing. The last thing we want to be doing is fighting among ourselves."

"I agree, Sam," said Bill, taking Carrie's insult personally, staring hard at an indifferent Steve Edwards. "Let's start discussing some solutions instead of levying accusations."

The detective recanted, "I apologize if I came on too strong. I want resolution as much as the rest of you. I know my stake in this, Detective Knowles and mine, is quite different from the rest of you, but I do want to bring an end to this. I'm just having a difficult time accepting this mumbo-jumbo. Is there anything you can tell me to convince me otherwise, something concrete?"

His question was directed to everyone, but Carrie took the lead.

"My word. A mother's plea for her children. The disappearances of long-time Raven residents for causes you and your office have been unable to determine. Detective, I know this is hard to accept. If I hadn't experienced firsthand what we are dealing with, I would be as skeptical as you. I'm asking you to open yourself to the possibility, the chance, that something outside our normal scientific understanding is out there, a living, functioning life form driven by the same primal needs as you and I. If I'm wrong, you go back to your legitimate kidnappings and drug trafficking. No harm done. You leave behind an insane woman and her demented followers. But if I'm right, and I know I am, you get to fulfill your calling - to serve and protect."

Carrie had hit Edwards at his core, opening a door he couldn't further refuse passing through.

"Are you a religious man, Detective?" she said.

"Not practicing," he said.

"Do you believe in God, *a* god?"

"Yes. Yes, I do."

"Then summon whatever faith you give to your god's existence and use it here," Carrie said. "It is out there, waiting for our response. We can't delay much longer."

■

"Anybody have an idea?"

Carrie had told them everything she had experienced, every impression she had of the entity, a label that each of them now used when talking of Raven's unwelcome guest. Their facts were clear - the entity was dying as the town died, its food source, the feelings that were expelled from human bodies like carbon dioxide, was steadily depleting with the population. Somehow those expulsions made their ethereal way to the entity, where they were used as energy. It had, therefore, found a way to enter the physical world of Raven, seeking out the source of its necessity, killing for the concentrated bursts of emotion that were released from its unsuspecting prey and, in Carrie's case, attempting to renew the town through deceit and intimidation, qualities apparently acquired through the long time exposure to the human animal. They reasoned that the entity crossed to their dimension, one that shared time and possibly space given Carrie's latest revelation, fixed on an isolated individual, absorbed him, and withdrew to its lair when necessary. The hasty conclusion that the entity could read anyone's thoughts at any time seemed doubtful after further discussion. Bill, who was proving to be a valuable commodity in this hypothetical sketch of their suspect, reasoned that if Carrie communicated with it after it made contact with her, the same type of contact Bobby Rollson described in Ramsey Peler's death, it stood to reason that the entity required a physical interaction. He added that Bobby made no mention of a personal, mental contact. He was strictly an observer.

Their last piece to a puzzle they knew might prove unsolvable was also the most heartening. The borders of Raven were apparently a cage that contained the creature, invisible walls that for whatever reason it couldn't traverse. Conceived in the dark reaches of the Other Raven, the entity was bound to it, like a fish to water or a worm to moist earth. Outside this confinement it would shrivel and die. They thought this might be valuable later. With this body of knowledge before them, the group prepared for its greatest test – how to end the growing carnage and eliminate the entity.

Knowles was the first to offer an answer. "Why not a mass evacuation, pull everyone out of their homes, establish temporary shelter in a neighboring community?"

"I thought of that," Carrie said, "and until last night, I would have believed that was our best choice. But having had conscious interaction with it, I gained a true feel for its situation. What we are talking about is like a wild animal backed into a corner, teeth bared, and ready to strike, but intelligent. It won't be cheated that easily. It's waiting, just under the surface, waiting to be appeased or rejected. The risk is death if it trusted me to comply now."

"I agree," said Sam. "If it is able to isolate its victims, it makes sense that it can judge the movement of us across the landscape when so inclined."

It all did make perfect sense, but of course, they had to remember they were dealing with the unknown. For all they knew, the entity could live indefinitely unfed, making Raven not only a ghost town, but one in a quarantined status. And for how long?

"Can it be reasoned with if it's so damned intelligent? Ms. Hammons, can you do your psychic link with the thing and manage some dialogue, some compromise?" Edwards couldn't escape his terminal logic.

"Please, call me Carrie, and no, it can't be reasoned with, I don't believe. No matter how developed it is intellectually, the facts remain: it must feed or die. It can't leave its home, and we can't ask a thousand people to move into town to help a supernatural being. It wants things the way they used to be, and we can't make that happen."

He wasn't used to a playing field without negotiation, and Edwards felt disabled in attempts at helpful suggestions.

Had anyone been looking at Bill at that moment, they would have seen the dawning of a workable yet dangerous idea. He appeared to be playing out the possibilities of its effectiveness in his head, his eyes darting in every direction as he measured the breadth of his brainchild. His left hand moved to his upper lip, pulling and lightly squeezing with the thumb and forefinger as his other arm offered support. Carrie noticed his intense internal studies eventually, and she recognized them for what they were. She had seen him in this posture many times before, the analytical gears turning at high speed. He had something.

"What is it, Bill?" she said.

"I don't know. Maybe nothing, maybe everything," he said, looking to Carrie, his eyes lit up in unparalleled understanding.

It's the same way Tim appeared when I was teaching him to read. It was like a revelation.

"If you've got an idea of what we can do, Mr. Curtis, I wish you would share it," said Edwards.

Bill dropped his hand, slapping his thighs in the process.

"Okay, but I'll warn you ahead of time, you're not going to like it, especially you, Carrie. What I'm going to propose scares me to death."

26

For the fourteenth consecutive day, forecasters had predicted temperatures would climb into the hundreds in Raven, forcing elderly and young alike indoors yet again to escape the stifling rays that beat perpetually on the area. The weather was working in tandem with the entity, concentrating its corrosive efforts on the structures of the town. Tar filler, coal black and liquefied, bubbled in the cracks of the pavement. Paint peeled and faded everywhere. Birdbaths, leaning heavily on the dry ground marred by fissures, stood empty near equally vacant homes, their life-giving moisture long evaporated. It was lifeless, a purgatorial weigh station of death. Had it not been for the occasional brave souls scurrying like mice in a barren field, proof of living, breathing habitation would be hard to come by.

One of these town dwellers was Dottie Pickering.

Regardless of the climate, it was guaranteed Dottie would be opening her antiques shop Monday through Saturday eight hours a day. Seventy-two, the widowed daughter of a strict Baptist farmer, she had learned from an early age the importance of hard work. Long hours caring for livestock, helping her mother in the kitchen, and tending to her younger siblings had taught her there was little room for idle hands in a world infested with depravity and sloth. She had managed a home of her own after marriage, raised four healthy, God-fearing boys, and devoted all her attention to the shop following John's death. A good man, John, loving and committed, he had gone to the Lord after a brave struggle with cancer. During his decline, Dottie had managed both the home and the small shop they had invested in following John's retirement from the glassworks factory in Davenport. And now, with the children gone and little to sustain her voracious work ethic, she continued the daily operation of the business, though its open doors rarely saw a customer enter these days. It did not discourage her. With plenty of money to live on (John had invested wisely and their home had been mortgage free for fifteen years), the shop was a diversion, a place to pass the lonely days and direct her vast energies.

While the morning progressed slowly to noon, Dottie had already completed her ritual of cleaning and straightening. She was forever amazed at the dust that found its way to her many shelves, populated with beautiful pieces of collectable glassware, rustic kitchen implements, and handmade novelties. The walls suffered equal attack, their array of farming tools and ranching devices were regularly in need of her feather duster.

Now, sitting in the back of her store, knitting a blanket for one of her thirteen grandchildren, Dottie noticed Joyce Keller leg her way past the display windows, pausing briefly to wave at her, turn over her empty hands, and move on. Joyce was Raven's post office. Like Dottie, her day was one of redundancy. She made deliveries on foot in the heart of town, drove to the mailboxes of increasingly isolated customers until lunchtime, and manned the small, postal counter in the old Chamber of Commerce until four o'clock. The chamber building, once the political hub of Raven, housing the town council assembly room, the mayor's office, a musty, box-filled records division, and various commercial offices, was a shadow of its former self, no longer a buzzing hive of activity. Other than the post office and the part-time presence of Mayor Tom Wilkey, the place was rarely in use. Joyce's non-verbal signal out on the sidewalk meant she had nothing for Dottie today, though when she did it was usually junk mail. With few visitors here or at home, she relished the short visits of pedestrians like Joyce, but so far, the day had been without interaction.

Getting back to her knitting, Dottie sat and hummed idly, contemplating whether to stop to eat the egg salad sandwich that awaited her in the small refrigerator that hummed gently in the opposite corner. As she came to an edge in her handiwork, Dottie remembered the letter that sat stamped and ready on the sales counter, and judged herself harshly for her forgetfulness. She had written to her son Thomas to let him know she would love to come out for a few weeks and spend time with him and the family. Shutting down the shop was no problem; any lost sales would probably amount to very little considering her weekly income. It actually cost more to cool and light the five hundred square feet of space then her register receipts could cover.

Dottie's arthritis had limited her spryness, and long periods in the same position left her stiff and slow. She set aside her yarn and needles, moved in successive hitches from the chair, and made for the door with the letter. Even if it was a slow mail day for Joyce, Dottie knew she could catch her before she was gone. Years of observation and discussion told Dottie that Joyce covered her side of the block first, crossed at the corner of Main and the highway, and made her way back toward the antiquary from across the street, a journey of over five minutes not including the mail stops. It had been just a few minutes since Joyce had passed.

Outside the sun was blinding, and Dottie squinted in response to its intensity. Her estimations placed Joyce still up the street moving toward her, but first glance failed to locate her. Dottie looked up her side of the road, sure the postal woman would already be through with that stretch, and saw no one. She looked back over Main, her stare running from the feed store, to Tucker's Insurance, and finally the shoe store. Nothing. She decided to wait and watch for the mail carrier, though the heat was already making the short vigil uncomfortable.

The sidewalk opposite the sentinel that was Dottie Pickering failed to transport any pedestrians for the next thirty minutes. Longing for the cool confines of the shop after ten minutes, Dottie continued her watch through the sparkling clean window inside. Joyce never emerged from a door or passed again. Positive that she had not had time to make the circuit so quickly, Dottie eventually relinquished her post, returning to the deep recesses of her shop bewildered and disappointed.

"Well, that's strange," she said aloud. "I wonder where she went." Her letter to Thomas would have to wait another day, she figured.

Intent on stopping Joyce tomorrow and asking about her miraculous race up and down Main, she picked up her knitting.

"Strange," she said again to no one.

■

For the next three days, the group went about their assigned duties. Having split Bill's idea into four areas of responsibility (Edwards and Knowles paired in their task), they went about their jobs with determination, but a hint of doubt clung to them like a ship's barnacle. They had discussed their misgivings, constructed a hypothesis, and were gathering the means to conduct their experiment. That they were dealing with something outside the realm of science and normal human experience caused their greatest concern. Their time frame relied on the skills and resources of every member, and even then they were unsure if the plan would work. So many variables, such a huge margin for error.

The plan was a shaky one at best, needing the concerted efforts of everyone, but none more than Carrie. Her commitment to Bill's idea, one that he openly feared more than she, required the same blind trust Carrie had asked of the rest of the group earlier.

"Let me start off by reminding everyone that we know very little about this entity," Bill had said as he shared his theory. "What we do know comes mainly from Carrie's psychic connection with it, and a witnessed death. I think it is fair to say that for the many blank spaces of understanding we have, the entity is far from an authority on our reality. It has spent its entire existence contently drawing from the wellspring of human emotion that has flowed freely from one astral plane to the other. But now, the creek is running dry, so the entity, by shear force of will, manages to breach the gap of our two parallel worlds to find a way to satisfy its need and restart its precious current. It has learned much from its intimacy with our feelings, gained a remarkable intelligence, registered an elementary construct of our language, way of life, and relationships. So what does it do?

"The entity gets the lay of the land, so to speak. Feels out these human bodies that are the source of its nourishment, notes the pleasures of destroying a few for a quick burst of energy, but at the same time recognizes its limitations, the depleting numbers of sources and its own physical boundaries. It eventually sees the need to harvest a new group of humans, those that will live here and provide for it. Enter Carrie, as the entity understands her, a deliverer, a waitress."

Bill looked at her with a shrug of the shoulders. Carrie cut her eyes in feigned anger.

"We know all of this already, Bill. Get to the point of your plan," said Sam.

"Okay, I'm getting there," Bill said, pushing his palms down in a repeated calming effect. "In both cases, Carrie's contact and Peler's death, a commonality exists – the entity creates a single link, a limiting bond."

He paused, the dramatic effect lost on his audience. "Don't you see? It separates individuals from the herd, like a feline hunter. Instead of isolating the weakest, it fixes on someone emitting strong emotional output before making its kill. But a problem exists - its rudimentary knowledge of our nature tells it we are capable of hysterical reactions, self-preserving bouts of fear that move us to run to safety when faced with danger. The entity can't survive a mass exodus, so it kills quietly when it feels the need."

"That would explain the lack of eyewitnesses to the attacks," Sam said.

"Right. Bobby Rollson just came upon what he saw, and I'll bet there have been others who have seen someone taken and either didn't believe their eyes or were too scared to report it," said Bill. "This and Carrie's encounters show the entity is not omnipresent. Like us, and as our creation it is going to share our qualities, it can only process within its proximity."

"Great, it's not friggin' Zeus. What does that do for us?" Edwards said, his attitude still less than appealing.

"It's the key to saving Raven, if what I want to try works," said Bill.

"Bill, I have to admit I'm confused about where you're going with this," Carrie said.

"What I am suggesting relies on the theory that the creature is limited in its psychic power, narrowed to the individual emotions and thought it is in touch with at the point of contact, physical contact. If we can establish contact with it, safe contact, and in so doing divert its attention from what is happening elsewhere in Raven, then we may just be able to beat it."

"But we can't throw someone out there to be in contact with this thing. It's sure death," Sam said.

Bill turned to Carrie. "Not just anyone."

"You can't be serious. I won't allow it," said a shocked Sam. "And you of all people, Bill. I had the impression you two were close, for God's sake."

Carrie stopped him. She looked at Bill with a clear understanding. "No, Sam, he's right. Who better to bond with the entity? I've had more contact with it than anyone."

"Yeah, but Carrie, the danger. I just..."

"I think Carrie is aware of the danger, but at the same time she knows that the entity has chosen to work through her, that her life will be spared as long as it believes she is doing what it has asked," said Bill, turning to her with a deeper look of compassion than Carrie had ever seen in his face. "Carrie, Sam's right. It's a dangerous thing that I'm suggesting, and you can say no without anyone here blaming you, but if I understand everything you have told me, you are safe as long as the entity is assured of your help."

"But you said this thing can read thoughts. If she joins up with it, she can't hide her deceit. It will know in an instant, and then what?" said Edwards.

"Carrie, this is where the real trust comes in." Bill had heard him, but his attention stayed fixed on her. "You can't hear the rest of my plan. If you know what is going on, so will the entity. What I propose is that I tell these gentlemen my idea without you here. If they agree, then we join up with you when your moment is at hand. The entity may sense some untruth, but it won't have access to anything."

Bill stepped to her, took her hands, and a deep seriousness covered his face.

"I will be with you, and if you can trust me, we'll walk away from Raven safely."

■

Carrie's role in the actual confrontation with the entity was not to be acted out until the final hour, so, as they had decided, she spent the first few days in normal activity, going to the office, showing homes in Raven (though she turned off her charm and encouraged her buyers to look elsewhere), and spending time with her kids in the evenings. She would have to trust that her compatriots could manage their affairs without her, but it left her feeling worthless and unneeded. She knew when the time came that her job was crucial to their success, but the fact that it was also the most dangerous did nothing to lighten her spirits.

She had instantly agreed with Bill's idea, regardless of the risks to her personally. She couldn't see that they had any other choice. Bill had immediately apologized for even suggesting his solution, encouraging the others to think of different ways the entity could be distracted while they carried out his logical, manageable plan. Carrie had rebuffed further discussion, eager to start as soon as possible. The sheriff, Detective Edwards, and Detective Knowles were sure they could carry their end of the load, though they would need time to get everything in place. The meeting broke with a confident air, and they decided to stay in regular contact, updating each other on their progress.

For now, Carrie had to curb her impatience and await her moment. In a matter of hours, she had a date with destiny in the shapeless form of a supernatural power few had confronted, and of those, fewer still who had lived to bear witness to its evil hunger. Fate was a constant traveler, showing its face at pivotal junctures, leaving in its wake both joy and heartache. Carrie willed Fate to favor her one more time.

She waited.

27

Bill spent the majority of the day in the town records room of the chamber building, sorting through the battered cardboard boxes stacked to the ceiling in an area too small for its purpose. Raven's population rolls, birth certificates, property deeds, marriage and divorce documentation, records of legal proceedings, and various maps outlining the township through its history were among the hundreds of boxes, labeled on their tight-fitting lids with contents and dates. Whoever had maintained the array of paperwork had long ago abandoned a system of quick retrieval, apparently returning papers to the wrong boxes, without concern for chronological order, and then dumped the boxes in the nearest space. It was a mess, and Bill hoped a full day was enough time to find what he was looking for.

He had gained access to the locked storage after he and Sheriff Butler had talked with Mayor Wilkey. During their meeting at Bill's, the group had agreed that the mayor would have to be informed of *a* situation, not *the* situation, before they put things into motion. His role in Raven was deteriorating with the town, so he was quick to support any action that may help, no matter what it involved. Sam assured Wilkey that he could coordinate the operation without his assistance, though they would need access to various materials housed within the records room. Wilkey, an impish, nervous man with an emasculating habit of nodding affirmation with each statement presented him, gave them his assurances that the town was at their disposal.

Bill had met with the building's caretaker, Eddie Dalton, a retired machine-shop worker, kind and grandfatherly, passing his declining years in part-time janitorial service. It was a good job for Eddie, slow-paced and undemanding, and he was content with the minimum wages he was paid, grateful for the opportunity to feel productive.

Eddie shuffled through the huge number of keys that hung from his belt, a weight that Bill imagined burdensome to the janitor's frail, slight frame.

"I sure appreciate your doing this for me, Mr. Dalton. I know this was sort of last minute."

"No problem at all. I was coming in soon after the mayor's call," Eddie said, still searching for the necessary key. Bill wondered how many of those he actually found the need to use. There must have been over fifty.

Ending what seemed an eternity, he finally separated what Bill hoped was a winner, inserted it in the doorknob, and pushed open the door. They were hit with the familiar odor of time and neglect.

"Not much call for folks coming in here any more. I've been in myself only a time or two."

Eddie reached around the corner of the doorframe and flipped on the light to reveal the mountain of chaos Bill was soon to climb. Records for the past ten years were being forwarded to the county for filing since Raven had found itself unable to maintain paid personnel for the job. In fact, the mayor's office served only as an overseer of public services, and those were nearing elimination, making even political office an extravagance. The town was destined for incorporation. It was only a matter of time.

"Well, I'm sure I'll find what I need. Now the mayor did tell you I could be here awhile?" Bill said.

"Yeah, not a problem. If you can't find me, just lock the door behind you when you leave," said Eddie. "I'll be out later this evening to shut everything down."

Bill made for the stacks of disarray. "Thanks again. I'll lock up when I'm done."

Eddie didn't stay around to detain Bill, for which he was thankful. As he started through the nearest boxes, using a long, rickety table to stack pages during each inspection, he realized the monumental task that lay before him. Nothing was where it belonged. What he was after could be anywhere, and he wondered whether more manpower was necessary, though he knew everyone else was tied up in their own duties. Bill's responsibility, which he had originally viewed as the simplest of assignments, was looking enormous in comparison.

He rolled up his sleeves and dug in, thumbing through every conceivable form of legal documentation, probing the detailed history of Raven's growth and emergence as a vital hub of agricultural life in this section of the state. The boxes looked to Bill to be duplicating themselves each time he turned his back.

Eddie may have to let me shut things down tonight.

■

"You want what?"

Steve Edwards had anticipated a negative reaction to his request from the State Director, the numbers he was wanting were staggering, but he thought under the circumstances it would be better received. It wasn't so much the availability but the time frame he was working with that was causing such a road block.

"Sir, I realize the extreme nature of what I'm asking, but it is paramount to my investigation that I have this," he argued.

"Extreme is putting it lightly, Edwards. I gave you until the end of the week to shore up your loose ends, get your house in order before the feds show, and you respond with this sideshow? What the hell do you hope to accomplish?" the director said.

A Vietnam veteran and twenty-two year member of the bureau, Larry Upton was a tough, no-nonsense director. Upton had revamped the entire bureau following his appointment. His decisive policies, implemented within days of his takeover, had created a stir in the department but proved to be immensely effective. He was a man that drew proponents and detractors alike, but no one denied him the deep respect that came with his leadership's successes, and it was felt his days as the state level were numbered.

Edwards feared the man, not due to any previous conflicts, but because of his power to make or break him. Upton could be a loyal ally or a brutal enemy, a Mengele-type who found no difficulty casting aside those he found problematic. Bill would have to be careful or he might find himself on the looped end of a short rope.

"Sir, we have narrowed our suspect to the Raven area, but we have been unable to locate him. With his knowledge of the town, and our limited manpower, we felt our best chance of apprehension would involve cordoning off the perimeters of the town and then conducting a sweeping search in hopes of flushing the believed perpetrator."

"What makes you think he is still in Raven, or will remain there until support arrives?" Upton asked. "This is preposterous."

Edwards was doing his best impression of solid detective work. "We have done a complete M.O. on the guy. He's indigenous to the area. Been here all his life."

Boy, if you only knew, Steve laughed to himself. He was enjoying this, despite the earful he was getting from his boss. When he had agreed to fulfill Bill Curtis' request, it was to prove his resourcefulness more than to help the town.

"Our sources indicate he stays on the move, lurking in the abandoned buildings and residences throughout town, coming out to take his victims when his crazed mind warrants the need. We have eyewitnesses, and we have been receiving reliable information that should lead us to the whereabouts of a victim or victims very soon."

"Serial killer?"

"Probably, sir. We have every indication that the kidnappings will continue."

"Why haven't you informed me of your progress until now with this bombshell? You must have needed assistance long before now."

The detective faltered briefly, but then gathered his courage. "This has all come together in the last twelve hours, sir. I wish I could have foreseen my request earlier, but like I said, we have only recently acquired this new information."

"Yes, but five hundred and guardsmen?"

Working up the numbers in their meeting that morning, the five of them had decided it was the smallest number they could get away with and still put their plan into effect. It was unprecedented, even for large metropolitan events, but what were they to do? They had no choice.

"The opportunities for a stealthy border crossing are immense. Too many dirt roads, creeks, and untended pasture land to ignore. I'll need over half that number to cover the perimeter while the remainder assists in the building-to-building search. I worked it up and have tried to be conservative in my estimates, sir."

Upton would appreciate the detail and thought put into his plans. The one thing Edwards had to guarantee should his request be honored was that he, Steve Edwards, had to be put in complete charge of the operation. If the military were given a measure of authority, their objective would be at risk.

"It is vital to my operation, sir, that I be given complete control over these men once they have been retained. Detective Knowles and I should be able to coordinate everything. We have the additional aid of the local sheriff. Too many cooks in the kitchen, you know?"

The director was less than impressed.

"Want the reins of this horse, do you, Edwards? Well, I can't blame you. It's your last chance to save the bureau's face and blow your own horn."

Upton had no idea how exposed to ridicule the bureau could potentially be.

"All right, Edwards, I guess I can talk to the Adjutant General over at the military department and see what he can do for us, but I can tell you now he won't like it. Major General Avery is a tough sell," Upton said. Edwards was surprised that the director found anybody a challenge, but he was confident in his administrative abilities.

"I appreciate it, sir. You can tell the major general we should be able to wrap things up within twenty-four hours of their arrival."

Edwards had already decided that if Bill Curtis' plan failed, he would instigate a token search as described to Upton and later try to explain away his initial use of the men. His former roommate Sheriff Butler would get the brunt of that blame if necessary. Edwards would not feel guilty if it came to that. Butler's career was headed nowhere - no harm, no foul. His, on the other hand...

Upton promised to notify Edwards the moment he had confirmation from Avery, at which time the detective could notify the proper military channels as to his desires. He hung up with the director feeling a pang of regret. His inability to solve the missing person cases in Raven would have been passed off as tough luck, the inevitable failure of even the best detective. Now, as he stepped to the smeared window of the sheriff's office and looked out upon the enigmatic town of Raven, he realized he had taken a grievous risk, one that could find him on the next rung of his career assent or send him crashing downward, his dreams of a federal position lost in the ruinous waste of this paranormal pursuit.

Edwards busied himself, trying not to await the call.

■

It was Sam Butler's position as sheriff of Raven that landed him the most detailed job, but it made sense that he and Cody Hawkins work with the residents, who would be more agreeable with someone they knew. Like Steve Edwards manipulation of the National Guard, Sam would have to be a great salesman, convincing the population of Raven that the story he was telling them was on the up and up. It was a huge undertaking.

The men had determined that at any point if one of them was unable to carry out his duty, Bill would be called and everyone else informed that the plan was a wash. Sam hoped he wouldn't be the one to topple the cards that were already precariously stacked.

The operation in Raven required the simultaneous gathering of every member of the Raven community, all three hundred twenty-two men, women, and children, at a central location in town within seventy-two hours of Sam's departure from Bill's office that Monday morning. After considering this aspect of Bill's idea, Sam had decided the site was workable and that notification would be challenging but possible. What stumped him and made the task momentous was devising a believable purpose for attendance. His concern was the real chance that some residents, especially the elderly and lone-wolf types, would ignore a call for a town meeting as either unnecessary or ridiculous. It was a valid point. A few were bound to stay away.

Bill's remedy to this potential ailment in his plan was to use fear and preservation of self and family as a motivation. Using the disappearances which were now common knowledge, he recommended that Sam and his deputy spread word through signs, the newspaper, and face to face contact that Raven has been declared the site of a medical emergency, requiring quarantine and immunization. The sheriff could explain that the findings of the SBI pointed to a rare strain of illness that had caused the death of those missing, and that due to fear of widespread panic or infection, authorities had kept their conclusions quiet until now. There would be the select few who would doubt the validity of the containment, question the cloak and dagger nature of law enforcement, but that should be expected. If their personal safety is emphasized, if their questions are promised detailed answers at the gathering, and, if necessary, the threat of arrest is levied to demonstrate the importance of their presence, one hundred percent attendance could be counted on.

Bill allowed for the possibility that someone may not comply, and for him or her he expressed heartfelt sorrow. His plan called for a final sweep of Raven to gather stragglers, but there were no guarantees. *There were no guarantees of anything*, he argued. They could be spitting in the wind thinking they could overcome a supernatural killer that had psychic and astral projection capabilities at its disposal, but it was the only chance they had. In a final speech full of fire and confidence, Bill had rallied them behind his idea, summoned their resolve, and given them hope.

Sam's job only started there, though.

Cody was in touch with the Davenport Sheriff's Department, inquiring about their ability to assist in the undertaking. Sam had hoped they would offer little resistance to the unusual request, which called for five of their officers and the use of some of the local school's equipment, gymnasium, and cafeteria. Being the summer, Bill had figured the invasion of the campus would be tolerable considering the urgency of their request. From the inside, the stories they had concocted, one involving a medical quarantine, the other a coordinated manhunt, appeared believable, but Bill's group couldn't be sure how outsiders would react to what was described as a volatile situation needing immediate attention. He had mentioned that there was always the remote chance that the various departments they were involving would want more information and discover inconsistencies, but there was only so much they could control.

Sam thought of Steve Edwards' final question, his defeatism rearing its ugly head yet again.

"All right, let's say everything goes as planned. How do we know the entity is destroyed, and what do we tell the federal authorities at that point? We are going to look like a bunch of fools when we tell them what we were really doing."

Sam could see the hard lines that converged at Bill's eyes as he turned to Edwards. They were all sick of his negativity, but as the legal authority in Raven, his presence was not up for debate. Bill looked tired, his face a broken topography of pain and worry, but he was still able to summon a loathing for Edwards' selfish manner. According to Carrie and himself, Bill had been a hard sell, but now there wasn't a stronger believer. Sam had recognized the closeness that Bill and Carrie had exhibited; their eyes had said volumes. His was a belief structure built on care, compassion, and most probably, love.

"If lives are saved, I don't really care what we tell them," Bill had said through the thin line that was his mouth. "The truth may be our best bet. If the feds want to test our theory, they are more than welcome to tramp into town and risk watching each other melt into the air. But I don't think it will come to that. Only Carrie will be able to tell us for sure, but I think after the chow wagon runs dry, this thing will be a memory."

After Sam talked with Jimmy Trathor and was promised a huge announcement for the front page of tomorrow's paper, he pondered the remaining items on his grocery list. The PA system would have to be pulled from storage, its use evaporated with the loss of Raven's school system and the occasional public gatherings. Banners and signs could also be created from long-stored materials in the Shed, a corrugated steel building that stood behind the sheriff's department that held everything from fencing and tools to picnic tables from the extinct Fourth of July celebrations that lit the skies of Raven so many years ago. He hoped his wife could put her creative touches to this part of his assignment. Sam found little use these days for the artifacts the Shed held but was glad he and others had had the foresight to retain everything. Little had they realized what events would drag the dust-laden treasures of the past from their confines.

Other items, a field marker with ample spray paint, sawhorse barricades (also found in the Shed), flood lighting to expose five football fields, walkie-talkies, and the names of a dozen dependable men in Raven rounded out Sam's responsibilities. With Cody's help and a three-day cushion, it was manageable, but the urgency kept him from pushing the doubt aside. He wondered if he was any better than Edwards, questioning the validity of their actions. What if Carrie Hammons was a fraud, if young Bobby Rollson had let his juvenile mind play tricks on him? Sam ignored his inner voice this time and went about the job at hand. He had lived his whole life in service to his fellow man, going to dangerous and often-questionable lengths when he determined a life lay in the balance. He would perform no differently now. The lives of hundreds of his charges were being threatened, and it ultimately didn't matter to Sam whether the culprit was natural or paranormal. He would answer the call.

28

Wednesday came with the searing force of a hundred summers, a debilitating, crushing heat that demanded the humbled posture of all living things. The penitent man was reacquainted with his secondary place on the chain of order on a day like this as Mother Nature expressed her aggressive rule over all things. Whether it was the climatic scourges of flood, fire, or wind, it wasn't long before she exerted her dominance. Yet this was somehow different. The conditions that persecuted Raven appeared to be of malicious intent, as if the gods on Olympus were playing with the lives of its inhabitants. Though the mercury hovered at record setting levels, it was more than temperature and humidity. There wasn't but a degree's difference fifty miles in any direction according to weather centers, but the quality of the heat was evident once the borders of Raven were penetrated. Raven was the definite epicenter of an unexplainable heat, one that suffocated, that drove the hardiest of creatures to seek shelter, withering and killing without regard.

Carrie had received the call an hour ago, the one she both dreaded and hoped for. Bill was to arrive at her house later that evening to join her for the final stage, her time in the spotlight. He had been noticeably excited, letting her know everything was in place, and she marveled at his boyish exuberance, though he had apologized yet again, a habit she jokingly told him would be broken if he expected to spend any future with her. They had decided that the children would be safer at the sheriff's office, where one of Edwards' men would ensure their transport out of Raven once Carrie established her psychic link with the entity. Now, having just returned from downtown, where a long, emotional good-bye had occurred, something Carrie had promised herself would not happen but had overcome her nonetheless, she concentrated on the job awaiting her.

Bill had stopped by frequently during the days leading up to this moment, telling her how things were progressing without divulging too much information. They had worried that Sam would run into a wall of problems, but he had mastered them beautifully. Bill had spoken highly of him, commending him on his resourcefulness and stubborn refusal to accept no for an answer. Though the group had every reason to doubt the reliability of Edwards, he also had delivered as promised.

Carrie found in those last few days that she and Bill had reached a level of personal comfort around each other, the carefully chosen dialogue of new relationships long forgotten. They relaxed in the other's company, leaning heavily without imposition. She had never felt this way with Walt and had not believed it was possible to fully open herself to anyone without fear. Bill was changing her whole outlook on the possibilities of a fulfilling life. There was the promise for a rewarding future, one that could be shared again, but this time, in earnest. An infinite amount of beautiful sunrises awaited them, and Carrie hoped that someday they would begin to welcome those together, but first, the entity had to be confronted.

■

She greeted Bill at the door with a reassuring moment of intimacy, searching for the same strength she always drew from him at trying times. It was there as usual, deep and invigorating.

"Well, how's my girl? Ready for this?" he said.

"As ever."

He studied her features, as if he were looking for something half-hidden in her show of confidence.

"Carrie, we can still put an end to this, call it off. There is no reason to jeopardize yourself. You've done more than anyone could expect," he said.

"No, it's the right thing. I feel it, and I'm not overly concerned about my own safety. Neither of us would have entertained this had we thought I was in extreme danger. It can't dump me now, we just started seeing each other," she quipped, though Bill could see her mask of bravado slipping slightly.

"It's just that everything up to now has been guess work. I can be here while you are linked with it, but will I be able to free you if something goes wrong? And how will I know you're in trouble? There are too many variables we didn't consider."

Carrie had failed to maintain a courageous front with her kids, but she tried again with Bill.

"Listen, mister, we can't start doubting our decision now. The lives of hundreds of people depend on our success, and we are the only ones who can make this happen. It will work. I have faith it will work. It's all we have had to go on from the beginning."

She was right, and Bill knew it. This was not a normal, ten o'clock news, front-page story dilemma. A supernatural creature, created unknowingly in the backwash of human emotion, was clinging to its bizarre existence at the expense of Raven's fathers, mothers, sons, and daughters. There was no means of compromise, no peaceful way to negotiate. Science, UFO researchers, parapsychologists, even cult leaders, argued incessantly over the possibility of an unknown life form, terrestrial or otherwise, living among us, entering our reality. Now that it was here, there was little hope that anyone would accept it as truth, until it was hopelessly too late. Something had to be done now.

They waited nervously for the seven o'clock hour to arrive, thumbing through magazines, exchanging small talk, and checking the wall clock every few minutes. Carrie had seen the full page ad in the local paper imploring everyone to attend the town meeting in Sumner's Park, a small, frequently used half block in the center of town that held a jungle gym, two stone picnic tables, and an overused charcoal grill leaning heavily on the chasmed ground. The notification read strongly as a demand, harboring the suggestion of grave consequences should anyone ignore the mandated order. She knew not to ask Bill about their intentions, though she knew he wouldn't tell her anything that could jeopardize her or their plan. The entity would be conscious of the concentration of human life in the park, but it would have to join with one of those attending to understand the purpose. Even then, nothing in the ad or the signs she had seen on the streets coming in and out of Raven explained any actions beyond the ordered time of arrival. If she had gained the attention of the entity while this and Detective Edwards' efforts were underway, there was no reason to believe their intentions would be discovered.

The hour approached slowly, and Carrie wished they could just get on with it, but she knew the time was conducive not only to maximum turnout to Sam's little shindig but late enough for Carrie to attain a restful state, one that would draw the entity to her. She had taken some sleeping pills earlier as Bill instructed, settled on the couch to relax, and tried to let the tension that pulled at her release itself. Bill checked in with Sam and Edwards every half hour on the walkie-talkie he carried obtrusively, never setting it down for more than a minute before possessively snatching it up and cradling it in his hands.

Once Carrie had begun her subconscious hunt, Bill would stay in touch with both locations, their coordinated efforts vital to the success of all their work. He figured he could commute from the living room to just outside her door so as not to wake her. It was his strong belief, one he emphasized in their meeting, that he would know when Carrie was with the entity. The account Bobby Rollson described was, he argued, an actual moment of contact, complete with visual proof.

As they agreed, Carrie went back to her bedroom a little before zero hour to complete a short period of intense thought directed at the entity. Like her last experience, if she fell asleep under those conditions, the entity was bound to come for her. Bill thought she looked sleepy, though he couldn't be sure if it was her mental exhaustion, something they all shared, or the pills doing their job.

Carrie stood wearily. "All right, Bill. Wish me luck. I hope I don't disappoint everyone. They've all gone to so much trouble, and on my word alone."

Bill took her arm and led her down the hall to her bedroom.

"It'll work, Carrie. It has to," he said, helping her into bed as she sank like a stone in the soft mattress.

"And you'll be here the whole time?"

"Right here. I promise."

"And you think I'll know when to end the contact?"

"If things go the way I think, the entity will break the link gladly. Then I will whisk you away from here and we can join the kids," Bill said, kissing her forehead and drawing the covers up under her chin.

"I love you, Carrie."

"Love you, and you better be here when I wake up. I've got plans for you, buddy."

"I'm in your hands."

Bill stepped out into the hallway and returned to the living room, where he grabbed the walkie-talkie and let everyone know the curtain had been raised - the show had begun.

■

The fading light of evening fought desperately to maintain its hold on Raven, casting its shafts of subtle glow toward every growing shadow, but darkness was finding purchase in the deepest corners, claiming its territory for yet another night. Carrie had closed the faux pas wood blinds that hung inside her bedroom curtains, which she drew together as well soon after returning home. She feared her troubled conscious would deny a heavy sleep entry, so she had taken every contingency to guarantee her rest. Waking very early that morning, long before the four-thirty alarm she had set welcomed her to that fateful day, she hoped sleep would come without too much trouble.

As she watched Bill walk out of her bedroom, now dark and tomblike, she wondered if she had done enough. She didn't know how long she had to let sleep take her, she hoped at least an hour considering the circumstances, but she tried not to add more pressure to her situation. People were counting on her, most without any knowledge of what she was about to do, and it was this responsibility focusing her mind on reaching out to the entity.

Her approach would be the same as last time, except instead of the hate-filled thoughts that preceded her to a restful sleep; she wanted to transmit a positive attitude, a kindly desire to be with the entity again. If she could summon in herself a longing, a need, maybe the entity would recognize this quality and more readily answer the call. The one thing that she had going for her was her importance to it, and she hoped to use this. *There was something more than her job that caused the strange union of human and supernatural being.* Carrie must possess some higher level of telepathic ability that would explain the ease of each of their meetings. She was never in mental anguish or physical distress during these; on the contrary, it was a sensually pleasant rendezvous, a nightmare in reverse. Though she awoke anxious and uncomfortable, the actually time in touch with the mind and physical manifestation of the entity was enjoyable.

Having spent what she considered some fifteen or twenty minutes in her mental pleading for the entity's return, Carrie turned her thoughts inward. She concentrated on a wave of warm relaxation, letting it flow slowly down her neck, across her shoulders, down each arm, through her torso, and eventually down each leg. The wave paused in intervals, loosening and freeing the last few weeks of tension that had burrowed there. It was a form of transcendental meditation she had found on the Internet. She had laughed at the irony of using a technique that was credited with allowing astral projection, the ability to leave one's body via the spirit or soul. Had she been able to secure a sensory deprivation chamber or some other form of reality escape, she would have jumped at the advantage. Instead, she was left with her own resources.

By clearing her mind and calming her body a part at a time, Carrie hoped to glide down into unconsciousness. She focused on a single point in her mind's eye and gradually everything fell away as she sloughed off the skin of wakefulness like a snake. She floated lightly for a while, soon losing awareness of the bedding that formed cocoon-like around her. The sense of falling was undeniable, and Carrie progressed further through the stages of mental processing until an observer would have been able to recognize the signs of REM sleep.

Not aware of physical time, Carrie would have been encouraged to know how quickly she attained a state of sleep and accompanied her subconscious down a familiar path, leading to the Raven of the future, the barren nothingness the entity projected as its unhappy hereafter without the help, whether extended or forced, of Carrie. Nothing had changed. The scene was a perfect reproduction of her last visit, and she registered the solitude. In the distance a sound rolled and rumbled its way toward her in perfect harmony with her memory, a juggernaut of unmistakable turbulence that encouraged her feeling of déjà vu.

Somewhere deep inside her hidden consciousness, she prayed with a fervor that belonged in this spiritual theme park, prayed that Bill was charging those in the real world to action. Just above the stark horizon, the cool blue emptiness distorted and impossibly dissolved, making a supernatural doorway for the approaching entity. She knew her time had come.

29

It was all Bill could do to keep himself in the living room and allow Carrie to fall asleep. He had felt uneasy with the whole idea since its inception, but the reality of losing her, now, after they had finally put things on a solid path, was overwhelming. Used to having things go his way for the majority of his protected life, the divorce and years of long nights at the office to avoid the painful return to an empty house had left him despondent and wallowing in self-pity. He had been unprepared for the cruelty of the real world, his parents shielding him from many of life's necessary lessons as they showered their only child with the best money could provide. In the face of adversity in his adult years, it had left him naïve and open to deep, unforgiving wounds. The chance to break the miserable cycle and return to a happier time lay agonizingly near, yet there was nothing he could do to protect that future. Carrie was readying herself for a confrontation in which he could be of no consequence. She would go there alone, further fueling his helplessness and exposing his raw emotional state to painful attack.

Thirty minutes into his wait, nerves conducting their frenzied dance across his entire body, Bill ventured down the long, forbidden hall to determine whether Carrie had established contact with the entity. Through the slightly ajar door, he could perceive a stillness and darkness unnatural for such an early time in the evening. Summoning a courage he found himself surprisingly in need of, Bill gently pushed the door inward, stopping just short of the threshold, and listened.

The room was cast in a minister's veil of shadow, the setting sun's final amber rays failing to penetrate the covered windows. The hallway light was off, creating a cavernous quality to that part of the house. As his eyes adjusted slowly to the nearly impenetrable darkness, Bill began to perceive the various pieces of furniture that crouched undefined along the walls of Carrie's bedroom, marked with pinpoint variations of their black background with drawer handles and ornate hinges that caught bits of light from unseen sources. In the king size bed to his left, he noted the soft curve of Carrie's sleek figure, almost lost in the bed's immensity.

Not wanting to enter the room for fear the slightest noise may break her apparent peacefulness, he remained frozen, letting his eyes do the evaluative work. Soon, Carrie mumbled gently in what Bill believed was a descending state of sleep, imperceptible syllables lost in the thickness of dark. He leaned into the room, straining to translate her jumbled dialogue, but it was impossible from his place in the hall. It was almost a total darkness, one that worried Bill, not because he feared night, but because of its implications. If he was going to determine whether Carrie was under the spell of the entity, surrounded in its projected form, he had to see more definition than this.

He hurried as quietly as possible back down the hall to the living area, turning on every light there and in the kitchen. It was his intention to allow the concentrated light to filter its way to the recesses of the back bedroom, shedding a soft but revealing glow on Carrie's progress. Should he be unable to positively identify Carrie in contact over the next hour and a half, the amount of time they figured Sam could control those crowded into Sumner Park, then they would abort the whole thing. Something else would have to be tried; what else no one could offer.

Returning to the open door, Bill needed only a few seconds for his pupils to find their maximum effectiveness, in a large part because there was now the perfect measure of light exposing the lines and dimensions of what was contained in the bedroom. He could see the covers that cascaded over Carrie like a waterfall, though her face was turned away from his side of the room. Bill was pleased with the contrast and felt assured that the light would not bother her even if she faced the doorway. Retrieving a kitchen chair and placing it in the hall, his eye line unobstructed but his presence not overbearing, he settled in, checking his watch frequently. At the other end of the house, the walkie-talkie lay discarded on the couch, its volume knob turned way down to mute static, prepared to broadcast instructions when the time came. Bill stared in deep concentration, focusing every fiber of his being on the air surrounding his future, and began his guardianship.

■

Sam had the assistance of Davenport's officers should the presently calm crowd turn into a mob. Their passive resistance to the situation was based on a lack of information, but the sheriff knew that in that mingling mass of Raven's own there had to be a few dissenters, doubting Thomas's that enjoyed stirring up a group such as this, using the convenient stage as a platform for their own performance. Sam had already isolated a few suspects with the help of Cody and a few reliable members of the community. Past experience told them who would start barking distaste in their self-ascribed need to know. Those individuals were now being given special attention as the eight o'clock hour neared.

A makeshift riser had been set up on the north end of the park where the crowd could still stand comfortably in attendance without rubbing too many shoulders. Sam avoided ascending the stage and taking up the bullhorn that waited patiently for him, choosing instead to walk among his neighbors, pacifying their concern without divulging too many facts. He knew he could chew up a large chunk of time in an alphabetical roll call of the families, and in so doing verify everyone's presence. There were of course a few people who were unable to attend, but their whereabouts were known and they would be joining the rest of the community at a predetermined location.

The neighborhood canvassing had gone well, with only three families actually failing to receive direct communication from the sheriff's department. Those individuals' homes and the rest of the town would be given a final sweep once Bill gave Sam and his team the word. He had dealt with the expected flurry of calls over what would be later described as the "potentially hazardous viral illness in Raven demanding immediate inoculations and, once determined, possible quarantine for ongoing treatment." It would be emphasized that though this strain of infection was not contagious, there was the threat of infection of visitors to Raven that could call for the closing of its borders.

As he surveyed those present, Sam hoped the demeanor of the crowd didn't shift to the negative. He would hate to use force to contain them, but he was prepared to do whatever was necessary to save lives.

Officer Joe Dugan, one of the five deputies he had asked for two days ago, approached him, a look of uncertainty on his face.

"Sheriff, I don't think a lot of these folks are happy with my answers," he said, his red hair and freckled skin signaling his Irish heritage. Dugan had arrived around six o'clock in Raven, not in the traditional patrol car, but as the driver of a bright yellow school bus, like his partners, in an unfamiliar summer procession. They had come early to receive their final instructions and get a marginally accurate account of their duty. Sam needed them for two reasons: crowd control, and if things went as planned, transportation. He felt guilty about offering little in the way of information to the townspeople, but keeping a fellow officer in the dark was unbearable.

"Well, Joe, like I told you when you got here, until the CDC makes their appearance, I'm not even sure what's involved in this."

It was a hard lie to spit out, but Sam knew the truth would not guarantee any assistance.

"I'm getting ready to run the names up front. Just tell the others to maintain a calm attitude, but be forceful about the gravity of our situation. It's crucial that we not have a riotous response from our invitation-only party," Sam smiled, slapping Joe on the shoulder as he turned and headed to the stage.

He could milk the roll call for thirty minutes minimum, maybe forty, but after that, he didn't know how much longer the crowd would stay agreeable. The fear of disease and lack of useful information might work against Sam, and as he climbed the steps to stand before his potential detractors, he touched the communication device that hung awkwardly from his police belt.

Come on, Bill, he thought, *make the call.*

■

Though the National Guardsmen, five hundred strong, had met on a remote stretch of Raven's border six miles to the east of Sam's location and were orderly and required little overseeing, they were nonetheless antsy for some action. They had positioned themselves as instructed, fanned out over a few hundred yards along a marked stretched confirmed through Bill's painstaking records search, and were now idly talking among their trucks, Hummers, and other transport vehicles as they had done for the past three hours. The beating sun had faded to a deep orange ball melting into the horizon, but the heat had already made some of the men irritable while awaiting their orders.

Stationed at one end of the military line was the SBI team, in complete command but feeling uncomfortable in charge of these homeland defenders. It seemed that government bodies, working for a common cause, never found coordinated projects appealing, and both groups had already expressed their distaste for the other.

"Damn weekend warriors. Dress them up like G.I. Joe and they get a case of the hard ass," Edwards spit. He had never been in the service himself, and his comments cut deep in the purple hearts of some of his detectives. "I wish this circus would get underway so we can be through with this God-forsaken town. I can't believe I agreed to this, Knowles."

He wiped his forehead that perspired freely.

"Just another hour, sir, and then we can send them packing."

Sergeant-Major Tom Billingsly had lead the entourage that descended on Raven early that day, striking Edwards as an intelligent man though too wrapped up in the rah-rah of military discipline. He had immediately passed the baton of control to Edwards as he had been instructed, but he did it grudgingly, almost distrustfully.

"Sir, may I ask the nature of our role in your operation?" he barked, chest out, eyes slightly off Edwards.

"Simple border control, and if necessary, civilian reconnaissance. Nothing taxing, though highly classified. I hope your men can perform as ordered?" Edwards said.

"Without question, sir, though I can't promise their undying loyalty to civilian police."

Edwards cut the sergeant a curt smile.

"I don't need their flag-waving, fight-to-the-last-man loyalty, Sergeant, just their attention. Do you think when I say jump, they can leave their feet?"

His famous patronizing tone did little to secure the faith or efforts of the angered sergeant.

"Higher than you wanted, sir. Higher than you wanted."

In his best swiveling spin, Billingsly left them, his hatred for Edwards obvious.

"Great, a supernatural killing machine and now the Third Reich. Curtis better get this over in a hurry if he wants to count on this band of white trash to be here come tonight," Edwards said, glancing at the silent walkie-talkie that rested on the hood of his car.

"In a hurry."

30

As the entity completed its existential transfer from one plane to another, Carrie took note of the pathetic state of the food flow that continued to occupy its place in the heavens above her. Though it seemed to be infused with occasional surges of substance, the length of the pipeline was suffering multiple voids. Like an electrical current misfiring, the life-giving supply of spectral nourishment was separated by huge gaps of nothingness, dry pockets where Carrie could see the sky hanging clearly. The transformed emotion lay almost stagnant, giving the illusion of a drying riverbed, spotted here and there with murky water. There was little proof that a self-contained, free-flowing tube of thick, dark gray matter had once embodied it. Carrie doubted if the entity could survive much longer on such a meager store, and she figured to verify her suspicions in the next few moments.

The entity had completed its crossing over and hung silently before her, its undulations as stunted as its food source. Carrie was quick to notice the change in the creature over the past few days, its color and activity paling in comparison. What presented itself to her now was lessened, dramatically altered in a way Carrie couldn't define in her limited experience. If she had to qualify this dream visitor of hers, she would have said at that moment that it looked sickly, as if infected in some way. It was sluggish, lacking in the rich colors and mesmerizing movements that had defined it in earlier encounters. The extensions that marked its borders in the past were no more than slight humps, marginal variations on the cellular wall that Carrie couldn't envision capable of reaching out to envelope her or touching the diminishing flow above.

Carrie stood expectantly, awaiting what she hoped would happen soon. Bill had told her she would know when to break her contact with the entity, but she wondered whether that joining could even happen with it so debilitated. It had made the trip across dimensions, probably expending a great deal of energy in the process. If it had any resources left to communicate with her, she couldn't say, but she was overcome by the sense of urgency that she had picked up from Bill earlier. He had impressed upon her the need to make contact and then end the telekinetic act as soon as she could.

Thinking that she would have to initiate the dialogue, Carrie stepped toward the entity, closing the distance between them gradually. She was offered no help or resistance, so she continued her progression. As she neared the wall of the entity, just a step away, expecting at any second that a section of the lithe creature would encompass her, she hesitated. What if it was so weakened that it would consume her totally in a last effort to stay alive, absorb her as it had Peler, maybe Walt? What if it was feigning in order to conserve all its strength, only to briefly revitalize itself with her emotional stockpile? These were the same what-ifs that had plagued the others - Bill, Sheriff Butler, even Detective Edwards - but they had carried out their duties without fail. She stared at the once viscous form inches from her. People were counting on her. Tim and Sara were waiting for their mother. Carrie stepped into the entity.

■

The complete darkness that had shrouded Raven over the last few minutes brought with it a sense of foreboding to those that kept vigilant watch both in Sumner Park and along the town border. Humid conditions that had assaulted them failed to disappear with the departed sun, lending to a growing apprehension and tide of unrest that was washing over the unwitting players in Bill's theater of horror. The confused, some fearful, residents of Raven were beginning to voice their discouragement, as were the guardsmen who shared in the frustrating wait. Running out of ways to appease the disgruntled groups, those in charge were wrestling with the plan they had supported earlier. If something didn't happen shortly, there was no guarantee their efforts would prove worthwhile.

Bill sat in his statuesque pose in the hallway, his eyes rarely leaving the still shape of Carrie in her bed. She had moved a few times in fitful rest, but little else had occurred. He knew she was asleep. Whether she was having any luck on the other end of her consciousness, he couldn't say with any confidence. He had checked his watch a hundred times, the anxiety unbearable. His plan had to work. They had put so much time and effort into it, risking their careers in the process, that nothing but complete success was acceptable. He knew the others had to be dealing with impatience, both their own and their charges, but there was nothing he could do until Carrie made her connection.

She moved slightly, a soft moan issuing from her burrowed mouth in the recesses of her coverings. Bill started, leaning forward to detect the smallest change in the air around her. There was nothing. The room remained unchanged, a still picture that had begun to burn itself in Bill's pupils.

He stood and stretched, moving ever so quietly so as not to disturb Carrie's sleep. If he were to awaken her now, all was probably lost. There was no way that Sheriff Butler or Steve Edwards could control their situations for more than another hour until questions and arguments would overcome them. A single clock chime earlier had sent Bill's heart skyrocketing into his throat, the real chance of Carrie waking up almost sending him over the edge. This had been his plan, and its success or failure would rest squarely on his shoulders. As a man used to having things go his way, failure stung him longer, losing hurt deeper. This pain could last a lifetime.

Sitting back down and crossing his legs, Bill checked his watch again when a flicker of movement caught his peripheral vision. Snapping his head toward Carrie, he squinted his eyes and sat motionless, poised like a retriever in a maze field, trying to discern the slightest change in the atmosphere. He allowed his focus to scan the circumference of her still form, the lack of light playing tricks in the recessed shadows. Bill circled the periphery slowly, with careful intent. And then, there, a small area just hovering above Carrie and yet somehow attached to her, a vague blur, an inconsistency. Concentrating every fiber of his being, willing the distortion to evolve into a greater scrambling of molecules, Bill saw what he had hoped for.

Within seconds, the change spread, and similar smears and blurs began in other locations surrounding Carrie. The urge to burst into the room and pull her away from the alien presence was tremendous, but Bill fought against the protective response to what was materializing. He was hypnotized, awe-struck by the vision he had only imagined. It was real, and in that moment, his faith was rewarded. Soon the abnormal air was all about her, and then even Carrie took on the same quality. She was in contact with the entity, and the need to act was now.

Bill knew he had to go, had to break the trance he was under and get to the living room where the walkie-talkie lay waiting. But he froze, absorbed by the image that coalesced in Carrie's bedroom. He had not known what to expect, how it would present itself, but here it was. It struck him as simple, unassuming, not the glorious, explosive quality he thought he would see. And in that brief moment, it made perfect sense. The entity, a creation of man, could ultimately be measured in human terms, not in the paranormal theatrics of history and best-selling fiction. Born of man, nursed on the milk of emotion, this thing they referred to as a creature, a beast, a killer, was human life personified, an individual driven to survive at all costs. In a world where brave, resourceful men fought Thomas' dying of the light, this life-form stood as a frightening admonition that Death was an unwelcome yet frequent visitor, and His arrival marked a battle line drawn. Bill couldn't hate the creature, but he had brought the fight to it. Now was the time to draw his sword. He tore his eyes from the panorama and sprinted down the hall.

■

Passing through the membranous surface of the entity, Carrie met no resistance. It was as if she had moved through an open doorway into a room full of sulfurous smoke, but the walls of this living compartment were highly transparent as she could still see the vast wasteland from which she had departed.

Her mind was immediately bombarded with an agonized pain, deep and unforgiving, though she felt no physical discomfort. The entity was crossing the final bridge to reach Carrie, bringing its mental anguish full bear on her in the process. It was a combination of chaotic desperation and an almost childlike fear, an aspect that the maternal side of Carrie was quick to recognize.

The voice that touched her was familiar, but weak, fighting to release each syllable.

"Sweet Carrie, why have you forsaken me?"

The rather Biblical reference did little to encourage a compassionate sorrow from Carrie, though she did acknowledge the continued attempts to affect her at a personal level. Her commitment to her hometown, a mother's protective nature, and now her very religious morality were used against her so that the entity might live. It was unforgivable, yet in the back of her repeatedly invaded mind, she understood the primitive will to survive.

"I've done what I can, but they are leaving faster than I can bring them here," she said/thought.

The entity's thoughts glowed with a fire Carrie had figured

impossible in what appeared this last, fading hour in its existence.

"You must bring them. Bring them now. I know you see what is left to me," it said, and Carrie understood the entity meant its food source that hung precariously above them. *"I must begin to take what vessels are here, and I will start with your children. You haven't done enough, and we've run out of time."*

Carrie jumped at the mention of her kids yet again, and she fought to maintain composure.

"No, you must let me keep trying. I have some families that I know will move here, but what you have asked of me can't be done overnight. There must be another way. Please don't destroy those that are here until I can think of something," Carrie said.

The entity expressed emotion with its mental vocabulary, possibly an offshoot of its creation, and Carrie could feel the sense of exhausted finality coming through. The flash fire of anger she had been sent earlier had been nearly extinguished.

"Carrie, I have no other choice, and I have perceived your intentions as deceitful, which I would expect having grown to know your kind. Even with the few that remain, I can't continue. Soon, I, we, will be no longer."

The entity was too resigned now, too done. It terrified Carrie.

"We are much alike, Carrie, you and I. In my existence I have felt the human joys of living, the happiness that love, friendship, and success bring. And I have known your darkest thoughts, the angry impurities that balance your lives - revenge, hatred, lust, and greed. In a large way I am a culmination of all these things, and to a lesser degree of my own design. With this, and much more, I have acquired your primitive instinct for survival. My reaction should be quite understandable to you."

Carrie wanted to argue for humanity, for reason, and the illogic of killing. She couldn't. The entity was not a creation of hers alone, but the offspring of all thought, both moral and immoral. It had learned not by observing, but by absorbing the good with the bad. The purest of emotions had carried them this far. The dark side of man was calling it quits.

"But there must be within you some guilt, some shadow of morality that won't allow this," Carrie pleaded her thoughts.

"Living supercedes regret."

"Killing is wrong."

"I have felt the joy that flows from your kind in the face of victory. I know of your wars, your brutality, the shedding of blood in the name of freedom. You celebrate the death of others, hiding your moral truths

behind symbols of patriotism and loyalty. Can you question my motivation with your history?"

There was nothing Carrie could argue in humanity's defense. The entity had arrived at a reasonable conclusion, using the faculties it had been so ethereally given.

"You and the others will join me shortly, and then I too will cease to be." Cold. Calculated. *"Don't you find it rather funny, dear Carrie? You shall soon meet your maker. I, on the other hand, have already met mine."*

Mankind had stood as a pitiful example of care and compassion, lending its selfishness and lecherous dark side as tools in the unknown rearing of this supernatural child. For Raven, the end of times was now; the apocalyptic signs had made themselves known and were steering toward Armageddon. Carrie wept for what was, and what might have been. She thought of Bill, her children, and the unfairness of it all.

She had run out of debate, almost resigned to the deaths that awaited all of them in the foreseeable future, when she felt a change in the link that joined them. Up to now the entity had floated in still repose, conserving what remained of it energy. A surge of motion, a perceptible physical reaction, was taking place. Carrie looked all around her, expecting to witness her own "absorption," the first play in what she figured would be a quick game of death. The entity was definitely in a state of contortion, urging itself out of its lifelessness. There was nothing different in its transparency, nor its shape, but something was happening.

She looked all about her, scanning the horizon for some explanation for what was starting the nearly dead engine of the entity. Looking upward, Carrie saw the reason for the change in its manner. The tubular food source, what Carrie had grown to understand as the depository of emotion that Raven emitted, had altered dramatically. The wisps of failing currents that had signaled its demise not so long ago had been replaced by a literal flood of activity. Thick, gray waves of surging matter moved in abundance, filling the length of the line. Carrie believed it to be many times fuller than when she had first seen it in past encounters.

The reason for its resurgence she couldn't figure, but she recognized this for what it was - Bill had put things in motion. He had somehow managed to bring what she herself had failed to supply, and she stood in awe of its timely arrival. Bill had told her she would know when the time to end her link with the entity would be, but it was taking care of that for her. As the rich supply of man's emotional discharge turned and rolled in its familiar pattern, the entity drew away from Carrie, leaving her alone on the barren ground. She watched it move single-mindedly toward the line, like a thirsty desert dweller faced with a vast oasis of cool, life-giving water. Its progress was slow, its strength greatly diminished, but Carrie knew it would reach its objective.

She stood transfixed, unable to rationalize what she was seeing, and would have remained there longer had she not heard the distant calling of her name. Behind her, the voice called, growing in volume. It was Bill, and he was commanding her attention, telling her they had to go. *Go where? Not now, Bill. Don't you see the beauty of life here, the gift of one creature to another?* They had been surrounded by death and heartache for so long. This was refreshing, proof of man's reclamation of his innate goodness. *Come, Bill, stand with me and witness humanity.*

But the consternation in Bill's voice was undeniable, and she felt herself being pulled away from the beautiful scene, swept along on an unseen conveyor. The setting soon dissolved in her wake, and she was accelerating upward through a dark tunnel, the sense of rising very real as she rocketed toward where, she didn't know.

A shaft of light illuminated a place far above her, and at her rate of progress she would come upon it quickly. As the orb grew, Carrie was able to make out shapes within it, indistinct colors and textures gaining sharpness by the second. And then, out of the blur of motion, there was Bill, wonderful Bill, telling her to help him, to keep moving. She was disoriented, not sure where she was or why Bill was being so forceful with her, but the cloud of ignorance was lifting. They were in her house, shuffling through it, she leaning heavily on his side, trying to find purchase with her weakened legs. Staggering out the front door, hit with a gust of hot air that took the breath away and gave little of itself in return, Carrie was shocked into a greater consciousness.

"Where, what...?"

"Come on, Carrie. We've got to get to the car and get out of town. We don't have much time."

Carrie complied not because she agreed with him but because she was still throwing off her incoherence. Bill helped her into the passenger's seat of his car, raced around to the other side, and spread rubber in an arching line down her driveway. Carrie stayed silent, lost somewhere between the reality of the lurching car ride and the euphoric vision of the entity, feeding in glorious rebirth.

31

When Bill's call came through in its muffled excitement, no one was more relieved than Sam Butler. He and six deputies had managed the swelling unrest of the once tolerant crowd to its breaking point. Two fights had ensued among the park's confines over petty issues, and a few disagreeable men, parading their attitudes like roosters in a henhouse, had needed forceful reminders of exactly who was in charge. Sam's announcement of a potentially harmful illness in Raven following the roll call had not been well received. He wondered what the next disruption would be when he heard Bill's voice issue from the receiver attached to his belt.

"Attention! Attention! This is Bill Curtis. Commence operation. Contact has been made. Repeat - commence operation! Go for it, boys!"

Sam had not needed to be told twice, nor did he stop to verify it with Bill. They were out of time, and the crowd, busting at the seams with their right to know more, had become dangerous beyond their control. He sprinted to the platform, pushing aside with a degree of patience the half dozen of his neighbors that approached him angrily, and grabbed the blow horn. His men had been briefed on this aspect of their duties, and Sam could already see them circling the entire crowd in a uniformed pattern. The sheriff had also authorized the demonstration of weapons for this phase, guaranteeing the cooperation of every last person.

With his first words from the blaring horn, the crowd turned as one, their angry conversations ceased in anticipation of an end to their ignorance.

"Ladies and gentlemen, can I have your attention please. I have an important announcement."

Sam paused to ensure the mass was tuned in to him.

"I have just been given word that the contagion affecting Raven and potentially its inhabitants is airborne, I repeat, airborne, so certain precautions will have to be administered to ensure the safety of everyone here."

There was a mumbling of shared thoughts among the residents, and a friend of Sam's, Carl Jasper, yelled out from where he was standing with his family.

"Come on, Sam. What does that mean?"

"From what I have been told, it means that the CDC will be here shortly to sanitize the entire town proper, a procedure that will require seventy-two hours. In the meantime, myself and the officers here will be escorting you and your families to Davenport where…"

The response was instantaneous, a combined moan from over three hundred voices. Sam only increased his volume and authority.

"…where the Center for Disease Control will check everyone and provide the necessary medications and preventatives. You will be housed in the school gymnasium, field houses, and classrooms until the threat of infection has passed, hopefully, in three days."

The combination of questions, complaints, and refusals emitted from the throng was expected, Sam was even apathetic, but he found his resolve, raising his hand in a call for silence.

"You will be well provided for. Shelter and food await your arrival. I am sorry that you cannot return to your homes to retrieve valuables. Let me assure you as one of your own that security will be at the highest level. In regard to your pets - I can't help those of you that left them behind, but I hope you return to find them healthy. This town is being shutdown until further notice. That is all I know at this point."

It was a great deal to ask of these people, and Sam expected further pockets of problems, but maybe they were too stunned to argue because no one voiced objection. He caught his wife's eye in the sea of faces, her commitment to her husband and his duty as strong as his own love for his career choice. She had accepted his story earlier without objection, their sixteen years together having forged a bond of trust unbreakable.

"I want you to know I have no control over the matter. Like you, I will be vacating my home with my wife and joining you in Davenport. This is now a federal situation. If, after you have been secured, you wish to level complaints, you may do so at that time, though I don't know why you would find fault in an inconvenience that is saving your life."

Sam let the crowd digest his last statement for a while, feeling like he may have put the final nail in the coffin of the muckrakers and complainers. When no one made challenge, he continued.

"At this time I need you to calmly load the buses behind me, taking as little time as possible. It is important that we leave as soon as possible. Thank you for your assistance in this matter."

214 • DAVID FRAMEL

Sam lowered the horn and looked to Cody Hawkins who immediately started encouraging those groups near him to head for the buses. Those beckoned looked lost, shaken by the commandments they had just heard, but also resigned to the inevitable. Maybe it was their lifestyle, maybe it was the destitution that plagued Raven, but whatever it was, this mass of humanity had learned to adapt to change. They had survived so much, this was but another hole in the road they forever crossed in their small town lives. Their strength, born of difficulty and years of challenge, had emerged to face yet more adversity. They would make it, and Sam was proud to call them his friends.

Within fifteen minutes the buses were full, and after calling Edwards to okay the transport, Sam signaled the deputies to begin the evacuation of the entire town of Raven. They were to disembark in Davenport, and Sam had kissed his wife good-bye, promising to join her there in a matter of hours.

He and Cody would make a final patrol of the town, checking the few houses that may hold residents adamant regarding the gathering in the park. If he had to, Sam had decided to take these individuals at gunpoint, but he expected little resistance. Those that hadn't been accounted for in the park, a small number, were probably out of town, and the barricading of all roads leading in and out of Raven later would discourage their return.

Sam heaved a great sigh of relief as the buses faded around the corner. So far Bill's plan was working, but the sheriff didn't want to wait around to see if there were going to be any ramifications from their actions. The consequences could be deadly. He waved Cody over to the patrol car so they could start the final leg of the crazy marathon they were in the midst of.

Pulling out of the parking lot, Sam checked his watch. Thirty minutes since Bill's call. He hoped time was on their side.

■

They had stood in a meandering, queue for an hour, mumbling their dislike of the SBI and, in particular, Steve Edwards. He had ordered this human picket fence with his surly, condescending bark over the public address system that was strung haphazardly across their expanse. The hours baking in the now departed sun had done little for their attitudes, and to have to obey the commands of some non-military pencil pusher only heightened their bitterness. Roughly three feet apart, the guardsmen crouched, swiveled, and stretched their tired bodies, wondering all the while what purpose they could possibly be serving.

Before them lay a continuous, single stripe of white paint, an oddity in this empty field that had gone unnoticed until they were instructed to stand a few feet from it. The white line didn't spare rock, brush, or bare earth in its coverage, and the emphasis given not to cross it made it all the more strange.

Many of them had served in their guard capacity at natural disaster sites and other locations where a show of control was necessary. None of them had ever been part of such a worthless endeavor. Word had circled quickly from those in the know that Raven was a sparsely populated town without need for such a military display, especially in such great numbers. The lack of solid information they had received from their temporary bosses only furthered the confusion, and they were disappointed in the evasiveness of the Sergeant Major, though he showed the same steaming anger they felt. Even now he was trudging along the disorderly line, barking his embarrassment over their lackluster performance.

"I don't care why or for how long, you will act like soldiers and dress this line," he bellowed, and the men formerly in his direct charge responded with each resounding word. "We have a job to do, gentlemen, and we will perform it to the letter."

In conjunction with Billingsly's boisterous one-man parade, the sodium lights behind them blinked on in rapid succession, casting long shadows every few yards over the painted line and illuminating the grounds that lay toward Raven.

The hour was growing late, and Steve Edwards had nearly reached the end of his rope with the whole ridiculous affair. How he could have allowed himself to take part in this ghost hunt was beyond him, but here he sat, the sweat having saturated every stitch of his clothing, wondering how he would ever live it down.

He had ordered the guardsmen to assume a position just outside the painted border almost an hour previous, and he feared that in the next hour he would be telling these same men to stand down without explanation. Billingsly was doing his part to keep the group sharp, but even Edwards could not help the pity he felt for them. This was a mad charade concocted by civilians keen on spooks and spirits. It had been desperation that pushed his inclusion, a last-ditch effort to solve a case soon to be the property of federal authority. *Damn his pompous will!* Curtis would never call, and when he did, it would be to report the plan a wash. Edwards could see himself dismissing the Guard without reason, followed by a lengthy investigation involving military and bureau heads that was sure to seriously jeopardize his future. His single-minded aim for the top was going to land him a desk job pushing papers in some obscure corner of the state.

His musings were interrupted by the forced whisper of Bill Curtis over the walkie-talkie that had held the same spot next to him for hours. He had wondered if the small town equipment wasn't broken, a sure death sentence to their plans, but they had field-tested fine earlier in the day.

Curtis was obviously excited, and Edwards couldn't help the rush of adrenaline that overtook him. It was clear Ms. Hammons was engaged in whatever supernatural rendezvous occupied her, and Edwards jumped from his leaning position on the front of his car and grabbed the PA microphone.

"Gentlemen, we are ready for the next phase of our operation. It is very important that you follow my instructions to the letter. Any derivation from it could cause irrevocable harm, and let me remind you that lives do hang in the balance."

The old sound system crackled and hummed with every word, and Steve fought his only source of communication with the long line of guardsmen to make himself heard. It was impossible to tell the quality of sound at the far end, but Steve imagined that the line that digressed from normal to miniature-sized soldiers more suitable for child's play could follow the lead of those before them. There was no time to question it now.

"All right, this is going to sound like a strange request, and I sympathize with your involvement, but on the count of three, I repeat, on the count of three, I need each of you to take a position ten paces inside the white line in front of you."

Edwards registered the faces of roughly seventy men he could make out that looked at him in utter shock. He envisioned duplication of these grave countenances down to the last man, but there was no show of refusal. Billingsly had done his job well.

"Once you have taken up your place ten paces inside the line, I will need you to remain there until further notice. If you will now move to a spot just before the line, we can begin."

The guardsmen shuffled their way sporadically to the line, and Edwards gave them a minute or two to settle in. He wanted to tell them the obvious insanity of what he was asking had not lost its effect on him, but this was not a friendly night on the town. He owed them nothing.

They were paid to serve, as he was, and their service was needed.

"Okay, gentlemen, on three. Ten paces forward."

The many faces looked to him expectantly.

"One,"

The faces looked down at their feet, at the line they were to cross.

"Two,"

This better work, thought Edwards.

"Three."

In unison, five hundred National Guardsmen crossed into Raven, bringing with them their anger, confusion, and expectations.

32

The last ones to join them in the temporary city of Raven were Sam Butler and Deputy Hawkins. The two arrived visibly exhausted but apparently pleased with the results. They had completed their canvassing of the few houses needing attention, finding no one, and followed up with a final check of all barricades blocking the roads into town that declared the area off limits by order of the Sheriff's Department. They could never be sure if someone strayed into Raven's borders, they didn't have the manpower to close it off entirely, but they hoped for the best.

Bill greeted them as they walked into the gymnasium in Davenport, alive with more noise than any basketball game was able to provide. There were people everywhere, including CDC personnel who flitted about in their completely unnecessary duties, taking blood and compiling family histories. Edwards had assured the group that after the agency's testing proved negative, the CDC would not pursue the matter. Budget cuts and a growing international concern limited the time and effort the center could afford on a dead end trail. His office could pass it off as what they considered a needed evaluation to eliminate possibilities in a difficult case.

Sam immediately started looking for his wife to assure her of his safety. Carrie and Edwards were nearby, the latter nursing a bottle of water and showing signs of mental fatigue. Sam felt little sympathy for the man, but knew his efforts could not be dismissed. Carrie glanced up at the sheriff with a forced smile. Of all the team, she looked the worst. He figured her experience, though the others would never know what it must be like, was the most taxing. If Edwards looked like he had just run ten miles, Carrie had just finished a marathon.

"Sheriff, thank God you made it. Detective Edwards said you had stopped to give him the all clear, but we worried anyway. Those boundary lines were suspect since the records were so out of date," Bill said, shaking their hands with genuine gratitude.

"We've got food and drinks over here if you need them," pointing toward one end of the gym where several long tables displayed various soft drinks, bags of chips, and meat trays. "The Davenport Ladies' Auxiliary did us right, don't you think?"

Sam half heard Bill's gesticulations, continuing to scan the crowd for his wife. Bill seemed to feel his urgency.

"She's over in the cafeteria, Sam, helping with the food. She's fine."

Sam smiled appreciatively, the tension falling from him like a dirty shroud, and he walked with Bill to the makeshift banquet.

"A drink sounds perfect," Sam said. He looked at the wall-to-wall bodies pressed into the small building. "Have they been told?"

"I thought we would let them get settled, put their children down. It's been a long day for all of us."

Sam nodded. "How's Carrie? She looks battered."

Bill spoke with an emotion reserved for the deeply in love.

"It was incredible, Sam. Incredible. I stood there helplessly while that thing surrounded her. I can only imagine the fear she fought back to connect with it."

"She's a remarkable woman."

"Don't I know it."

While Sam went off to join his wife, Bill returned to where Carrie and Steve sat silently as a world of chaos buzzed about them. He sat next to Carrie, his arm finding its way across her back in affectionate support.

"Better?"

She took a deep breath. "Much."

Bill had launched them out of town without delay, stopping only after they had passed the sawhorses and placards on Main that warned visitors of Raven's circumstance. Coming to a skidding stop, Bill had checked on Carrie, who sat slumped but coherent on the seat next to him, assuring him she was all right. Only then had he radioed Edwards to let him know they were clear, and having confirmed the safety of Carrie's children, they headed for Davenport to join the others. Edwards was satisfied with the news, though he had still needed to hear from Sam Butler before his job was done.

"When can we be sure it's over?" Edwards asked, always the optimist.

Bill was ready for that question. His conversation with Carrie on the way to the school had confirmed his final suspicion.

"I'd say no more than a day. What Carrie described seeing demonstrates to me the entity's inability to survive cold turkey."

Edwards looked at him quizzically.

"Now you've got the damn thing eating turkeys?"

"No, no, you didn't hear me. I think it is safe to assume that the entity's life force is in direct proportion to its food supply. No food, no entity. When Sam let you know he was through, and you gave the order for the guard to step out of Raven, the gravy train was derailed."

"How can you feel safe assuming anything? We know nothing of this thing. Couldn't its latest feast support it for weeks?" Edwards said, his question carrying merit.

"It's like I told Carrie. In her sojourns with the entity, she saw an obvious change in its appearance, felt its limited strength, while at the same time seeing the corresponding depleted energy supply. It's like a car running on gas. You can go on fumes only so long, and the change is dramatic, before you come to a stop. Killing gave it the bursts of fuel it needed to carry out its functions both here and in its world. But now, with the neighborhoods and streets of Raven empty, with the emotional bait of almost a thousand souls ripped away simultaneously, the pump, my friend, is dry."

Bill made perfect sense, and Carrie's account of her final meeting with the entity supported him. He had hit on everything to this point; there was no reason to doubt his conclusions now.

"But we need to be sure. I can't in good faith allow these people to return home if a threat still exists. What would we say then?" Edwards said.

"We make sure it's gone."

Sam had joined them from the cafeteria, holding a sandwich and bottle of pop.

"Edwards, if I thought for a minute your concern was for these people, I would accept your attempt at concern." He was angry, and it was probably the events over the last three days that pushed him to speak.

"You're so concerned about your career, your position in the bureau, I think you would sacrifice the whole lot if it would benefit you."

Bill stepped in, "Now, Sam, I don't think this is the time to…"

"This is the time." He looked back to Edwards. "I can't judge you too much. You helped this community as much as I did, but I know your motivation was in the wrong place. We're officers of the law, to serve and protect. That is our number one priority. Personal goals should never," and here he was emphatic, "*never* stand in the way of that duty."

Edwards sat motionless, his lack of response only furthering his discomfort and confirming his guilt. All he could manage was to shake his head and stare blindly between his feet.

"We do have to know for sure," Carrie said, a silent observer of the awkward moment. "That's why tomorrow morning I will have to return to make contact."

Bill and the others looked at her with a shared perplexity.

"No way, Carrie, no way," Bill said, his head moving vigorously side to side. "We never discussed that. Detective Knowles was to cross the threshold three days from now. That was the plan. If we saw him being invaded in any way, we were going to yank him back to safety. End of story."

"Bill, you know as well as I do that the entity could ignore the detective for any of a number of reasons. It may be too weak to take him, it may kill him, or it may be dead. We can't be sure until I see it for myself."

Carrie's determination was inarguable, her resolve a foundation from which she would never sway. This had really been her show from the start, all the business with the entity, and she wanted to see it through.

"But, Carrie, the danger."

"You can do the same with me as you were with Detective Knowles." Carrie was pleading her case to Bill with a talent only he could appreciate. "You've seen the event. You'll know when it is with me. There's no other choice."

She was right, and everyone's reluctant compliance confirmed the correctness of her argument. They couldn't ask innocent people to return to the death chamber they had narrowly escaped today on an assumption. The morning was guaranteed to bring the sweltering heat, and now with it, a return to Raven.

■

The four returned in Sam's patrol car with the dawning of the fateful day. Everyone inside knew the implications of what they were about to do, the risks they were taking. Sam was getting ready to watch a friend sacrifice her safety and possibly her life in an attempt to determine the condition of a supernatural being that had invaded their hometown. His career meant nothing to him now; the efforts of this one woman paled in comparison.

Steve Edwards would be able to salvage his position in the SBI if Carrie could confirm the death of the entity. A quick call to his superiors relaying news of the end of Raven's problem with the promise of a complete report upon his return would stave off federal intervention and give him time to prepare his story. He planned on telling the truth, to an extent. The four had agreed upon a story that would feasibly satisfy the most stringent inquiry, though Edwards had promised a cursory review.

Initial interviews, crime scene investigations, and lab work had pointed to the outside possibility of a potentially deadly contagion effecting residents of Raven. When SBI lab results proved negative, as had all the materials Edwards had sent in the past weeks, exhaustive police work allowed him and local authorities to focus on a vagrant, who they pressured in lengthy interrogation, and eventually they were able to affect a confession. Seems the homeless figure had brutally murdered his victims, stuffed their bodies in the furnace of an abandoned fertilizer manufacturing building at the far end of town, and burned them beyond recognition. His own fate was sealed when he broke from officers while showing them the still burning interior of the furnace and leapt through the open door, a portal too hot to allow his retrieval. No one present felt the urge to extinguish the flames, and with that, the disappearances had ceased. The elaborate tale would also satisfy military involvement, though the manner of their role was highly suspicious. It had its holes, Edwards admitted, but it could be managed. "You'd be surprised what we can manage," he'd said.

With Carrie sitting with him in the back seat, Bill held her hand fiercely as he agonized over her intentions. Though her encounter with the entity yesterday had been dangerous, there had been the comfort in knowing that there was something to draw it away from her. She represented the only source of survival to the entity when she bridged that gap this morning. It was reckless and foolhardy, but at the same time unavoidable. The fate of so many lives hung in the balance, and Bill was forced to honor her commitment though he was nearing a state of hysterical panic.

Even though it was morning, Carrie was unconcerned about her potential to fall asleep to gain access to the entity's world. Once inside the town border, she would simply relax her mind, using the same methods that had assisted her last night, and reach out. She had confided in Bill that during her experience she didn't believe she actually "slept," but instead had projected herself to the same dimension she was prepared to seek again. Astral projection was a theory at best, a Far East sideshow for mystics and Himalayan Mountain dwellers, but given the recent events that would forever test their rational metal, they had to acknowledge the potential of Carrie's special gift.

They pulled up to the spot that not twelve hours ago had been besieged with military trucks, jeeps, and personnel, the white paint still visible on the parched terrain. Reluctantly stepping from the patrol car, the four shuffled over to the boundary between salvation and hell and gazed at the land beyond, more deserted now than ever before. Bill could almost feel the void and was sure his voice could carry for miles unimpeded across its hollow expanse. Edwards was his dismissive self, doubt forever his companion.

Sam went to the rear of the car and withdrew from the trunk a heavy rope and rescue harness that he brought back around with him. The idea was almost laughable in its intent. They would secure the harness to Carrie, allow her twenty feet of rope as she entered Hell's Gate, and with a measure of luck could pull her back to them like a trophy bass to shore. Like everything else they had taken part in, it was ludicrous to believe in its success, but the surprises kept mounting. Sam would tie the other end of the rope to the front bumper of his car in case their tug-o-war method failed to retrieve her.

Bill had covered things a million times, but while Sam secured the harness to her, he reviewed it yet again.

"Remember, you don't have to make contact to assess the situation. Just find out what its condition is if you can and work your way back. If we see the slightest disturbance in the air, we are dragging you back."

Behind her Sam was yanking the straps tight, jerking her unsteadily.

"Bill. I'll be fine."

"I know, but I can't help the worry."

Sam looked at Bill over Carrie's shoulder.

"Ready. How's it feel, Ms. Hammons?" the sheriff said while he tugged at various points for security.

"Uncomfortable, but I guess I am in no position to complain," she said. Carrie looked up at Bill, his face riddled with lines of regret.

"I'll be right back. Don't go meeting other women while I'm gone."

"I love you," he said.

"Love you."

■

Bill checked his watch, unable to believe only ten minutes had passed since Carrie had entered Raven. It was true what they said about painful experiences seeming to extend normal time; he had ample proof of that wives' tale. Carrie sat cross-legged in front of them at a distance that Bill perceived as infinite, the rope lying slack on the ground as it led back to the patrol car. There, Edwards was propped against the hood, his arms folded in a posture of annoyance. No one spoke for fear of disturbing her.

Carrie's mental trek proved relatively easy in the light of the conditions by which she was attempting to travel. The sun demanded moisture from her hydrated form, bringing beads of perspiration along her forehead and upper lip. Relaxed and within minutes unaware of her earthly discomforts, Carrie's mind's eye spiraled down through the familiar dark tunnel that linked her world with that of the entity. She felt weightless and alive, the fear that had gripped her heart all morning releasing its heavy hold. The sensation was indescribable, and when fully conscious she could only liken it to a roller coaster ride in sheer darkness, the thrill overwhelming.

In time she recognized a soft glow of light ahead of her, its subtlety spreading with her approach. She had learned not to fear these cosmic adventures, trips she had taken many times, and wondered whether this might be the last.

The light soon revealed the ever-present setting of Raven, either past or future, though this time there were surreal changes to the landscape. As Carrie settled upon the usual empty plain of Raven's fateful tomorrow, she felt like she was looking at a painting yet completed. The ground was patchy, its former covering lacking in many places in detail and color. Where the earth was unfinished there rested blotches of white nothingness, and Carrie saw the sky suffering from the same malady. But none of this was the most clear difference in the entity's manufactured future: the narrow river of emotion was indistinguishable in its place above her, its shell empty save for a few minute wisps of smoky waves that faded with their laborious movement. Carrie surveyed this with a deep-seated apprehension. The entity had not made its timely entrance, and she wondered if what she was seeing might be a trap, hiding a greater enigma.

She moved forward, avoiding the stains of white that pocked her way, wary of the slightest movement or rush of sound. For many steps there was nothing but the incomplete setting, but as she made her way further along, she saw an irregularity on the horizon, an almost imperceptible change where the earth and sky bonded. She hurried her pace, eager to be done with the entity's fantasy world but in need of an answer as well. As she neared the distortion, stepping here and there, afraid to drop through the white trap doors that could take her away forever, she saw the shape for what it was. Here, collapsed on the surface of its own creation, was the entity, its form nearly lifeless as it lay like a discarded plastic bag. Its coloring was opaque; its exterior showed no movements.

Carrie stood over it for a time, taking in the state of the fallen creature. It had lived on the forces that define man, his ambition and will, and it was dying as a result of the same. Carrie pitied the loss, not because she felt any bond with it, but because she was naturally compassionate. Maybe this had been the trait she emitted that had drawn the entity to her in the beginning. Whatever it was, the battle was over, and here lay the aftermath.

Driven by an unexplainable desire to know, something that Carrie would look back on later with satisfaction for who she was as a person, she knelt down and let her hand brush the creature's transparent surface. Her skin was caressed and warmed even now by the dying entity, and in that moment of contact, though brief, Carrie's questions were answered.

Somewhere parallel to Carrie's final contact, Bill, Sam, and Steve Edwards measured their individual time in personal pursuits. The detective remained fixed to the vehicle, his face turned away from the solar blast that was making its presence felt yet another day. Sam stood with Bill, who was transfixed on Carrie, the sheriff occasionally grasping his shoulder or giving him a look of friendly confidence. With her back to them, the two men failed to see the liquid change in the air on and about her hand, its waves never venturing farther than her wrist. Her hair shone in auburn radiance, its strands soft and unmoving in the stillness, but the area surrounding her right hand was alive with vibrancy.

"She's a tough girl, Bill. She'll be fine," Sam whispered, not sounding like he really believed it himself.

"I know, but I can't relax until she is back over here with me," Bill said.

They regarded her immobile figure.

"How long has it been?" Sam asked.

"Thirty-five minutes, give or take. It has to be soon. Maybe she can't make contact. What if the thing is dead and gone? What then?"

Bill was frantic, his normally calm, business-like demeanor overshadowed. Sam didn't know what to do other than wait out the seventy-two hour time frame they had originally given themselves and try again.

"If she doesn't have an encounter, I see it as a good thing. Could mean it's gone," he said.

Carrie leaned forward ever so slightly, her back rigid. Bill started, moving precariously close to the painted line.

"Wait, Bill. Give her a chance. We've got the rope in case anything happens," Sam said.

She continued the gradual waist-high bend, and when it seemed her lips would kiss the ground, her legs unfolded in one lithe motion, and she stood.

The three men stood frozen, unsure whether to take up the lifeline that bridged them. After what seemed forever, Carrie turned and walked back toward them, the rope trailing her like a useless umbilical cord. Her face was expressionless, its smooth lines denying access to her state of mind, her eyes glazed over as if she were autistic. And then she was with them, as was now Edwards, who had joined his allies in the formation of a semi-circle about her.

Carrie continued to stare vacantly, her focus on a sight the others knew they could never see themselves.

"Carrie? Are you all right?" Bill pleaded, his hands taking each of her shoulders gently. "Carrie?"

The deep, introspective stare slowly faded, and Carrie was able to look into Bill's eyes with a recognition he feared forever lost.

"Carrie?"

"It's over," she said, and fell heavily into his arms.

Epilogue

An orange ball of sun nestled gently into the deep purple clouds of a western sky over the distant horizon. The evenings were drawing their shades earlier with each passing day as summer drew to its close, and the winds of fall announced its imminent arrival in sharp gusts of cool, welcome air. Though failing to equal the intensity of a year past, the season supplied its share of oppressive reminders that Nature was truly above everything else. Those in Raven and other communities were intimately aware of its devastating potential and were quick to offer the respect it deserved.

Carrie had found the move into the huge home she and Bill now owned in one of Paul's Valleys' newer developments challenging but at the same time providing a pure satisfaction. After a whirlwind courtship and marriage just three months previous, Carrie had packed up the kids and their lives in Raven and joined Bill, eager to put behind her the past riddled with disturbing memories. Bill's practice had attained its original healthy status, allowing Carrie to tend to the house and kids without needing real estate in her life. She had been able to say thank you and good-bye to Shephard's prior to her wedding, grateful for the opportunity provided her. Carrie believed she was good at the job she had done, managing her properties at a professional level, but she would not miss that undeniable anxiety every time she entered a vacant home. She was only now able to get through an entire day without thinking of Raven, it and her final contact with the entity.

She told them everything on the drive back to Davenport that morning, a day still so prominent in her mind that it seemed like yesterday. With Bill's gentle urgings, she had been able to recount what was for her a very spiritual moment.

With her hand having broken the surface of the entity, moving dreamily within its decaying form, Carrie had pushed her thoughts out to it. With what Carrie perceived as an incredible effort, the entity shared itself for a final time.

"So this is death, sweet Carrie. You failed to show me its true face."

"Death is a permanent visitor we can never describe," Carrie said, her heart torn for the sufferings of this, a living creature, regardless of its history.

And what of that history? she had concluded. The entity had not asked for life; it only fought to maintain it with the only knowledge it possessed, the primitive, often barbaric instincts of man.

"I was your enemy, using you for my own good, and yet you are here feeding me with compassion. Why do you come here, Carrie?"

"I had to know, had to be sure that we could be safe again," Carrie said, "but Death is not a thing I cherish, no matter whose door it enters."

"I know the truth in what you feel," the entity said, its thoughts losing their strength. *"Tell me - what will become of me, Carrie? To what do I go?"*

Carrie's religious upbringing provided her with no real answers to the query, a fact that left her empty inside.

"I can't say," she said, her response calculated. "We die, and with faith, we live on elsewhere."

"I know not of an elsewhere. I have only known here. Does faith allow for ignorance?" the entity asked.

Carrie could feel its sorrow, and though she couldn't be sure of anything she promised, her heart was the guide.

"Faith *requires* ignorance. It's our belief in what we can't see or know that makes it real. If you believe, then it will be."

"Then I believe," it said. *"Thank you, Carrie. Thank you."*

These last words were faint and barely distinguishable, and as Carrie knelt there, trying to hold the entity with her longer, she felt it slip away, a complete stillness of the rippling surface marking its passage.

She had stood in helpless isolation, now alone on the deteriorated astral plane, weeping inside for the loss of a being she had only recently feared and wished dead. Carrie searched her battered soul for some measure of good that may have come from this, but found only regret at the loss.

The spirit of Raven, its decades of hopes and dreams, was gone. There was no satisfaction in its demise.